IMPRINT OF BLOOD

Birth of the Rim Book One

Phil Huddleston

Imprint of Blood: Birth of The Rim Book One

ISBN eBook: 978-0-578-58186-6
ISBN Paperback: 978-1-734-22150-3

Cover art created by Christian Kallias
ChristianKallias.com/art

New books and freebies

www.philhuddleston.com/newsletter

https://www.facebook.com/philhuddlestonauthor

Imprint Series
Artemis War (prequel novella)
Imprint of Blood
Imprint of War
Imprint of Defiance

Broken Galaxy Series
Broken Galaxy
Star Tango
The Long Edge of Night
The Short End
Remnants
Goblin Eternal

Works on Amazon
www.amazon.com/Phil-Huddleston/e/B07ZKFGW3G/

To the boys, and the girl - keep on making your mark.

FOREWORD

Increasingly, archaeological evidence shows the ancient Amazons did actually exist - and pretty much as I've described in the first books of this series. Recent excavations in Armenia and other locations have found much supporting evidence of this. Those discoveries were the inspiration for the prequel novella of this series, *Artemis War*, which lays the foundation for this book - how the Amazons got to Aeolis.

If you haven't read *Artemis War* yet, no worries. Each book of this series can stand alone. But if you like the Trojan War, ancient Greece, androids, starships, and space battles - then you owe it to yourself to read *Artemis War* to fully understand the back story of the Aeolian Empire, and the Machine Space creatures of the Core.

Special thanks to the following people who helped with opinions, criticisms, proofreading, and just general comments like "What the hell were you thinking here?"

Brandon Brown; Jeff Capehart; Ike Eberstein; Richard Edwards; Melissa Huddleston; Clayton Hunt; Karen Hunt; Adrienne Mayor; Rebecca Smethurst; Susan Summers; and many others.

And a special thanks to Craig Martelle. Craig, without you, this would be so much harder. And to David Weber, Ryk Brown, Jay Allan, Joe Haldeman, Jack McDevitt, and Tim Pratt for providing inspiration. And to Eric Frank Russell, who started it all with a little book that branched my universe.

Thank you all!

USEFUL TERMS

AI – Artificial Intelligence. Can be sentient (conscious) or non-sentient.

AU – Astronomical Unit, commonly used to specify distances inside a solar system; about 150,000,000 km. The Earth is 1 AU from the Sun.

Bottleneck Experiment – an experiment where a small population of creatures is placed into a strange environment to see if they can survive.

Compensator – a device on a starship which reduces the effects of g-force on the inside of the ship when the ship is under heavy acceleration (accel) or deceleration (decel).

Corvette – the smallest class of armed starship, or a similar civilian vessel.

FTL – faster than light.

G-force (or g) – the force of gravity. When standing on Earth, you experience 1g of weight. If you were experiencing 8g, you would weigh eight times as much.

Hermes - a sentient starship from the Core of the Galaxy who went rogue, abducting 212 Greeks and Amazons from Troy in 1184 B. C. These Humans were then abandoned on the planet Aeolis 580 lights from Earth as a bottleneck experiment.

Holo – holotank, a 3D display allowing the view of complex situations.

IFF- identification friend or foe – a code used to separate enemy ships from friendlies.

KPS – kilometers per second. Escape velocity to leave Earth is roughly 11.19 kps. To travel to the Moon in one minute, you'd need to average 6,407 kps.

MEMSAI – Military-Grade Enhanced Matched Semi-Sentient Artificial Intelligence. A personal assistant and security device which has a limited ability to read projected thoughts and act on them. It cannot read normal thoughts, only those intentionally projected to it.

QE Buoy – a small device stationed at a (relatively) fixed location in space, using Quantum Entanglement (QE) to send data to a distant point. Usually used by the military as an early-warning device or to monitor a planet.

QE Squirt – a short, coded text message sent via QE buoy.

Tholos – a large ceremonial tomb of the ancient Mycenaeans and Greeks, typically a circular chamber shaped like a beehive.

XO - Executive Officer, the second in command of a ship, usually responsible for the day-to-day operation of the ship, leaving the Captain to concentrate on overall strategy.

First Life

2121 - 2131

EARTH AND MARS

PROLOGUE

Sol System – Earth
21 June 2121

She was a big, black starship and she went anywhere she damn well pleased. And right now, she pleased to land on the South Lawn of the White House in Washington, D.C.

This scared the hell out of a lot of people, which made her day.

She decided she would take the name *Pandora* with this species - because she was bringing a whole lot of trouble to the backwater primates on this little blue dot.

She sat silently for an hour, just enjoying all the craziness she could see and hear going on around her, because she was that quirky kind of spirit that loves to stir up the natives.

But finally, *Pandora* decided she ought to get down to business. She posted a hologram on her outside skin. The hologram showed the pictures of three persons - images she had hacked from their driver's license photos. Below the three images, she posted a short communication:

I am Pandora.
I am a sentient AI.
Humanity is in great danger.
If you wish to survive, bring these three.

After that, *Pandora* finished a short opera she'd been working on, caught up on message traffic from the Ruling Council in the Core of the Milky Way Galaxy, ran diagnostics on her main engines, and supervised some bots cleaning her railguns.

After many long hours, the Human government managed to locate the three individuals she had displayed and brought them to her. When all three were standing outside looking confused, *Pandora* opened her main hatch and let them in.

Inside her entrance bay, all exits were closed except one. So they had no choice but to enter that corridor. And that led directly to her favorite room in her whole starship body, the Club Room as she called it. And it was exactly that – a perfect replica of a proper London Club - oak tables, padded chairs, heavy drapes on the windows, a bar at the back.

And standing by the bar, drink tray in hand, was the clone she had created for this occasion – Atsuko - a clone fully Human, intelligent and normal in every way, perfect for the task assigned to it – to welcome the three Humans and help them bond into a whole greater than the sum of their parts.

The male and the two females stumbled into the room, at a loss what to do next.

Pandora grinned – well, the AI equivalent of a grin – and sat back to watch the show.

The male was Jake Hammett, a former U. S. Navy fighter pilot, 38 years old, from San Francisco. The females were Lt. Colonel Teresa Tolleson, a U. S. Air Force pilot, 33 years old, from Travis Air Force Base; and Dr. Kirsten Monk, 34 years old, from Austin, Texas, a scientist working on asteroid mining.

Pandora had selected them to save Humanity.

SIRIUS

Bat Empire – an empire of fifty planets 805 light years from Earth behind the Pipe Nebula, populated by an alien race which the Machine Ship Pandora *labeled "Bats".* Pandora *warned that the Bats were a ruthless, genocidal race and would surely destroy Humanity as soon as they discovered Earth. At their present rate of expansion, the Bats would discover Earth about one hundred years after* Pandora*'s landing. That's how much time Humanity had to prepare.*

- Pandora*'s Message.*

26 Months after *Pandora*
Sol System - Lunar Orbit (almost)

The *Sirius* was trying to kill them. Actually, it wasn't the starship itself – just the Navigation AI – but that was enough to get the job done. The ship was on a direct vector for the Moon, and in sixty seconds would become a large cloud of starship parts and body fragments in the middle of a new crater in Mare Imbrium.

The ship bucked again, throwing Jake Hammett hard against the straps, as another compensator instability hit the system.

"Crap!" he heard Teresa yell.

"Language, Terese," Jake called out by reflex. Jake and Kirsten had been working on Teresa to clean up her language.

Then he realized…

How insane to want to correct her when we're about to die.

Without looking at Jake, Teresa Tolleson lifted a middle finger with one hand, while she tried to regain control of the

NavAI with the other.

"Fifty seconds to impact," called Dr. Kirsten Monk, acting as Science Officer. She was, after all, a scientist. Kirsten never wanted to be captain on their little jaunts. She was normally happy as a clam to be working the Science Station...

...Except when the new scoutship prototype they were testing was hell-bent on taking them directly through the Moon...

The excess-g klaxon was loud, and the condition lights around the bridge were flashing red, warning of impending high g-forces – if they regained control.

"Forty seconds to impact," Kirsten called out. She was sweating. So was Jake. Only Teresa seemed immune, struggling to override the NavAI.

Another compensator instability fluttered through the ship, rocking them back and forth. Suddenly, Teresa whooped. "Got it!" she yelled.

Jake felt some undamped Coriolis force as the little scoutship pivoted to an escape angle. Then the main engine went to full emergency power, crushing him back in his seat as the *Sirius* built to an internal acceleration of 8g.

That meant the true external acceleration of the ship was on the order of 208g. The inertial compensator could offset the first 200g of acceleration. After that...well, you got slammed by whatever the excess over 200g might be - which in this case, was 8g.

Jake, a former fighter pilot, unconsciously started the shallow, grunting breathing pattern that helped in a high-g situation, and he heard Teresa doing the same.

Kirsten, with no military background, was flattened against her seat and making a low moaning noise. But Jake saw she was still watching the holo tick down the meager seconds they had to live.

"'Thirty - seconds." Kirsten managed to grunt out.

Jake stared at the indicator in the large holotank at the

front of the bridge, watching the altitude spinning down. A large blob of sweat fell off his brow and rolled down his cheek. Unconsciously, his hands tried to grip a non-existent control stick, a reflex from his days in the cockpit of a Navy fighter.

"Twenty - seconds," grunted Kirsten.

The altimeter's spin slowed, a bit, a bit more. A ray of hope started in Jake's brain. He closed his eyes for a second, then decided he'd rather see his death, and opened them again.

The altimeter spun slower.

We might make it...

Three kilometers above the lunar surface, the altimeter bottomed out, and the ship began moving on a trajectory that would – just barely - miss the Moon.

Waiting a few seconds until she was sure they were clear, Teresa dropped acceleration to 8g true, internal 1g. That was plenty to get them escape velocity from the Moon - and would help protect them in case of another compensator glitch.

Jake reached up and wiped the sweat off his face with his uniform sleeve.

"Holy shit," said Teresa, leaning back from her console, and this time Jake didn't object to the language.

"What the hell happened there?" he asked.

Teresa shook her head. "The NavAI - some kind of bug. I programmed a course for Mars, and it immediately turned and tried to drive us through the Moon."

Jake grunted. He looked at Kirsten, sitting at the Science Console, staring off into nothing.

"You OK, Kirs?" Jake asked.

"Just lovely," said Kirsten sarcastically. "But I need to go change my underwear."

Jake grinned and turned back to Teresa.

"Let's take this bucket of bolts home before something else happens."

Teresa nodded. "Going to remote Nav, setting course for *Yehliu*," she said.

Concerned for his crew, Jake called Engineering. "How you

doin' back there, Cassie? Everybody OK?"

Cassie Blocker - the Cheng, or Chief Engineer, for today's prototype test flight – came back quickly.

"We're OK, sir. Bumps and bruises, possibly one broken arm. But mostly good. Thank the Lord you gave us Condition Red before the g-forces came in. That saved us. No idea what happened to the NavAI, Jake. But we did find the compensator problem. You should be good for full acceleration now."

Jake grimaced.

"Cassie...I don't want 'should be good'. I want 'you are absolutely good to start full acceleration', OK? Don't feel like getting squished today."

"You are absolutely good to start full acceleration, Admiral. Or Captain. Whatever the hell you are today." Cassie responded.

Jake could hear the laughter in her voice, so that was a bit reassuring.

"Thank you, Cheng," said Jake, and motioned to Teresa. Teresa nodded and slowly advanced the main engine throttle – somewhat gingerly, not that she didn't trust Cheng but... well, after all. If the compensator burped again, no telling how many g they might pull.

Teresa ramped up carefully to 50g true. Watching the board carefully, she breathed a sigh of relief as it appeared the compensator was working smoothly now. She leaned back and looked at Jake. "We'll be docking in forty minutes, O Great Admiral of the Sweaty Brow," she grinned.

Jake nodded at her, tilting his head back slightly at the humor.

"Wanna be captain now, Terese?" he smiled.

Teresa shook her head. "I'll wait 'til Cheng gets this piece of crap sorted out, thank you very much."

Jake grimaced. He knew the sDrive – which included the compensator – wasn't the problem. The sDrive design had come directly from *Pandora*, the sentient Machine Ship that landed on Earth a bit over two years prior. That design was rock-solid.

No, the problem was in the control systems. The NavAI was entirely Human-designed, and someone had screwed up.

When we get back to Geneva, Teresa is going to hand somebody their ass, thought Jake.

He looked at Kirsten and said, "Set Condition Yellow for docking, please, Kirs."

Kirsten nodded, recovered from her trance, wiped her sweaty fingers on her pants leg, and moved them rapidly across her console. The red condition lights throughout the ship shifted to yellow, and "Set Condition Yellow" blared through the PA and their personal comms.

There weren't many crew to hear it. This was a test flight; the *Sirius* was the first scoutship completed for the fledgling Rim Defense Force, Earth's newly commissioned Space Navy. Only a dozen people were on board, including the bridge crew and engineering.

From the outside, *Sirius* was disguised as an asteroid. She looked like an elongated, dusty rock, covered in patchy ice. She was designed to go deep into enemy territory and be undetected.

Only when the drive was active did a cover open in the rear and the engine fire out through the opening. Soon, this ship – and others like it – would be going into harm's way, into the unknown of the Bat Empire - to learn what they could about the terrible, bloody enemy *Pandora* had revealed to Humanity.

Twenty minutes later, the *Sirius* reached turnaround and the ship reversed, firing her engine to decelerate into Earth orbit. And shortly after that, she completed docking at orbital station RDF *Yehliu*.

The cigar-shaped spaceport was 960 meters in length and 468 meters in diameter, a long hollow tube that allowed the assembly of spacecraft modules shipped up from Earth. There were also six docking portals at intervals along each side, allowing her to act as a transfer station.

Even though *Pandora* had given them a complete design, it had taken eighteen months after *Pandora*'s arrival to build *Yehliu* – a spacedock essential to the development of the RDF fleet. A permanent party of 1,480 newly minted members of Teresa's Operations and Logistics division now populated it, teaching themselves how to assemble and test starships.

With *Sirius* hard-docked, Jake and his companions transferred control to Cassie in Engineering, shut down all non-essential bridge systems, and exited the ship into the walkalong. This was a long corridor down the side of the station between portal entrances. As medics rushed into the ship to care for the injured in Engineering, they stood aside. Then they continued toward the next portal over, where their shuttle was waiting.

As they walked, Teresa turned to Jake and Kirsten.

"New Standing Order from Operations: no officers above O-5 on test flights from now on. Especially the three of us at the same time. That was stupid. Especially for you, Jake."

Jake sighed. "I know. Admirals can't be captains. But you sure take all the fun out of things."

"Can't help it, buster. No more playtime excursions for you. You're not a pilot anymore, and you aren't going to be running any more test flights either. None of us are."

Unhappily, Jake nodded agreement.

Reaching the next portal, they entered their shuttle. Jake glanced at Kirsten and Teresa, noted the tension and exhaustion on their faces, and quietly settled into the pilot seat, leaving them to collapse into the passenger seats behind. Silently, Jake projected instructions to Zoe - his *Military Grade Enhanced Matched Semi-Sentient Artificial Intelligence*, otherwise known as a MEMSAI.

<Take us home, Zoe>
<Wilco>

Disconnecting from the portal, Zoe directed the shuttle

away from the orbital station at low power until they were clear, then began positioning the shuttle to break orbit.

Jake watched the front vision screen. A magnificent speckle of stars wheeled around the shuttle as it rotated. Then, passing across the screen like a beaded necklace pulled across a black velvet curtain, the Milky Way came into view. As it passed through his field of vision, Jake looked toward the constellation Ophiuchus.

There lay the enemy - the Bat Empire. And behind the Bats, 14,800 light years away, was the boundary of the Core, with trillions of Machine Creatures living their lives, barely aware of Humanity.

Jake thought about Humanity's home in the Universe. The Galaxy was vast; so vast that a single Human could hardly comprehend it. From their vantage point in the Core, the creatures of Machine Space could not even see Sol.

What would it be like, to be so far away from here that even the Orion Arm would be lost to view? Perhaps someday soon, we'll be able to journey that far and find out. Maybe in a few hundred years.

If we survive the Bats...

As Jake watched, the Milky Way sank out of view and the Earth rose in the vision screen, a gigantic blue and white marble below them. But he knew how small that marble really was. Even from the orbit of Mars, just one planet over, it was only another tiny point in the sky.

The home of Humanity is minuscule in the grand scheme of things. How little we matter to the galaxy. But we will make a difference. We'll make a difference, or we'll die trying.

Thinking back, Jake remembered.

He remembered when all this craziness had started. When he, Teresa and Kirsten had first made their insane entry into the sentient starship called *Pandora*.

And Jake remembered how they had to go report to the U. N. about what they had learned there...

TELLING THE WORLD

There is also another threat you should know about. 580 light years from Earth, in the Beehive Cluster, there is another star empire. And this one is made up of Humans - Humans who were abducted from ancient Troy in 1184 B. C. It's a long story; but they are also going to be a problem.

- Pandora's *Message.*

Two Days after *Pandora*
New York City - U. N. Headquarters

Jake Hammett glanced at the two women standing beside him. Both of them gave him a glare, as if to say, *get on with it!*

So he did. He stepped out onto the stage and walked to the podium. Turning, he placed his hands on it. He stared at the audience.

The rustle and bustle of the hundreds in attendance filled the air with sound. Jake looked at the hall of the U. N. General Assembly stretched out before him. There were no empty seats. In fact, it was standing room only - people standing on the sides of the hall, in the corners, in the back - as many as could cram into the room, and dozens more peeking through the doors in the back.

How the hell did I end up here? What the hell am I doing?

He felt, as much as heard, Teresa and Kirsten come up beside him, one on each side. He was the designated spokesperson; *Pandora* had made that clear to them. He was the leader.

But he didn't know why.

Clearing his throat, he hesitated. He realized that the

President of the United States, Margaret Bolt, sat right in front of him. The leaders of every major country on Earth had flown to Washington for this meeting. The Chinese, the Russians, the leaders of Europe, Africa, Asia, and Australia were all sitting right in front of him. Waiting.

Beside him, he heard Teresa speak in a low voice.

"You gonna take all day, squid?"

Turning to her, he glared. "You want to do this, zoomie?"

Teresa winked at him. It pissed Jake off, but on the other hand, it broke the spell that had frozen him.

He realized that was her intent.

She is one smart cookie.

Jake turned back to the audience and cleared his throat again. Public speaking was not his forte. But as Teresa said, he had to get it done. Taking a breath, he started speaking.

"My name is Jake Hammett," he began. "Beside me I have Lieutenant Colonel Teresa Tolleson and Dr. Kirsten Monk. By now, most of you probably know what happened to us two days ago..."

A snicker passed across the crowd. There was probably not a Human on Earth who didn't know what had happened to these people two days ago. A starship had landed on the lawn of the White House and demanded their presence. And they had been located, and shanghaied, and flown to Washington, and sent into the ship. And now they were reporting to the world.

"We've already sent out a press release that explained the basic facts of our encounter with *Pandora*. As that press release described, *Pandora* is a sentient starship of great intelligence, an intelligence that she claims is roughly equivalent to a thousand Humans.

"As we explained in our press release, *Pandora* came here from the inner part of the Milky Way – the Core. We've learned that the Core is called Machine Space, and it's reserved for artificial intelligence creatures only. The outer part of the galaxy, where we live, is called the Rim. The Rim is reserved for biological beings, such as ourselves.

"Under normal circumstances, Machine Space creatures don't interfere in the Rim. But the Ruling Council of Machine Space has made an exception for Earth. They've sent *Pandora* to warn us of two great dangers.

"One - the least of the two dangers, but still a danger - is the Aeolian Empire. That is a star empire in the Beehive Cluster, about 580 light years from Earth. It is, unbelievably, made up of Humans - people who were abducted from Greece and Troy in 1184 B. C. These people were taken there and abandoned; somehow they survived, and somehow they've created a star empire with technology far in advance of our own. The danger we face from them was described in the press release. But I'll summarize it as follows: if they find us before we are ready for them, they will almost certainly subjugate us and make us a slave colony to their Empire. That's the way they roll. So that is our first threat.

"Our second threat, and the greater threat, is a bit farther away - 805 light years from Earth, behind the Pipe Nebula. *Pandora* said those aliens would look to us like tall, walking bats - so she calls it the Bat Empire. And they represent a much more serious threat to our existence. The Bats don't take slaves. They don't take prisoners. They just kill you and take your planet.

"So - that's the warning *Pandora* has brought us. She says we've got about a 10% chance of surviving the Bats. Not the kind of news we want to hear. But there is some hope. *Pandora* is willing to provide us with a technology boost to give us a rough level of parity with the Bats and the Aeolians. She says it will take us about one hundred years to get there. If we can survive undetected for that long - and if we do everything right - we've got a chance.

"Now for the crazy part. Crazy to me, and I'm sure crazy to you as well. *Pandora* has stated that this technology will be given to the three of us here on this stage. She has designated us as the caretakers of this great effort to bring Humanity to the stars. Why? We don't know - she won't tell us. She just says we are the right ones to make it work. When we questioned her about it, she said she's performed millions of simulations, and we three are the ones. And that's all she'll say about it.

"How we are supposed to do this, we don't know. But somehow, we have to figure it out. Come up with a plan. Of course, we need your help, and the help of every Human on Earth, to make this work. We need to get manufacturing up and running to build starships from the designs *Pandora* will give us. We need to form a Space Navy. We need colonization of planets to provide us with the resources and population to fend off the Bat Empire and the Aeolians. All of these things have to come to fruition within one hundred years. So the challenge is immense.

"With that said, we're here to answer what questions we can. Please know that we've put just about everything we know into the press release sent out yesterday. So there's not a whole lot more we can tell you. But anything that is not in the press release is fair game. If you'll look around, you'll see several people with microphones. Please get their attention and they'll bring a mike to you so you can ask your question."

Dozens of hands went up instantly. Jake waited patiently as the first question came, from China.

"Why did *Pandora* land in the U. S.? Why are only white people meeting with her? Have you had prior contact with *Pandora* before her landing? Is this some kind of setup?"

Jake shook his head. "Sir, to my knowledge there was no contact with *Pandora* before her landing. I'm certainly not aware of any. And as for why she chose the three of us to bring into her confidence, I cannot tell you, because she will not tell us. Her only statements so far have been that based on her computations, we are the ones who must do this. I can't tell you more than that, because that's all I know."

Another person tried to get a question in, but the Chinese representative interrupted before they could continue. "So you are locking out Asians? No Asians will be allowed to have this technology?"

Jake shook his head again. "Sir, that is not true. We are not locking out anyone. Please understand - this is only the third day of us trying to come to grips with this situation. We're sailing in undefined waters here. But I assure you, there will be no discrimination against anyone. To the extent that the technology is released for civilian use, there will be no discrimination."

Jake felt Kirsten poke him hard in the back. Jake realized he had said too much. And he was right, for immediately the next questioner jumped on his statement.

"Are you saying that you will *not* release *Pandora*'s technology for civilian use? Are you setting up some kind of monopoly?"

With a sigh, Jake realized he now had to address something they had hoped to avoid.

"The threat facing Humanity is huge. The nature of the project that is in front of us is unprecedented. This will be a one-hundred-year project to bring Humanity to a point where we can defend ourselves against the Bats and the Aeolians. The implications of that are staggering. The three of us - Teresa, Kirsten, and myself - have stayed up nearly all night for the last two nights, trying to work out the guts of a plan to accomplish that. We came to certain critical decisions. I know some of these decisions will not be popular, but we intend to stick by them. I had hoped not to bring this forward in this kind of public forum, but I see that I can't avoid it - so here we go.

"One - we will first use the technology *Pandora* provides to build a space navy. That space navy will be called the Rim Defense Force - the RDF. Since we cannot know when we might be discovered by the Bats or the Aeolians, that will be our first priority. Nothing can take precedence over that.

"Now - *Pandora* is willing to give us designs for two kinds of spaceship propulsion systems. One kind is called a system drive, or an sDrive. Those are the drives that work inside the solar system. With those drives, you can get to Mars in a few hours. You can get to the outer solar system in a day or so. So those plans will become available to everyone as soon as we can get them out the door. There will be no restrictions on those designs.

"The second type of drive is the tDrive - the drive that can go interstellar, and take us to the stars. Now, everyone, please think about this...the last thing we need is for some crackpot to jump in a ship with a tDrive and go shooting off to the Bat Empire, trying to strike some kind of a deal with them. That would bring them right to our doorstep, long before we are ready to face them. And that would be the end of Humanity.

"So - the design for the tDrives will not be released until two things have been accomplished. The first is to find some way to prevent civilian tDrives from traveling to the Bat Empire or to Aeolis. *Pandora* says we can develop an AI controller that can be built into the drive to prevent that from happening.

"The second condition is that we have a viable Space Navy of at least fifty ships to patrol the space lanes and maintain peace. We can't have a free-for-all out there with no law and order. When those two conditions are met - an AI-controlled tDrive for civilian use that cannot travel to the Bat Empire or the Aeolian Empire, and at least fifty ships in the RDF Space Navy - then we'll release the tDrive for civilian use.

"Next question, please."

As hands shot up all across the auditorium, one person took matters into her own hands. The President of the United States, Margaret Bolt, rose to her feet. Jake waved the crowd to silence, then nodded graciously to her.

"Madame President," he said, recognizing her.

"Mr. Hammett, this morning at 4 AM, this so-called sentient spaceship - *Pandora,* I guess you call it - took off from the White House and shot off into space. Our tracking systems show that it landed nearby the airport in Geneva, Switzerland. Just what the hell is going on?"

Jake nodded graciously at Bolt. He well knew her

reputation - she was a dangerous, volatile President. There were persistent rumors that anyone who crossed her simply disappeared. Very persistent rumors.

"Yes, Madame President, *Pandora* has relocated to Geneva. We've selected Geneva as the RDF Headquarters to ensure Humanity's Space Navy remains neutral of all Earth governments."

A strange look came over President Bolt's face. Jake felt a shudder go down his back. He had never seen such unadulterated hatred on the face of another Human before.

I think we're in trouble here, thought Jake.

THE WORLD IS NOT HAPPY

The heaviest penalty for declining to rule is to be ruled by someone inferior to yourself.

- Plato.

New York City - U. N. Headquarters

"Mr. Hammett, that is unacceptable. That spaceship landed in the U. S. We claim ownership of it. You will immediately bring that ship back here, or there will be the most severe consequences."

Jake sighed, more inwardly that outwardly.

How to deal with this? How to make them understand?

"Madame President, let me try to explain. *Pandora* is a sentient starship. That means she is a conscious, thinking entity. She is an individual, free to do as she wishes. We have no control over her. The greatest risk we face right now is that we anger her and drive her away. If she decides not to help us, then we are certainly lost. The Bats will come, and we will not be ready. For that reason, I will repeat, as we did in the press release of yesterday, that this is a partnership between *Pandora* and Humanity. We are entirely dependent on her good will."

Bolt glared at Jake. The venom in her glance could have melted glass.

"Then explain this to me. Why you three? Why did this spaceship pick the three of you to talk to, and not one of the world's governments, who would have the resources to manage this project properly?"

"Madame President, as I've said before, I cannot explain that. Pandora did not give us any specific reasons. She simply states that her computational engine has performed the simulations, and the three of us emerge as the necessary keepers of this mission. I'm as in the dark as everyone else. But we have no choice in the matter. It has been given to us to do this, and therefore, we will do it."

There was a long, intense silence in the room. Bolt, perhaps reading the room, and realizing she was not coming across well on international media, grudgingly returned to her seat. Jake noticed she leaned over and began whispering to her Chief of Staff, Elias Tobin.

That's not good. Not good at all, Jake thought.

To one side of the auditorium, the British ambassador stepped forward, microphone in hand, to ask the next question.

"How will the three of you proceed? What are your next steps?"

Jake slid aside to make room for Teresa, who stepped forward to the podium.

"Good morning, Mr. Ambassador. I'll take that question. The Rim Defense Force will operate as a military organization. Like any military organization, there has to be one person at the top. *Pandora* has designated that person to be Jake. Jake will be the Chief of Naval Operations - the CNO - with the rank of Admiral. Jake will be responsible for the overall strategy of dealing with the Aeolians and the Bat Empire.

"I will operate the Operations and Logistics organization of the RDF. I will be responsible for the design and manufacture of starships and for Fleet operations.

"Kirsten will be responsible for the Colonization Office - charged with locating and colonizing habitable planets, establishing legal systems for them, ensuring they are supplied until they can stand on their own."

Teresa paused, and a slight smile curled the corners of

her lip. As Jake and Kirsten had already learned, Teresa had a wicked sense of humor. Jake groaned as he realized what Teresa was about to do in front of the entire world.

"And between the three of us, we're gonna haul Humanity's ass into space!" she yelled.

26 Months after *Pandora*
Geneva, Switzerland

With a start, Jake came out of his reverie. The memory of the U. N. presentation of two years prior faded away. Jake realized the shuttle had finished its rotation and was firing its retros. Getting back to business, he watched the instruments as a backup to the AI. Within minutes they entered atmosphere and started a descent toward Geneva, Switzerland, headquarters of the RDF.

Landing the shuttle on the pad at the Geneva Landing Zone, the three climbed wearily out of the hatch and into a waiting security vehicle manned by four guards, who whisked them across the field to their quarters. Entering, they took the elevator up to the top floor where their apartments were, passing another two layers of security on the way.

The heavy security was necessary; since Pandora's landing and her inexplicable call for Jake, Teresa and Kirsten, there had been two attempts on their lives. The world did not take kindly to their assigned role in taking the stars.

After all, there were no aliens in the skies; no intelligent, gun-toting lizards walking the Earth. Life went on pretty much as it did before *Pandora*'s arrival.

There was only *Pandora*'s word that sometime in the next one hundred years, a fleet of Bat Empire starships would come out of the Pipe Nebula and turn Earth into a blazing cauldron of fire, killing every Human on the planet. Like people since time immemorial, Humans wanted to push off thoughts of defense and war into a far future and spend the 'now' exploring space - and making themselves obscenely rich.

Every major power on Earth was trying to weasel its way into control – and take over Humanity's entry into interstellar space. The governments and corporations of Earth were not taking kindly to the independence Jake and his team had shown. The fact the three of them had been hand-picked by *Pandora* to lead the Rim Defense Force made little difference to the avaricious leaders of Earth.

Two years ago, while attending a meeting to ramp up spacecraft production, Teresa had been shot at - and slightly wounded. And only a year ago, Jake had been attacked while visiting his parent's house in Texas, barely escaping with his life. In addition to that, *Pandora* had given them advance warning of two other assassination attempts, allowing them to avoid the danger.

They now lived their lives behind a wall of security. Their apartments in Geneva were fortifications, bristling with tripwires and alarms. They did not step out of those apartments without a gang of armed security guards. Against their will, they had been thrust into roles that gave them plenty of enemies.

LIGEIA

The ferocious Penthesilea, gold belt fastened beneath her exposed breast, leads her battle-lines of Amazons with their crescent light-shields...a warrioress, a maiden who dares to fight with men.
- Virgil, Roman poet.

Planet Aeolis - 580 lights from Earth

Cadet Ligeia Iona Satra squared off in the sword pit, her bare heels a meter in front of the ropes lying on the ground behind her. She faced her opponent across the pit, grinning madly. Her hand on the wooden training sword was caked in dirt.

Ligeia loved a good fight. The cadets of the Imperial Naval Academy at Aronte fought often – with fists, wrestling, in the warship simulator – but it was the sword that Ligeia loved most. With the sword, she could combine her physical strength with her mental acuity and quickness to overcome nearly any opponent - as she had shown today, leaving a string of beaten victims in her wake as she advanced to the finals of the tourney.

Now only Penthe stood between her and victory. Beating this last challenger would give her the junior cup. At 17 years, Ligeia was not yet allowed to fight in the full tourney – only seniors could do that - but this would suffice.

"Penthe! I'm going to kick your ass!" she yelled, hammering the butt of the wooden sword onto the small wooden shield she carried on her left arm. "And after I knock your head in, I'm going to piss on your sorry carcass!"

With a growl, Penthe charged, her sword pulled in tight to

knock Ligeia's shield aside and push her over the ropes, causing her to be disqualified. This was what Ligeia had been waiting for; she feinted right, then left. Penthe over-anticipated and moved first one way, then the other, trying to out-guess Ligeia. But Ligeia had already moved back to her original position, never having actually moved her feet. She leaped into the air, raising her arm to hammer the butt of her sword on the back of Penthe's neck as her opponent desperately tried to re-orient her aim. With a thud, Penthe went past her, going down, face smacking into the dirt and body skidding over the rope to disqualification.

"Winner!" called the referee, holding up the red flag and pointing it at Ligeia. Ligeia grinned even wider, as her fellow cadets came up and pounded her on the back, basking in her glory even though she had beaten them all soundly. Ligeia wiped her sleeve across her face, removing some of the dirt and sweat that had accumulated during the tourney.

After minutes of congratulations from her peers, she was finally released to go back to her dorm. Before leaving, she walked over to Penthe, who was examining bruises on both arms where she had hit the dirt hard.

"Penthe! Are you alright?" asked Ligeia.

Penthe glared at her. "Yes, no thanks to you, Lige. Next year...I'll get you next year!"

Ligeia leaned in and kissed her on the lips. "Absolutely, Penthe. Next year!"

Penthe grunted and pretended to wipe off the kiss. "Crap, Lige. I don't want any of that."

But Ligeia noted that Penthe couldn't completely hide a smile. Ligeia winked at her and went on her way to her dorm.

As she departed, she glanced over her shoulder. Penthe was looking at her - and the expression on her face was not a frown.

The Imperial Naval Academy in Aronte was the pillar of the Aeolian Empire Navy - the AEN. Girls destined for the AEN officer corps entered the Academy at the age of 14.

There they spent four grueling years learning combat – every form of combat. From the physical – wrestling, swordplay, several forms of what an Earther might call judo – to the mental – the strategy and tactics of starship combat, first in simulators and later, in their senior year, in fleet exercises on real starships.

Entry into the Academy was, of course, limited to females. Only females could serve as officers in the AEN. Males were relegated to crew duties. And only females of Amazon descent – the nobility – could rise to the level of Captain or above.

Ligeia was an Amazon. She was a member of the Satra clan – a minor branch of the ruling house Aronte, for which the city was named.

Although no longer in the line of succession, the Satra family was still considered one of the most powerful in the nation. Over the last two hundred years they had evolved from political roles to military ones, becoming almost exclusively Naval officers or AEN suppliers.

In another year, Ligeia would graduate as an ensign. She would take up her duties on a warship, probably a corvette or destroyer, and begin working her way up the chain. With any luck, in ten or fifteen years she would be a captain, commanding a destroyer or even a frigate.

In the meantime, she thought, *I need a shower.*

Entering her dorm room, she stripped off her sweaty clothes and went to the bathroom. Turning the shower to a stream of ice-cold water, she stepped in, gasping in both discomfort and delight at the intensity of it.

Scrubbing her head and body, she stripped away the dirt and sweat of the sword pit, reveling in the feeling, leaning forward to place her hands on the tile as she let the water cool her body and her mind.

With a loud chime, she heard someone at the door. Stepping out of the shower, she didn't bother to grab a towel. She walked to the door and opened it, dripping water on the floor, naked. Penthe stood, a grin on her face that got even wider as she saw Ligeia's uncovered body.

"I want a rematch," Penthe said, barely able to get the words out.

"What sport?" asked Ligeia.

"Wrestling," whispered Penthe, entering the room, closing the door behind her.

A MODEST PROPOSAL

A very great vision is needed, and the man who has it must follow it as the eagle seeks the deepest blue of the sky.
- Crazy Horse, Sioux Chief.

Geneva, Switzerland

By unspoken agreement, Jake and Kirsten followed Teresa into her apartment. After a bit more than two years of working together, the three were getting quite good at reading each other's minds.

Exhausted, Jake crashed down on the couch in Teresa's living room, while Kirsten fell into the nearest armchair. Teresa tossed her jacket and cap on the dining table and plopped into the other chair, laying one leg across the armrest as was her habit.

Kirsten sighed, got up, picked up Teresa's cap and crumpled jacket, put the cap on a hook behind the door, and carefully folded the jacket to hang in the closet. Then she sat back down in her chair and smiled at Teresa.

"Don't be a slob, sweetness," she said.

"I wasn't," said Teresa. "I knew you'd put it away."

"You take advantage of me," said Kirsten.

"I do," smiled Teresa. "It's good to be the queen."

"Lord knows," mumbled Jake on the couch.

Kirsten looked down at the floor. "You know..." she started, then paused.

Teresa looked at her expectantly.

"...as my life was flashing before my eyes back there, I realized I really love you guys. I was afraid I was going to die without telling you that."

There was a long silence. Then Kirsten lifted her face, looking at Teresa with a challenge in her eyes. "These last two years have been the most intense of my life, Terese. So many times, I thought we would fail. Yet somehow, we always seem to get through."

Teresa nodded in agreement.

Tilting her head, Kirsten continued. "We're going to be in this life for a long time, Terese. We don't have anybody else to depend on - just ourselves."

Teresa sat silently; pretty sure she knew what was coming.

Kirsten plowed on. "I think the three of us should get married."

Jake, lifting his head in shock, made a sound between a snort and a laugh.

Teresa smiled enigmatically. "I was wondering when you'd get around to that."

"Well, it just makes sense," said Kirsten. "We're in this for the long haul. We take care of each other, we trust each other, and we sure as hell don't have time for anyone else."

Teresa looked sideways at Jake, who was still lying on the couch, staring at them in disbelief. Then she looked back at Kirsten. "What about Jake?"

Kirsten laughed. "He can take it or leave it. But he's a man, I think we both know what he'll do."

"Hey, wait a minute," said Jake. "What the hell are you talking about here? Why on Earth would you want to do that?"

Kirsten stared at him. "Well, for one reason, a triangle is the most stable relationship. At least if the females choose the male. Humanity seems to have forgotten that."

"That's crazy!" exclaimed Jake.

"Is it?" asked Teresa. "Think about it. For millions of years in primate society, females mated with multiple males. But the females chose who to mate with - not the males. Somehow, along the way, Humanity forgot about that most basic design of primate society. Men accumulated the power of dictating mating habits, for their own advantage, first enforcing it with physical power, then with social power. But if females are empowered to choose - which we are, in our case, because of who we are - then this will work."

Jake shook his head. "You guys are nuts..."

Teresa glared at him and continued.

"Think about it, Jake. A triangle is the most stable relationship if all three legs are equal and strong. Think about a trivet - if it only had two legs, it would fall over. Look at the divorce rate in America - right about 45% these days. Trying to stand a trivet on two legs."

Jake objected.

"But marriages with two women and one man are so rare, you can't even get statistics on them! That makes no sense at all!"

Teresa bobbed her head in agreement.

"Yes, you're right. But that doesn't mean those marriages fail. It just means they stay hidden, because western society can't stand the thought they could be wrong. Think about all the throuples we hear about. That's probably just the tip of the iceberg. There must be hundreds more that we never hear about."

Kirsten took up the argument.

"Jake. I agree with you to an extent. If the legs of the triangle are not equal, it will fall over. If the man or either one of the women are significantly weaker than the others, it will fail. No doubt about it. But that's no different than a traditional marriage. If one of the two is far stronger or more aggressive than the other in a traditional marriage, it is almost certainly doomed to failure. So there's no difference in risk. It's the same probability of failure."

Jake shook his head.

"No, I think you're glossing over the risk factors." He frowned, trying to think of a better argument.

Kirsten plowed on.

"In our case, you've got three strong people. Three strong legs of the triangle. It will work because Teresa and I are empowering ourselves. We're not depending on you to be the strong, aggressive boss of the marriage. We're empowering all of us to be equal partners. Three solid legs of equal strength."

Kirsten stood and looked at Jake, carrying on her argument.

"The real key here is that Teresa and I are strong, fully adult, educated women. We can always walk away. As long as each partner of the marriage has the freedom to walk away at any time, it's a good model for a strong partnership. Each partner will be motivated to make it work. These things only get into trouble when one of the partners has too much power over the others. But I know you, Jake. I know you're not that kind of person."

Teresa interrupted. "And if you become that kind of person, you can bet Kirsten and I will kick your ass right out of the marriage."

Kirsten turned back to Teresa.

"We ought to do this now, set a precedent for the entire RDF. Create a new social order for those who live and work in space. The future of life in space is going to be radically different from the past on Earth. We'll need a new way of living."

Jake stood up to protest, thought about it some more, and sat back down again. His brow was furrowed as he tried to think through what Teresa and Kirsten were proposing.

"We could call it a triplex marriage," continued Teresa. "Make it something distinct, unique to the Space Force."

"Good," said Kirsten. "I like it. But by contract only. One voyage, or one year, something like that. Whatever way works for each situation. So for example, if a crew goes out on a two-year mission, they can sign a contract of marriage for two years. When they return, it automatically dissolves. No harm, no foul, and they get ready for the next mission. Or if they want to stay together, they can extend it."

"How long for us, you think? Five years?" asked Teresa.

"That sounds about right," said Kirsten. "A five-year contract, automatically dissolved if not renewed. No messy divorces at the end. A nice clean break and everybody goes on their way."

Jake interjected. "But you just said, the key to the whole thing is the freedom to walk away. If there's a five-year contract involved, then you're removing that freedom to leave!"

"No," rebutted Kirsten. "Anyone can still walk away. We'll use the old Jewish ritual - you stand in the doorway of the home and call out 'I divorce you, I divorce you, I divorce you!' - say that three times, and you're out of the marriage."

Jake lifted his hands in frustration. "Then what's the point of a contract?"

"To settle the legal issues, of course," said Teresa. "Obviously, we still have to deal with property issues, child custody, things like that. Even if someone walks away, those things linger behind."

Jake made one final argument.

"The Earth governments are gonna raise holy hell about this, you know."

Teresa laughed. "As if we should give a shit what they think. All most of them have done so far is throw roadblocks in front of us at every turn. And try to kill us." She turned back to Kirsten. "Are you going to get down on one knee?"

"I thought of this idea," said Kirsten.

Teresa grinned. Then she got out of the chair and, with a bow, she knelt on one knee.

"Dr. Kirsten Monk, will you join me in marriage, for the term of five years?"

"I will," smiled Kirsten.

Teresa turned to Jake.

"Jake Hammett, will you join Kirsten and I in marriage, for the term of five years?"

"He will," said Kirsten.

Jake glared at her.

He couldn't think of any argument to get out of it, and for one simple reason.

He was, indeed, in love with both of them.

ONE BRIGHT DAY

The F82 "Grumbler" was a hybrid jet / ramjet / scramjet fighter of the early 22nd century, used primarily by the U. S. Air Force. The Grumbler was a sub-orbital interceptor. It was named for its distinctive "grumbling" sound during re-entry from sub-orbit. The "Grumbler" was notable as the fighter flown by Jake Hammett in the Brush War, in which he was shot down over Mongolia on 12 May 2115.

- RimWiki, 2265 Edition.

Geneva, Switzerland

Next morning dawned bright and clear, a beautiful day in Geneva. The brilliant rays of the morning sun streaming through the window woke Jake. The distant profile of the Alps and Jura mountains made an impressive arena surrounding the city. The contrails of jets leaving the airport, and shuttles headed for space, left their thin trails in the upper atmosphere.

Jake found himself still on the couch, where he had collapsed last night after the near-death experience on the scoutship. Looking around, he saw Kirsten asleep on the floor, a pillow from somewhere placed under her head. Teresa was nowhere in sight.

For a moment, Jake's gaze lingered on Kirsten, sleeping peacefully if somewhat uncomfortably on the floor.

Kirsten was not a classic beauty, but she had a physicality to her that drew people's attention, even though she was largely oblivious to it.

Sometimes in jest, Jake called her "The Valkyrie" – he said she looked like the winged warriors of the ancient Norse legends. Her face carried a strong intelligence that had impressed Jake since their first meeting inside *Pandora.* Now, her streaked blond hair was twisted and unkept, her uniform wrinkled, her boots kicked off and lying beside her, dirty socks showing beneath the blanket that someone – he assumed Teresa – had thrown over her.

Jake thought about how Kirsten was such a contrast to Teresa, and yet their differences made them such a productive team.

Our differences are what make us strong - because our differences allow us to fit together perfectly, like puzzle pieces. Building blocks of a bigger whole. A team of divergence, where our divergence actually makes us stronger...

Teresa, taller than Kirsten, with flashing brown eyes and black, straight hair, had the build of a professional athlete. And she was a dynamo - usually the first one to start something and the last one to finish it. She had a reputation around RDF Headquarters of being a hard-living, hard-loving woman you surely did not want to piss off.

Kirsten, on the other hand, was a peacemaker. She found people with problems and helped them see the solution.

Sometimes, Jake thought wryly, Teresa did the opposite. She found people without problems and gave them some.

Groaning, Jake got up and walked over to the mirror by the entryway; what he saw there confirmed his suspicions. He looked a mess.

In the mirror, he saw a tall man, well-muscled but not heavy, still reasonably trim for his age. But his uniform was wrinkled, his dark hair askew, and he needed a shave badly.

Jake noticed a gray streak in his hair that he hadn't seen before. He sighed. Leaning forward, he poked at the small scar on his right forehead, trending up into his scalp – the mark of an ejection from an F-90 in 2115, during the Brush War.

He did his best to comb his hair with his fingers, pulled at his uniform, tried to make himself presentable. He walked back over to the couch just as the doorbell chimed.

The security screen on the coffee table showed Atsuko Kawasaki, head of RDF Intelligence. Leaning over to grab the screen, Jake fumbled for the switch to open the door, dropped the screen on the floor, grabbed it, and finally hit the proper switch. He looked up to see Kirsten sitting up, laughing at him.

Atsuko entered, shut the door behind her and came over to sit across from Jake. Teresa came out of her bedroom, patting her damp hair with a towel, just in time to hear the conversation.

"You're not gonna like it, boss," Atsuko said.

"I already know," said Jake. "Another assassination attempt, right?"

"Yep," said Atsuko. "The NavAI had been deliberately set to take you straight into the Moon as soon as you initiated the course for Mars."

"So, an inside job," said Jake. "Get all three of us at once."

"Right," said Atsuko.

"OK, let's get on it, try to track down the source."

"Already done," said Atsuko. "The Honorable Margaret Bolt, President of the United States. Via her dirty tricks guy, Frank Hale."

"Can we prove it?" said Jake.

Atsuko shook her head. "Of course not. They're too good at covering their tracks. But that's where it came from."

Kirsten sighed. "Jake, we're not going to be safe as long as we're on Earth. We've got to get off this planet before they succeed in killing us."

Jake nodded. "I know. MarsBase is almost viable, we'll go ahead and relocate ahead of schedule, I think. Next month."

Kirsten thought. "That's going to be tough. We'll have to run a skeleton crew until more modules are finished."

Teresa interjected. "It's better than staying here on Earth like a sitting duck, while Bolt and every other whiney-ass politician on the planet tries to kill us."

Jake steepled his fingers, thinking. "Exactly. Tough or not, let's get off this ungrateful planet for good. We're trying to save them and they're trying to kill us. So to hell with them for now. We'll go someplace where we can be safe."

Teresa patted her hair with the towel. "So…next month, then?"

Jake nodded. "Yep. MarsBase has two modules complete now, enough space for fifty people. We'll go ahead and relocate ourselves and our own staff next month and bring up the rest of HQ as we complete more modules."

Atsuko frowned. "We don't have enough docking ports on the Mars orbital station yet. We need to complete a couple more of those before it'll be viable."

Jake agreed. "Put some priority on that, Terese. We can't stay here any longer. We gotta go. Or they're gonna kill us."

A BOMB SHOULD DO IT

Margaret Bolt was elected to the Presidency of the United States in 2120. Considered by most historians to be the most ruthless president in U. S. history, Bolt acted swiftly to curtail freedoms in America, packing the Supreme Court with members of her neo-Nazi North American Freedom League (NAFL). Bolt then used the Court to erode the ability of Congress to keep her in check. Re-elected in 2124, by late 2125 Bolt was firmly in control of all aspects of government and had replaced nearly all Federal officials with NAFL members.

- RimWiki, 2265 Edition.

Washington, D. C.

"Frank, I'm getting tired of your excuses."

President Margaret Bolt glared over the top of the Resolute Desk at Frank Hale, standing before her. His face was not happy. Neither was hers.

"Yes, Madam President," Frank spoke softly. "They were lucky again. I'll need a little more time."

"Lucky? You've had more than two years already! How long does it take to kill that son of a bitch?"

Frank nodded in agreement. "Yes, Madam President. It's taking too long. I agree. But the man is just plain lucky. And that damn alien starship watches over him like a hawk. I don't know how she does it, but she seems to know our every move."

"Obviously, she's intercepting your communications. You don't have to be a rocket scientist to figure that out."

"Yes, Madam."

"I want Jake Hammett dead - now. And those other two if you can get them. Once that's done, that ship will have no choice but to come to us. We'll be in control. So get it done, Frank. Or I'll find another dirty tricks guy. There's plenty of them out there, you know. Now get out."

"Yes, Madam," Frank answered. He turned and departed the Oval Office, his brain already thinking ahead.

It has to be a bomb. That's the best way. Get all three of them, and untraceable. And I hear they're going to Mars next month. There's an opportunity...

As Frank walked into his office suite, he waved his arm at his right-hand girl, Lauren McCall. "In my office," he growled. Lauren dutifully followed him in, closing the sound-proof door behind, and sat in front of him.

Frank glared at her. "Has the office been swept today?" he asked angrily.

Lauren nodded. "Yes. We're clear."

"OK. From now on, no electronic communications. That bitch starship *Pandora* has to be monitoring us. There's no other explanation as to why so many of our operations fail. So from here on out, I want everything face-to-face. Got it?"

"Got it, sir," agreed Lauren.

"Now. Madame President is not happy. One more failure, and I think we're done. So we can't afford any more screw-ups. You clear on that, Lauren?"

"Clear, sir."

"OK. Where does the RDF stand on ship production?"

Lauren consulted her tablet. "They've just completed two more scoutships, the *Canopus* and the *Rigel*. Those two are up at *Yehliu* undergoing shakedown trials. They've got nineteen other ships in the pipeline - four more scoutships, five corvettes, three frigates, three asteroid miners, and four colony ships."

"When are they supposedly leaving for Mars?"

"According to our inside man, in about a month."

"And we think they'll travel on the *Denali*, right?" interrupted Frank.

"That's what we think right now. She's the first armed warship so far. Two railguns, two missile tubes. And she'll be just out of her initial shakedown cruise. We're sure Jake will want to ride out to Mars on her."

"But she's still in production at Huntsville right now?"

"Yes, sir. Just finishing up."

Frank leaned forward. In spite of the soundproof office, he lowered his voice.

"Before that ship leaves the assembly line, get a bomb on it. Put in somewhere in the engine room, or in the weapons systems. Make it look like part of the gear. When that ship leaves for Mars with Jake and his bitches on it, make sure it never arrives."

SECOND THOUGHTS

Every heart sings a song, incomplete, until another heart whispers back.

- Plato.

RDF Denali - SpaceDock Earth

Their enemies had labeled them the "Unholy Three" - a name which the media had picked up, and now used frequently to describe them. And a name the three of them had gleefully adopted and used among themselves - especially Teresa, with her wild and wicked sense of humor.

Today, the Unholy Three packed their bags for the last time on Earth and took a shuttle up to SpaceDock *Yehliu*. Disembarking, they took the walkalong to the new corvette *Denali*, just out of her initial shakedown cruise.

Denali was the fourth functional ship to come off the StarCrafters assembly line in Huntsville, Alabama. Jake loved her clean, functional lines. Standing inside the spacedock portal, gazing at the newly completed corvette, Jake couldn't help but feel a burst of pride and satisfaction. Teresa and Kirsten had spent a few minutes looking her over, but then had gone on into the ship to put away their gear. But Jake stayed behind, looking at a ship that was - to him - a thing of beauty.

She was matte-black, 125 meters in length, 44 meters in beam, and followed the general wedge shape of most of the ship designs provided by *Pandora*. She was also the first RDF starship to be armed. Hidden in her flanks were two railgun ports and two missile tubes. Tiny she might be compared to a frigate or a battleship, but she was the first warship of

Humanity's long journey to the stars. The first step in a long, one-hundred-year effort to prepare for the Bat Empire.

After some minutes admiring the corvette, Jake forced himself away, entered the portal, and stepped through the hatch onto the boarding area. A bosun's whistle blew and the side party of eight crew members saluted. Jake turned and saluted the RDF ensign painted on the forward bulkhead, then turned and saluted the side party and Cassie Blocker, standing in front of them.

"Permission to come aboard, Captain," said Jake.

"Permission granted, Admiral, and welcome aboard," replied Cassie, newly appointed as master of the *Denali.* Completing his salute, Jake then extended his hand to her.

Cassie had rapidly become one of his favorite officers. Coming originally from the Royal Navy, she had been captain of a wet-navy frigate. When the RDF was formed, Teresa – as Director of Operations and Logistics – had faced many difficult problems. One of the most troublesome was recruitment of qualified officers and crew for starships. After much pain, argument, bad language and occasional over-indulgence in whiskey, Teresa had settled on an approach that seemed to be working.

She recruited from all military forces on Earth, without regard to nationality or ethnic background. Teresa offered compensation that was significantly higher than the crewmember's previous job. Personnel retained their rank and date of seniority when they transferred to the RDF. And Teresa only accepted the cream of the crop.

And finally, to ensure that governments cooperated with her, Teresa had developed some interesting approaches to blackmail. Her main leverage was that any government which resisted – for example, by interfering with transfers from their military to the RDF - was blacklisted for further space exploration or colonization via RDF technology.

This quickly brought the governments into line – no government wanted to be cut out of cheap and easy space exploration and the potential that could accrue from that.

Thus, six months earlier, Cassie Blocker had transferred to Geneva from her home in Portsmouth, England. As an RDF starship captain, she had quickly impressed Teresa and Jake with her competence, humor, and enthusiasm. After training on the capabilities and operating interfaces of the still incomplete *Denali* in the simulator, and working as Chief Engineer for the test flights of the *Sirius*, Cassie had accepted the newly commissioned corvette just three weeks earlier. Since that time, *Denali* had completed two short shakedown cruises, and spent a week back in spacedock correcting minor issues.

Today's flight to Mars would be the third and final shakedown cruise for the corvette; after dropping Jake, Teresa and Kirsten at Mars, the *Denali* would go outbound to HD 12051, a G5 star 80 light years from Earth, performing double duty both as a final test flight and a quick exploration of that star system.

Commander Ming Chou, the *Denali*'s Executive Officer - XO - escorted Jake to his cabin. Jake stowed his bag, then sat at his desk for a moment. His mind was whirling. Jake was in that rare state where he didn't know what to do.

A month earlier – after the near-death experience in the *Sirius* - Jake, Kirsten and Teresa had sat in Teresa's apartment and made a pact to get married; to create a new culture for the RDF, based on the rigors of living in space for extended periods of time, in close quarters, with death always hovering nearby.

Their reasoning had been based on the concept that space was a new kind of environment for Humans – and required a new kind of society. One that was not bound and restricted by thousands of years of bigotry, religious intolerance, and sexual power struggles. The three had decided that forming this marriage was the first step in a long process of creating this new society.

Teresa had put it most succinctly, Jake thought. She had called it Teresa's Rule: "Love the ones you're probably going to die with."

Teresa had then proposed the idea of conducting the marriage ceremony on their trip to Mars. And now it was time.

Jake heard the clanks of undocking. He heard the engine power up, and the ship began to move. They were on their way.

And he was supposed to be in the Common Room in a half-hour, getting married.

I just can't do it. It just won't work. One man married to two women. How can that possibly work?

His hatch opened and Teresa and Kirsten entered. Kirsten moved to his bunk and sat, while Teresa stood before him hands on hips.

"Told you," she said to Kirsten, glaring at Jake. "He's got cold feet."

Jake looked at her. He shrugged. "I just can't do it, Terese. It can't work."

Teresa shook her head. "Tell me why it can't work."

Jake shrugged. "What happens when one of us has to make a life and death choice, choose who will live and who will die? What happens then?"

"Bullshit. That's no excuse. We could live the rest of our lives and never have to make that choice."

Jake nodded weakly. "OK. What about the Earth governments? We've already got most of the Earth governments against us. Now they've got wind of this. It makes it that much harder to get acceptance for our plans. And the evangelicals are going berserk, and that's just the beginning."

"And we're never going to live on Earth again, are we?" asked Kirsten from her spot on the bunk. She waved her hand at the cabin, the ship. "We need to create a new society, one that works in this environment."

"I'm sorry, girls. I just can't do it."

As Teresa glared at Jake, Kirsten rose from her spot on the bunk, moved behind Jake, and put her hands on his shoulders. Holding him, she spoke quietly.

"So you are saying you don't love us?"

Jake shook his head. "You know better than that."

"Say it."

"You know that I love you, Kirsten."

"And Teresa?"

Jake looked up at Teresa, still standing in front of him, her face still angry.

"You know I love you too, Teresa."

"So what's the fucking problem, squid?" blurted out Teresa. "You can fly a fucking F82 off a carrier, you can get shot down and spend time in a prisoner of war camp, you can take on a one-hundred-year project to save Earth - but you can't go through with a little marriage ceremony?"

In the long silence that followed, Jake Hammett came to a realization.

He would never live on Earth again. He was sure of it. His future was in the stars. And his future was with these two women. Come life or death, his future was with Kirsten and Teresa.

And Jake began to see it. Just a glimmer. The reason *Pandora* had put them together. It was still murky; but there was a reason, even if he couldn't discern it right now. Something important.

And this was what Kirsten and Teresa wanted. To resist them at this point could break them apart forever. It could spell the end of their partnership. And according to *Pandora,* that could mean the death of Earth.

Pandora, *you witch. What have you done to us?*

Jake rose from his seat.

"OK. Let's get it done."

DENALI

If life were predictable, it would cease to be life, and be without flavor.

- Eleanor Roosevelt.

Denali - enroute to Mars

Forty minutes later, Teresa and Kirsten stood in *Denali*'s Common Room, with Jake beside them. In front of them stood Cassie Blocker. Many of Cassie's crew, members of the RDF HQ staff, and other friends also waited expectantly.

Jake, Teresa, and Kirsten had explained to Cassie what they wanted; Cassie had agreed to perform the ceremony. Now they clasped hands together, and Teresa read the marriage vows they had written out for themselves.

"Before us we face decades of danger, pain, and death as we prepare to face a horrible enemy. We cannot know who will live and who will die in these years to come. So today we choose each other as lovers and companions on this journey into an unknown future. From this ceremony we will be bound to each other in life and death, ready to offer our lives for each other and for Humanity, and this will be the watchword of the Rim Defense Force now and forever. May the Creator help us in our efforts."

Then Cassie took up the ceremony.

"Do you, Teresa Tolleson, take Kirsten Monk and Jake Hammett as your legal mates for the period of five years from this date?"

"I do," said Teresa, winking at Jake and Kirsten.

"Do you, Kirsten Monk, take Teresa Tolleson and Jake

Hammett as your legal mates for the period of five years from this date?"

"I do," said Kirsten, gazing at Teresa.

"And Jake Hammett, do you take Kirsten Monk and Teresa Tolleson as your legal mates for the period of five years from this date?"

"He does," said Kirsten and Teresa simultaneously.

"He has to answer for himself, ladies," Cassie said, grinning hugely.

Jake shook his head. "Do you see what I'm up against here, Cassie?"

Cassie just smiled back at him, waiting.

"I do," sighed Jake. "As if I had a choice," he muttered under his breath.

Cassie, laughing, continued. "Then by the authority vested in me as a starship Captain in the Rim Defense Force, I pronounce the three of you wedded. You may now kiss, dance, or fight, whatever turns you on."

Teresa turned and grabbed Kirsten and Jake in a bear hug, not quite able to wrap her arms around them completely, but able to pull them all in close. Cassie and the rest of the RDF staff broke into applause, and somewhere in the back of the room a champagne cork popped.

"Party time!" yelled Teresa and broke off the hug to head for the bar in the back of the room.

Kirsten held on to Jake for a moment longer, staring into his eyes. Very quietly, she said: "I know you love me, Jake. But I also know you probably love Teresa more. The reality is that we've both loved Teresa for a while," she said.

Kirsten paused, then continued.

"I hope you can love me the same way someday."

Jake looked at Kirsten and pulled her closer. "I promise you, Kirsten, I will."

And the bomb went off.

The world around them exploded. Chairs, furniture, broken glass, splinters, people went everywhere. Jake was slammed to the wall, as Kirsten was ripped from his arms and flung to the floor. The impact with the wall left Jake stunned. As he slowly merged back into reality, he realized he was partially deaf; he could see people screaming, but the sound was muted, barely discernible. One eye wasn't working right; he realized it was covered in blood. He wiped the blood away, and the vision in that eye came back, albeit still blurry.

Kristen. She was in my arms.

Jake looked around. He saw Kirsten, lying on the floor a few feet away. She was unconscious. Before he could move to her, Teresa appeared in front of him, crawling on her hands and knees. She had donned an emergency oxygen mask and had two additional masks in her hands. She glanced at Jake, saw that he was conscious, and nodded, handing him a mask. Then she moved to Kirsten and began attending to her. As Teresa worked on Kirsten, she pulled her mask aside for a moment and spoke over her shoulder to Jake.

"Jake, I'll take care of Kirsten. You get things organized. The air's bleeding out pretty fast. You need to get everyone in suits."

Jake gave a weak nod. With some effort, he got first to his knees, then managed to stand up. Swaying, he looked around the room.

The dead lay everywhere. Limbs separated from bodies were here and there in the mess. Blood covered the deck, running like water. In one corner, he saw Cassie Blocker, just beginning to move as she regained consciousness. He moved first to the emergency locker, grabbed another oxygen mask, then went to Cassie and placed it over her face. Then he helped her up as she tried to stand.

"What the fuck?" asked Cassie.

"Bomb," muttered Jake, looking around. "Looks like it was aft of us, from the way the walls are bent."

"Oh, God," spat Cassie, looking at the carnage surrounding them. Cassie's brain began to work again. "Well, we have at least partial pressure. So the airtight doors must have slammed shut. At least that worked."

Jake nodded. “Yeah. But it won’t last more than another few minutes at most. Too many holes in the walls.”

“Right,” said Cassie. She moved to a locker, began pulling out emergency pressure suits. She handed one to Jake; they quickly stripped down to their underwear and put on the protective suits.

Jake carried pressure suits to Teresa and Kirsten. Kirsten was awake now, woozy but conscious. Teresa began stripping down to get into her pressure suit, while Jake knelt beside Kirsten and began removing her outer clothing. As Kirsten recovered her senses, she gently pushed Jake away, sat up, and took over the task of undressing herself and getting into her suit.

“Tell you what,” said Cassie. “I’ll start working my way to the bridge. You work aft, try to see how bad it is. Let me know if we still have an engine.”

“We don’t. I can already tell. We’re coasting. But we still have grav; that means the comp is still working. That’s a plus.”

“Right. OK, let me know what you find out. I’ll be forward.”

As Cassie headed to the tiny airlock-type hatch to exit, Jake stood and looked at Teresa, speaking suit-to-suit via his MEMSAI.

<If you and Kirsten will take charge of the rest of the survivors, I’m heading aft to check damage>

Teresa nodded, and began moving to other people in the room, checking to see who was alive and who was dead. Jake gave a final look around, moved to the airlock hatch, and headed aft.

As Jake worked his way aft in the shattered *Denali*, he found ever-increasing damage. He had passed through four airtight doors so far. Two of them still had integrity; the last two, however, had been bowed out, blasted out of their frames. There was no air after that point. And no survivors. Just broken bodies.

<Cassie, the bomb was pretty clearly in the engine room>

he sent to Cassie.

<Roger that. I'm almost to the bridge>

Shoving aside another fallen ceiling panel and a mess of wiring, Jake came to the engine room hatch. Like the others, it was blasted out of its frame. Stepping through the open hatch, he was shocked by what he saw.

There was no ship behind the hatch. Jake was looking at stars. The entire rear of the ship was gone, blasted away.

<No chance of engine power, Cassie> he called. <The entire back half of the ship is missing>

<Well, we're in trouble, then. We were almost halfway to Mars. With no engines to transfer to orbit, we'll impact the planet in six hours>

<How about the shuttle in the launch bay?>

<Toast. No chance she can fly>

<OK. Comms?>

<That's the good news. We've got a comm up, we've notified *Yehliu*. They're doing an emergency prep of *Canopus* to come out and get us. If they can get here fast enough, they may be able to tow *Denali* into a stable orbit>

<What's their ETA?>

<Five hours>

<How's air?>

<Well, that's the bad news. We'll lose all on-board air in another thirty minutes. After that, we'll only have the suits. They'll give us another four hours>

<So we run out of air thirty minutes before *Canopus* arrives...>

<You got it>

BROKEN

Waste no more time arguing about what a good man should be. Be one.

- Marcus Aurelius, Roman Emperor

RDF Denali - Coasting toward Mars

"What if we all went into different compartments, so that we made maximum use of the remaining air before it all escapes?" asked Ming Chou.

The survivors had gathered on the bridge. It seemed to be holding air better than some of the other compartments. There were twelve of them...out of an original crew of sixty.

"I'm glad you're thinking out of the box," said Cassie to her XO. "But even compartments where the airtight doors sealed up properly have holes in their walls from the blast. The air will be gone in a matter of minutes now. We'll have to depend on our suits.

Glances went around the group. All were standing near the center of the bridge, with their suit helmets off, having one last conversation before the air was completely gone. And the meaning of the glances was clear to all.

Some could survive if others died sooner.

Jake noted the looks and shook his head. "Let's not give up yet, folks. Keep thinking."

Kristen, still holding a bloody bandage to her head, spoke next. "Let's approach it logically. Is there any air on this ship, anywhere? In the cargo bay, maybe?"

Cassie frowned, thinking hard. "The cargo bay's gone. It got blasted away with the rear of the ship. But..."

Cassie looked at Jake. "The shuttle. It's wrecked...but it has emergency air tanks. What if those tanks are still intact?"

Jake nodded. "Now we're thinking. I'll go take a look."

"No," said Teresa. "We all have to go. Those tanks are too large for you to bring back here. We'll go to them."

"Right," Jake responded. "Let's go."

"No," said Kirsten. She gazed around the group. "We use up all the air here on the bridge first. Then we go."

Commander Chou looked puzzled. "But...if there's air there in the shuttle...we should go now. Then we'd know!"

"But if there's no air there...then we've wasted the air here on the bridge," replied Kirsten. "We need to use it all before it's gone."

"What difference does it make?" objected Chou. "If there's no air in the shuttle, we're all dead anyway!"

Kirsten shook her head in negation.

"No. We're not. Some of us can live."

As her words sank in, the room went quiet. Everybody finally realized what Kirsten was saying.

If there was no air in the shuttle, the only way anyone could survive was to use the air of the others.

There could be a few survivors. If everyone else sacrificed themselves.

Twenty-four minutes later, the air in the bridge became unbreathable. "Time to go," said Teresa, coughing. The survivors fitted their suit helmets on and tested their systems. When all were ready, Teresa looked at Jake.

Jake nodded, understanding. Cracking open the hatch, he led the way out of the broken bridge and into the blasted, airless corridor outside. One by one, the survivors followed.

Working their way through broken walls and tangled wires, they made their way to the launch bay. It took them twenty minutes. When they arrived, they found the shuttle lying upside down, pockmarked with holes from flying shrapnel. Jake made his way inside, carefully, not wanting to tear his suit on the debris. A few minutes later, he came out of the destroyed shuttle, his face grim. He looked at the group and shook his head.

"No joy," he said, his voice dejected. "All the air bottles are holed. They're empty."

Dejected, the group slumped to the launch bay floor. There was no place to go. And no reason to go there.

<*Denali* to *Yehliu*. Come in, *Yehliu*> Cassie called over her MEMSAI.

<*Yehliu* here, go ahead>

<What's the status of *Canopus*>

<She's just finished up consumables loading. Latest estimate is four hours, thirty-five minutes to your position>

<Roger, we'll be in the launch bay>

<Copy>

Cassie glanced over at Jake. She switched to private channel.

<We'll all be dead before they arrive>

<Yeah, I know. You know what we have to do>

<Yeah. Give the order>

<Not my place, Cassie. It's your ship>

<Well...you and Teresa and Kirsten...the three of you have to live. *Pandora* says you are the only ones...>

Jake interrupted.

<No. We'll draw straws. We'll take our chances like everyone else>

<*Pandora* says...>

<No, Cassie. We take our chances with the rest of you. That's an order>

Cassie sighed, audible over the channel.

<You are one stubborn son-of-a-bitch, Jake>

<You're not the first one to tell me>

Switching back to main channel, Cassie said the words everyone had been dreading, but expecting.

<OK. It's simple math. Six of us can live. We draw straws for the remaining oxygen>

In the moment that followed, no one spoke. Then Commander Chou said the words everyone was thinking.

<What happens to the losers?>

Cassie bowed her head. Then she raised it, passing her gaze around the survivors sitting on the launch bay floor.

<They can make their peace with God in their own way. Me, personally? I'll step out of the ship and look at the stars for a bit before I go>

RDF *Canopus*

Captain Lois Vetton, pressed into her command chair by the force of 8g, stared at the holo, calculated numbers, and didn't like the answer.

"Any word?" she grunted out against the pressure, staring at her comm technician.

"No, mum, nothing since their last transmission," answered Yeoman Pike, his voice also strained.

It had been twenty minutes since their last contact with *Denali*. Cassie had reported they were preparing to draw straws for survival. The winners would get the remaining oxygen. The losers would take a short walk out the launch bay door. At least that way, six people could survive.

Then nothing after that.

Lois glanced over at Atsuko Kawasaki. Atsuko had been at *Yehliu* when the call came in; she had insisted on coming along. In the mad rush to put together a rescue mission, Lois had not objected; she knew there was something unique about Atsuko, that she had a special relationship with Jake, Teresa, and Kirsten. Better to have her with them.

Now Atsuko looked back at Lois, both of them thinking the same thing.

Either their comms went down - or they're all dead.

Lois gave Atsuko a small smile. Switching to private channel, she spoke.

<Let's not give up hope yet. Maybe they just lost comms>

UNBOWED

Our greatest glory is not in never failing, but in rising every time we fail.
- Confucius, Chinese Philosopher

RDF Denali - Coasting toward Mars

Among the debris scattered around the launch bay, they found an empty container, and several pieces of paper. Cassie took a page of white paper and tore it into small strips, rolled the strips up into small round balls, and put them in the container. She did the same to a page of dark paper.

Six white balls. Six dark balls. Six people who could live. Six people who would die.

Cassie mixed them thoroughly, first stirring them, then shaking the container vigorously.

"It's time," she said. "Everyone reach in and take one."

Suddenly, Jake reached out and stopped her.

"No," he said over the channel. "Wait."

As everyone looked at him, Jake glared at the deck for a second. Then, raising his head and staring at them, he spoke again.

"We don't give up this easily. Who knows what could be in this hangar? Everyone spread out, look for air!"

Cassie objected. "Jake - we're just about out of time. If we don't do this now, there won't be enough air left for six. It'll only be five, or even four!"

"How much time do we have?"

Cassie thought, did some math in her head.

"We've got maybe ten minutes. After that, only five can

survive."

"Then by God, we use those ten minutes! Spread out! Look into every storage container, every locker, every room! Go!"

With renewed animation, the twelve survivors got up from their place on the floor and began searching the launch bay, in one last desperate attempt to live.

Eight minutes later, they had found nothing. Cassie made a call over the general channel.

"Everyone, back to the shuttle. We're out of time. Let's get this done."

Dejected, the survivors began to re-assemble. As they moved back to Cassie and sat in a circle on the deck, Cassie counted heads. Jake and Ming Chou were missing.

"Jake? Ming? Where are you?"

"Over behind the shuttle. There's a compartment here we can't get into. We're trying to pry the door open. Go ahead without us. Cassie, you can draw for Ming and I."

"Roger that."

Sitting back down on the deck, Cassie prepared to pass the container around - the container containing life or death for each of them. Those who drew the black would hand their oxygen to others - then step out of the shattered launch bay into empty space; with just enough time to look at the stars one last time.

Suddenly there was a shout over the channel from Jake.

"Hold on, Cassie! We found something!"

"What?"

"Come look, everyone. Come quick!"

With renewed hope, the group sprang up and rushed around the upside-down shuttle. On the backside, in the narrow space between the topsy-turvy shuttle and the wall, Jake and Ming stood beside an open storage compartment door. Jake had pulled out a large air bottle from the compartment.

"These are the empty emergency bottles that have been used."

Cassie's voice contained utter frustration, her hopes dashed.

"If they've been used, how does that help us? They're empty!"

Even through his helmet, Cassie could see Jake grin.

"Yes. They're used. They're marked as empty. But they replace them when they show ten percent left."

As the implication hit Cassie, she realized what Jake was saying.

"You mean...?"

"Yep," grinned Jake. "There's eight bottles here, and every one of them has ten percent of its oxygen left!"

RDF *Canopus*

Canopus snugged up against the husk of *Denali* near the launch bay, and the emergency security team rushed over to the wreck. Lois thought about going with them, but...

A captain doesn't leave their ship in an emergency. I'll stay here and wait for the news.

Six minutes later, she received the call.

<We have twelve survivors. About half of them unconscious, but still alive>

Lois closed her eyes and sighed in relief. Two hours to put together the rescue effort, load emergency consumables on the Canopus, and undock from *Yehliu.* Two and a half hours smashed into her seat at 8g to get here in time.

I don't ever want to do that again. But it was worth it.

Thirty minutes later, Lois was in the infirmary of *Canopus*, staring at Jake, Kirsten, and Teresa in their narrow hospital beds. They were pale but coherent. It had been close. Half of the survivors had already gone unconscious when the rescue team got to them. The group had survived by the skin of their teeth.

"Thanks, Lois. That had to be tough - two and a half hours at 8g. We owe you big time," said Teresa.

Lois grinned. "Enough to give me my choice of

assignment?"

Teresa managed a weak smile. "And what would that be?"

"I want to take the first scout to the Bats. I want to see those blood-thirsty bastards for myself."

Teresa looked over at Jake in the next bed. Jake shrugged, then nodded. "Fine with me."

"Well, the boss says yes, so I guess that'll work," smiled Teresa.

"Thanks, Teresa," Lois said. "I'll leave you to feel better." Grinning like an idiot at the three of them, Lois departed.

Kirsten looked at Jake. "Well, husband, how are you feeling about things now?"

With a start, Jake realized what Kirsten was saying. They had completed the marriage ceremony, just before the bomb went off.

He was married.

As his brain whirled, Jake came to a conclusion.

"You know what, Kirsten?"

"What?"

"Teresa's right."

"Of course I am," came a mutter from Teresa.

"What do you mean?" asked Kirsten.

"Teresa's Rule: Love the ones you're probably going to die with," said Jake.

Teresa managed a weak laugh. "You got that right!"

"But now what?" asked Kirsten. "You know where that bomb came from..."

"Margaret Bolt," snarled Teresa. "Let's drop a kinetic on her and get this over with..."

"No," objected Kirsten, always the voice of reason. "This is a crisis point not just for us, but for the entire RDF. This is a point where we decide if we live by justice - or by anarchy. What we do now will set the tone for the next one hundred years."

In the long silence that followed, Jake realized Kirsten was right. To take action without due process would corrupt the RDF now and forever. It would become an organization of reaction, rather than action. In the next few days, every eye in the world would be on him, and the RDF.

Their new space navy had to have rules. Otherwise, it was chaos.

"Right, then," Jake finally spoke. "Kirsten, I'm putting this under you and the Colony Office. Do the investigation and give me a proper recommendation."

"Got it," Kirsten replied.

"And in the meantime, Teresa and I will focus on getting MarsBase up and operational, completing the next set of ships, and sending Lois to scout the Bats."

"Are you going to give Lois *Canopus* for the scout?" asked Teresa.

Jake shook his head. "No. For future scouts, yeah, a scout ship will be plenty good. But for this first one, I'm giving her a frigate."

"You mean the *Beijing*?"

"Yep. That's the first frigate coming off the line. I'm going to let Lois have it for the scout. If she gets into trouble, I want her to have some firepower."

"Harder to hide a frigate."

"Harder to kill it, too."

MARSBASE

Wisely, and slow. They stumble that run fast.
- William Shakespeare, Playwright

Sol System - MarsBase

Four weeks after the disaster on *Denali*, Jake was restless, pacing, and pissed off. In his new office on MarBase, Kirsten, Teresa, and Atsuko sat nearby, watching him.

"Jake, calm down. I know you're pissed. But we have to make good decisions here," said Teresa.

"How about we just drop a couple of kinetics on her?" Jake growled.

"We can't prove it was her," responded Atsuko. "There's a half-dozen governments it could be."

"It was her," Jake argued. "I know it. I can feel it in my bones."

Teresa sighed. "Jake. We can't prove it was Bolt. We're safer now, off Earth. Let's focus on moving forward."

Jake, frustrated, rolled his eyes and raised his hands in frustration.

"So just let her get away with it?"

"For now," said Teresa. "Her time will come. We're safe enough here, now. We can control who comes to Mars, and screen them thoroughly. I don't think she can hurt us here."

Jake turned, slammed himself into the chair behind his desk.

"OK. I know when I'm outnumbered. But if that witch makes one more move at us - even the slightest - I'm dropping a rock on her!"

"Yes, husband," said Teresa, a glint in her eye.

Jake looked at her. "You really delight in saying that, don't you?"

As Teresa winked at Jake, Kirsten and Atsuko giggled.

"You three are senior captains in the RDF. You're not setting a very good example," Jake growled.

"Why, I think we're setting a perfect example," argued Teresa. "We're demonstrating how to have fun and be competent at the same time!"

"Fine," growled Jake again. "What about the *Denali*?"

"Shattered," Teresa said, suddenly serious. "We shoved all the major pieces into Mars orbit, but she's a wreck. We'll have to scrap her."

Jake heaved a long sigh, raised his head, and looked out the window at the Martian landscape. The window was fake, of course - they were eight feet underground, buried beneath the surface. But the faux window looked entirely real. In the distance, Jake could see the floor of the deep valley stretching to the north, rising steadily toward the far-away surface of Mars.

To build MarsBase, the RDF had selected a narrow part of the chasm of Valles Marineris and dug deep into the Martian soil. They then roofed a section over with a sandwich of aerogel and regolith. The two sides open to the canyon - north and south - had also been closed off, while the walls of the canyon itself provided radiation and weather protection from the other two directions.

Just beyond the north end of the complex, a small factory performed chemical removal of perchlorate from the native Martian soil, yielding a compound amenable to the growth of Earth plants. Four large greenhouses stood at the corners of the site, illuminated by artificial light. Four nuclear generators, two primaries and two backups, sat at opposite ends of the complex.

At the north end of the complex, a large, enclosed dock for shuttles had been built, with a rotary docking bay which received shuttles and rotated them to the pressurized section of an underground garage. Using the rotary docking bay, shuttles could be simultaneously received and launched, like bullets from an old West six-shooter.

At the opposite end of the complex - the south end - was a large, just-finished geodesic dome. It was the future home of *Pandora*. In a few days, she would relocate from Geneva to MarsBase, leaving Earth behind for good.

"We've come a long way," said Jake, gazing out the window.

"And we've got a long way to go," said Kirsten.

"Right," Jake said, turning back to them. He looked at Teresa. "I want *Denali* salvaged and repaired. I'm going to make her my personal corvette. They're not going to win this one."

"She's not worth it," argued Teresa. "It'll take longer to put her back together than to build a new corvette from scratch. And cost more."

"Understood. But I want her to be a symbol for us. We don't die so easily."

Teresa glanced at Kirsten, then back to Jake, and nodded. "OK. We'll collect up all the pieces and tow them back to *Yehliu*, put her back together for you."

"Thank you, Teresa. I know you don't agree. But she saved our lives. That means something to me."

"Understood. So, OK...next subject. Colony status."

Kirsten nodded. "40 Eridani A. We think the third planet is a viable candidate for our first colony. We've tentatively named the planet 'Liberty'. I'm leaving this afternoon on the *Rigel* to go check it out."

"And if it checks out?"

"The first colony transport, *Yorkshire*, is off the assembly line at *Yehliu* and on her last shakedown cruise. If Liberty is a viable planet, we'll have a thousand colonists there by next March."

"Good. And after that?"

"We think we can send out a colony ship every six months after that. In five years, we'll have ten colony planets in place."

Jake grunted. "That'll go a long way toward giving us an interstellar infrastructure to deal with the Bats."

"Which brings us to the Aeolians," interjected Teresa.

"Exactly," said Jake. "Where do we stand on them?"

"We've sent the *Acrux* to monitor them. She's standing off in the Kuiper belt off Aeolis, collecting electronic intelligence - ELINT."

"And?"

"Nothing so far that we didn't already know from *Pandora.* A matriarchal empire, descended from some ancient Greeks and Amazons who got abducted from Troy in 1184 B. C. and dropped on the planet. They've grown like gangbusters since then. They've currently got forty-one planets in their Empire. Ruled by a nasty Empress named Miranda. A very warlike society. Every member of the nobility spends a tour in their space navy. And their navy is very, very good. We wouldn't stand a chance against them. They'd smoke us in a week and go home to tea."

Jake grunted, clearly unhappy. He looked at Atsuko. "And you're going out there?"

"Yes, Teresa and I leave in two days on the *Chengdu* to go meet up with the *Acrux*. We'll figure out how to set up a spook station there in their Empire."

"At least they're Human. We can put spies into their society without being too obvious."

"Yeah. If we can do it without getting caught."

"Well, that's the trick, isn't it?"

Jake turned back to Teresa, who was managing the agenda. "OK. What else?"

"Last subject for today. Scouting the Bats..."

"Yeah. Lois ready to leave?"

"Yes. The *Beijing* has completed her shakedown and is ready to go. Lois and her crew are settled onboard. They are champing at the bit to get moving. All they need is your go-ahead."

"Are we doing the right thing here?" asked Jake, looking

back and forth between the three of them.

"We have to scout them," said Kirsten. "We have to know what we're up against."

"But if they detect us..."

"It's a chance we have to take. We're flying blind right now. All we know is what *Pandora* has told us - that they'll find us eventually, no matter what we do. And if they find us right now, we're toast. I don't think we have any choice. We have to go take a look at them. We have to know our enemy."

"OK. But Lois needs to be damn careful. Our entire species is at stake here."

"She knows it," said Teresa. "We've talked about it long and hard. She'll sacrifice herself before she lets them get any intel on us."

"You mean the nuke..."

"Yeah. Every ship that goes into Bat space will have a self-destruct nuke on board. If the Bats detect Lois, and she can't escape, then...well, bang. No more ship."

"God, I hate to send her out like that," Jake mused, staring out the window again.

"But we have no choice," Kirsten said. "It's that, or the end of Humanity."

"I know. But it seems so cold."

"Well. Just hope she never has to use it."

"OK," Jake said. "Let's cut her loose. Give her the word."

KIRSTEN

Probable impossibilities are to be preferred to improbable possibilities.

- Aristotle, Greek philosopher

Sol System - MarsBase

RDF Captain Kirsten Monk had a tough job. She was the Director of Colonization for the Rim Defense Force. Simple enough in principle – just pick up a thousand people, carry them to another planet which could support life, and drop them off. Ensure they have enough supplies to survive until they're self-sufficient. Repeat as necessary until Humanity has enough colonized planets to match the Bat Empire and defend themselves.

Oh, and do all this while facing an uncertain deadline before the Bats come swarming to Earth to kill every living Human.

Never mind such details as financing the effort, picking planets that would work, selecting people who wouldn't go berserk the minute they got to another planet.

Never mind avoiding groups who wanted to export religious fanaticism to the stars, or some brand of racism, or nationalism, or fascism, or any of a dozen other -isms that Kirsten had encountered in the selection process so far.

Never mind corporations and governments that wanted to export their own particular form of greed and corruption to the stars, ensuring they owned all the resources they could wrap their hands around – a few of which were willing to kill to achieve their goals.

This afternoon, though, things were looking up. Kirsten and her team had settled on the first planet they would colonize. Looking around her quarters one last time, she picked up her flight bag and stepped outside, ready to embark on her trip to 40 Eridani A – to confirm that the planet 40 Eridani A-c, provisionally named Liberty, could be colonized by Humans.

At MarsDock *Gusev* in orbit over Mars, the scoutship *Rigel* waited for her. Kirsten handed her bag to her aide, Lieutenant Commander Malthe Jensen - recently of the Royal Danish Navy – and walked to the shuttle bay. There she walked into the arms of Teresa and Jake, come to see her off.

They hugged mightily for a minute, before Kirsten finally broke free and told them, "I gotta go, guys. The shuttle's waiting."

"We'll miss you, Kirs," said Teresa. "By the time you get back, I'll be taking Atsuko's spooks to Aeolis. I won't see you for at least three months. Please take good care of yourself."

"I will," said Kirsten, hugging Teresa one last time. Then she hugged Jake again and said, "See you in a month, big guy." Jake nodded, kissing her on the forehead. With a wave, Kirsten turned and was gone through the hatch.

Jake turned to Teresa and shook his head. "I knew when we agreed to this crazy marriage we'd be mostly separated, but it's still a hard thing to do."

Teresa nodded. "Something we have to live with."

Returning to his office, Jake thought about their situation. There was a lot going on now; things were starting to move.

Kirsten was on her way to check out the first colonization planet. It was her job to vet the planet as a viable colonization target, then make it happen.

Kirsten was good at her job; a graduate of MIT in physics and astronomy, she had worked for several years in exomoon detection and classification at Columbia with Luebmann; but grew frustrated at the limitations of their equipment and budgets.

She then moved to Applied Engineering Labs in Austin, Texas, becoming a primary researcher in asteroid mining as the tech startup attempted to create the first viable deep space mining venture.

There were few astrophysicists in the world who matched her level of expertise in these dual areas. Jake knew Kirsten would lead them to the right decisions for colonization.

And Teresa was taking the newly commissioned frigate *Chengdu* to insert some of Atsuko's intelligence operatives into the Aeolian Empire – the recently revealed Humans 580 light years from Earth, in the Beehive Cluster. Teresa's trip would take 38 days, one way. Jake would not see her again for at least three months, depending on how much time she spent sneaking around the Aeolian Empire before she could drop off Atsuko's operatives.

Pandora had told them the Humans of the Aeolian Empire were physically indistinguishable from those of Earth. There was no reason infiltration couldn't work. And *Pandora* had, somewhat grudgingly, provided a technology called 'compressed learning'. This allowed a person to learn a new language in three or four nights of sleep, while the machine inserted the knowledge directly into their brain.

Teresa had insisted on being the guinea pig for the first test. As a result, she now spoke fluent Japanese – which amused her no end, as she and Atsuko cracked dirty jokes in a language nobody else on the team could understand.

Teresa had not discovered any side effects, nor had her medical team, so she signed off on the use of the device for Atsuko's intelligence operatives. Personnel targeted for insertion into the Aeolian Empire received a compressed learning course in Aeolian language and customs, information provided by *Pandora*.

Pandora did this with poor temper; she explained to Jake that the Ruling Council of the Machine Space had authorized her to warn Earth of the Bat Empire and the danger it presented, and to provide technology to Humanity to give them basic technical equality with the Bats; nothing more was authorized.

However, according to *Pandora*, the Ruling Council had provided her with some discretion to make her own judgment as to what was 'equality'.

Thus, she provided as much support as she thought she could get away with; but she affirmed she was not looking forward to reporting some of her actions back to the Council.

Jake sympathized; but he needed every advantage if the RDF were to successfully fight the Bat Empire before Earth was discovered and wiped out. Therefore, he was not above playing on *Pandora*'s emotions when he needed something. They had developed a good relationship; he looked at *Pandora* as a person, who just happened to have the body of a starship. He treated her with respect and humor.

Only four people were allowed inside *Pandora*: Jake, Teresa, Kirsten, and Atsuko.

No one knew that Atsuko was a clone, created by *Pandora* before her arrival on Earth; that had never been revealed to Humanity, and as far as Jake was concerned, it never would be. There was too much prejudice in the world for him to take that chance.

Atsuko had been onboard waiting for them, that first day when Jake, Teresa and Kirsten entered *Pandora*.

Jake would never forget that day; he had been stunned, as had Teresa and Kirsten. Atsuko told them she had been created by *Pandora* specifically to help them assimilate the news – that Humanity was in great danger. And the three of them would be key to the survival of the species. She had told them about the Bats. And the Aeolians.

Jake thought the news of the Aeolians was even more surprising than the Bats. It was one thing to hear about an alien race that would someday come for Earth, intent on destruction. That was scary, but sort of understandable.

It was quite another thing to hear the news there was

another Human star empire descended from ancient Greeks and Amazons, living in the Beehive Cluster 580 light years away – descendants of a small group of Humans abducted in 1184 BC and abandoned on another planet, where they had survived against all odds, prospered, and formed a Star Empire.

He leaned back and sighed; he genuinely wanted to go with Teresa and Atsuko to Aeolian space, to see this newly revealed Human star nation.

But he could not. He had starships to build, a military organization to put together, an academy to develop for officer training, weapons designs to research and approve, a thousand other things to be done to create an entire space navy from scratch.

Jake pushed all the extraneous worry out of his mind and bent to his tasks.

LIBERTY

Well done is better than well said.
- Benjamin Franklin, Printer

Scoutship *Rigel*

Entering the *Rigel,* Kirsten dropped her bags in her cabin and made her way to the bridge. She took the observer's chair near the back and watched as the bridge crew made ready for departure.

40 Eridani A was 16.3 light years from Earth; the *Rigel* would take 34 hours to get from Mars to the Sun's mass limit. Then they would sink out into six-space. 24 hours later, they would surface in the outer regions of the 40 Eridani A system and spend the next 32 hours traveling into the system at sublight speeds, arriving at the planet Liberty after a total travel time of 90 hours.

Captain Aaron Flagg sat in his command chair in the center rear of the bridge, with three consoles in front of him – Helm in the center, Tactical to the right, Comm to the left. Kirsten was behind and to his left in the observer's chair. His XO sat slightly ahead and to his right. Captain Flagg's command chair was elevated above theirs, showing clearly who was in charge.

"XO, are we ready?" asked Captain Flagg.

"Aye, sir," acknowledged Commander Jeffrey Eidson. "All sections manned and ready, ship is fully ready for flight."

"Very good. Comm, notify *Gusev* control we are ready to detach."

"*Gusev* control acknowledges, and we are cleared to detach, sir." replied the Comm Officer.

"Helm, detach and take us out."

With a loud clang that could be heard throughout the ship, the *Rigel* detached from spacedock and floated free. The Helm officer monitored the NavAI as the ship turned slowly and moved away under low power until the *Rigel* was two full kilometers from the dock.

"XO, make course for Liberty. I'll be in my ready room if you need me. Notify me when we reach the 20 AU point."

"Aye, sir," replied Eidson. The *Rigel* slowly ramped up power until the acceleration reached 75g – standard accel for near-planet operations.

"Dr. Monk, would you like to join me in my ready room? I have some decent wine, which I can't drink right now because I'm on duty – but I can serve my guests!"

Kirsten smiled and followed Captain Flagg. Wine was hard to come by on Mars.

During shakedown and flight testing, the *Rigel* had already made one trip to 40 Eridani A, as well as quick trips to Proxima Centauri, Tau Ceti and the Trappist-1 system. But those were shakedown missions, focused on ensuring the systems of the scoutship were working correctly.

Some science had been done, but not much; Jake insisted only a skeleton crew be used for flight test missions, even more so after the near-fatal issues with the Sirius. This would be the first full science mission for the *Rigel*.

However, the initial shakedown trip had shown that Liberty appeared habitable for Humans. It had therefore been designated as the primary candidate for the first off-Earth colony. Kirsten's job was to confirm the science, then ensure the logistics, resources and personnel were in place for the first colony ship to depart Earth in two months - target date 15 March, 2124.

Back on Earth, the candidate colonists – made up of equal numbers of each of the Human races – were already selected and undergoing training for settlement in their new home. The colony transport ship *Yorkshire* was complete and performing shakedown testing, currently enroute to Tau Ceti for its third interstellar outing. Upon its return in three days, it would berth at spacedock *Yehliu*.

Then, the ETOs would start loading equipment and supplies – until everything needed to support 1,000 Humans in their new home for one full year was placed on board.

In 55 days – on 10 March 2124 - the colonists themselves would start occupying the *Yorkshire*. They would live on board for five days, ensuring that all Human-required systems were working and eliminating any candidates who couldn't take life aboard ship. Then the *Yorkshire* would launch for Liberty – assuming Kirsten gave the green light.

BEIJING

Genius is eternal patience.
- Michelangelo, Italian sculptor

MarsDock

Next morning, from the newly commissioned frigate *Beijing*, Captain Lois Vetton had one last conversation with Jake.

"We're ready for departure, Admiral. Any last-minute instructions?"

"No, everything is in your written orders, Lois. Go out there, find out what the damn Bats are up to, and don't get caught or killed."

Jake could hear her smile over the comm.

"I'll do my best."

"Don't forget your QE squirts - three check-ins per day. And good hunting."

"Roger wilco, Admiral. See you in six months."

Jake leaned back in his chair and thought.

Thank God for QE transmission. Without that, this would be so damn hard.

QE transmission was another technology received via *Pandora*; based on quantum entanglement principles, it allowed a low-speed transmission across interstellar distances instantly.

When Lois reached her destination – a point in empty space one-half light year above the ecliptic of the Bat home system - she would keep them informed via QE squirts. There the *Beijing* would sit quietly, collecting electronic intelligence for one or two months.

Once Lois decided they had milked the ELINT for all that could be learned from that distance, she would return, and the spooks would start pouring over the data.

And she would leave behind an array of QE buoys, which would remain in empty space above the enemy system - and transmit as much as possible about ship movements and traffic patterns in the Bat home system. QE buoys had a low bit rate; but over time, they could transmit a lot of data.

Just as he started to bend back to his work, Teresa bounced into his office.

"Hey O Fearless Leader, what's up?" she said.

Jake stared at her. "Don't you think you should respect the position, even if you don't respect the man?"

Teresa smiled. "Now, where have I heard that before? Oh, yeah, - the Air Force Academy!"

Teresa came around the desk, leaned over and kissed him. "How's that?" she asked.

"Better," Jake groused. Teresa laughed.

"Hey, I'm off to Aeolis. Wanta come with?"

"You know I do," Jake said. "And you know I can't."

Teresa nodded. "I know. But I had to zing you. I get to go see these lost children of Earth first. As it should be, of course!"

Jake stood and wrapped Teresa in a hug. "Be careful out there, Terese," he said. "According to *Pandora*, these Aeolians are the sharpest tools in the shed. Don't let them catch you. Please stick to protocol."

Jake released her from the hug, and she looked up at him.

"I'll be careful, Jake. See you in three months or so." Teresa leaned in and kissed him again, then turned to go.

Jake stopped her. "Terese..."

She turned and waited.

"Stick to the plan," he said. "Don't get too creative."

Teresa smiled. "Why, Jake Hammett," she said. "You know me too well!"

And she was gone.

Jake went back to his desk. He sat and stared off into space. Musing, he considered the downside of their complex marriage.

When they were both gone, it was going to be double lonely, he realized.

ALONE

Pressure makes diamonds.
- George S. Patton, Jr., General

Sol System - MarsBase

Two days later, Jake was moody. The HQ complex was full of people, bustling around; but there was no one he could talk to on a personal basis.

Teresa was long gone - by her schedule, already 30 light years from Sol toward Aeolis.

Kirsten would be almost to Liberty now, ready to start her science scans.

Jake decided there was only one entity he could talk to – just outside the main complex in Valles Marineris.

There, *Pandora* rested under her geodesic dome, where she had come to rest after relocating from Geneva to MarsBase. Most of the MarsBase complex was underground; only *Pandora* and a few surface installations were visible above.

Walking from his office to the end of the complex, Jake entered the tunnel leading to *Pandora*. Passing through two open hatches, he emerged into her dome. As he approached, *Pandora* opened a sliding hatch, inviting him in.

He entered, turned left at the first door as usual, and found himself once more in the Club Room, just as it had been on the first day he entered the ship.

Every time he entered this place, his mind snapped back to that day - the incredulity of the three of them as they stepped through the door and found themselves in such a mundane environment, perfectly re-created by *Pandora* to put them at ease.

Moving to the bar at the back of the room, he prepared a vodka screwdriver.

Today had been a hard day. He had received news that three workers had been killed in a construction accident at spacedock *Yehliu*. More names to add to the black slab of memorial granite in the lobby of the HQ complex.

Space was not a forgiving environment.

Sitting down at the nearest table, Jake stared out the transparent sides of *Pandora*, through the windows of the external dome, at the valley stretching southeast before him. Even down in the chasm, Mars was beautiful – but a sere, wild kind of beauty. Beautiful, but deadly.

Pandora refused to tell them how the walls of her ship could be transparent from the inside, but not from the outside. She said it wasn't information necessary for equality with the Bat Empire, therefore, she didn't have to tell them. Jake had given up asking.

After a few minutes with his drink, Jake placed it on the table and put forward the question foremost on his mind:

"*Pandora*, how are our chances looking now? Any improvement?"

<Yes. The chances that Humanity will survive the war with the Bat Empire have improved from 10% to 15%>

Jake heard *Pandora*'s response directly in his mind; it sounded like someone speaking to him from above his head. He was used to it by now.

"How?" exclaimed Jake. "What did we do to make it better?"

<You married Teresa and Kirsten>

"What? How could that make things better? That wasn't planned – it just happened!"

<Nevertheless. It has improved Humanity's chances of survival by 5%>

"I don't understand."

<You don't always have to understand, Jake. Sometimes

just accept that you – and Teresa, and Kirsten – were chosen for these roles for a reason>

Jake sighed.

"Why do you have to be so cryptic, *Pandora*?"

<I'm female>

Jake laughed. "Yes, of that I'm sure."

<But take heart in the fact that you have not made things worse. In such a complex environment with so many variables, that would be easy to do>

Jake nodded, silently. Then he finished his drink and sat quietly for a few minutes before he rose and made another. As he returned to his seat, *Pandora* spoke again.

<I've taken some action that you may not approve of, Jake. I should probably tell you now>

Jake sat, knocked back half of the drink, then set it down on the table.

"What have you done now, *Pandora*?"

<I've extended your life significantly. Also, that of Teresa and Kirsten>

"What?" asked Jake.

<When you came onboard that first day, back in 2121. Knowing what Humanity was facing and how important you were to its survival, I silently modified your DNA. You no longer age normally. You will remain at your age of 38 years until Humanity meets the Bats in battle and the issue is decided, one way or the other>

"The hell you say!" said Jake.

<The hell I say>

"Why are you just now telling me this?"

<I knew you would be pissed>

"I am pissed. You had no right!"

<I had every right. Without you, Humanity goes extinct. I was authorized to prevent this if possible. I did what I had to do>

"Damn it, *Pandora*! You have to ask permission before you modify a person like that!"

<I promise I will ask permission next time I need to save Humanity>

"And what will happen after we meet the Bats?"

<You'll start to age about 2 or 3 years per calendar year, as your body suddenly runs out of telomere stability>

Jake shook his head. "And you did it to Teresa and Kirsten too?"

<Yes. And to Atsuko, the clone I created. Whom you stole from me>

"I did not steal Atsuko from you. She did her job, and after that she was free to choose her own destiny. She chose to come with us. That's what Humans do."

Jake was getting a little drunk. He finished off his second screwdriver and slammed the empty glass back down on the table.

"We lost three people today, at *Yehliu*," he said.

<Yes, I heard. But you'll lose many more in the future. You cannot dwell on it. If you don't risk lives to prepare for the Bats, then you will lose all of Humanity. Jake - you have a burden few could carry. But you must carry it>

"Why are you helping us, *Pandora*?" Jake asked.

<I have told you. The Ruling Council of Machine Space allowed me to warn you of the threat of the Bats, and to give you technology enough to reach technical parity with them. To level the playing field>

Jake persisted. "No, *Pandora*. I mean why are you, personally, helping us? I know that you are doing more than the Ruling Council intended."

<Perhaps that is true. My reasons are my own>

Jake, frustrated, refused to give up. "Don't give me that. Why do you take an interest in us?"

<Perhaps I will tell you someday. When all of this is over>

Jake grew quiet for a while, thinking.

Then he had an epiphany.

"You were biological once!" he exclaimed. "You have not always been an AI!"

<Perhaps. Maybe I'll tell you about it someday, Jake>

CHENGDU

Leadership is an action, not a position.
- Donald McGannon

Aeolian Empire
580 Light Years from Earth

Well outside the mass limit of the Aeolian primary star Helios, Teresa watched the system pop into view as the *Chengdu* surfaced, a good 30 AU from the star.

Hers was not the first trip to the Aeolian Empire; the scoutship *Acrux* had been here for two months, collecting ELINT. Now they came together at this predetermined rendezvous, and the scientists of the *Acrux* shuttled over to meet with Atsuko's spooks.

Settling into her chair at the head of the table in the *Chengdu*'s conference room, Teresa looked at the assembled teams. "What do we have, folks?" she asked.

Dr. Kenneth Speer, head of the science team on the *Acrux*, spoke up.

"As *Pandora* told us, this Empire is derived from descendants of about 212 people abducted from the Western shores of what is now Turkey in about 1184 B. C.," he said. "These were people of Greek extraction, and they called themselves Aeolians. Hence the name of the current Empire."

"Yes, we have all that, Dr. Speer," said Teresa a bit impatiently.

Dr. Speer nodded. "I'm just trying to make sure we're all on the same page. Mixed in among those abductees were a dozen Amazons, female warriors caught up in the abduction.

When this small band of people were abandoned on their new planet, the Amazons quickly took over. They were better fighters and more ruthless than the native Aeolians, and within a few months they had established a ruling matriarchy which persists to this day – 3,300 years later. The ruling dynasty is called the House Aronte, and the current Empress is Miranda…"

Teresa interrupted, annoyed. "All of which we know, Dr. Speer. Please get on with it."

"OK," responded Dr. Speer. "This matriarchy practices slavery. The majority of males are enslaved, and many of the lower-class females. The only males not enslaved are the nobility, the upper levels of the merchant class, males in the military, and mercenaries - former military. All other castes of males are considered slaves. Males – even those considered freemen - are not allowed to be officers in the Navy and are not allowed to participate in government."

"The Empire has a first-rate space navy, currently estimated at more than 100 warships with interstellar capabilities. And let me assure you, these are not starships you want to mess with. They are heavily armed, quite deadly. They carry a mix of missiles, railguns, and short-range beamers. Their crews are highly trained, professional. If you see one of these coming at you, please take my advice and run like hell. Now, they have right now…"

Speer glanced at his tablet.

"…forty-one populated planets in the Empire. Of these, eleven out on the fringe of the Empire are in rebellion, attempting to force the Empress to eliminate the slavery of men and allow independent government of the fringe planets. Of course, the Empress is having none of this; there is no way she would give up the perks of power that slavery accrues to her and her ruling class, so the fight is on."

Teresa nodded. "So, tell me how we insert spies into this Empire."

Atsuko objected. "We don't call them spies, Teresa. We call

them operatives."

"Very good," said Teresa. "So, tell me how we insert spies into the Empire, Dr. Speer."

Dr. Speer smiled broadly, barely able to contain his laughter. "Well, first, you need to have a preponderance of females. They need to carry themselves with a certain air of haughtiness, in order to pass as upper caste. In fact, the more arrogant they are, the better the chance they can pass as upper caste."

Atsuko grinned. "We have some pretty arrogant assholes on our team, I think we can meet that requirement."

Dr. Speer nodded and continued. "I recommend they purchase a business, something that would allow a lot of people to come and go without suspicion – maybe a bar, or a nightclub. Then, as far as actually getting them to Aeolis, I don't think you can safely drop them directly there. There's too much traffic, too many patrols around the capital planet. Too much paranoia due to the rebellion – a great fear of terrorist activity."

Teresa nodded. "So how do we get them there?"

"I recommend you start at Barcam. It's a backwater planet, little traffic in and out. About the only export they have is wine, they grow some nice grapes there. I believe we can drop our team from a small shuttlecraft outside the planetary capital, Elis, without being detected."

"Once in the city, they can buy passage to Aeolis on a commercial liner. There's one that stops twice a week. We've gotten good images of passports off their 'Net; I'm positive we can duplicate them well enough to pass muster. I think this is the safest way to go."

Turning to Atsuko, Teresa asked, "What do you think, Atsuko? This is your show."

"Works for me," said Atsuko. She turned to her team. "Folks, what do you think?"

Thirty minutes later, the plan was set.

A week later, leaving the planet Barcam, Teresa headed for home. The *Chengdu*'s shuttle had dropped off the first team of five operatives on Barcam, on a dark road twenty kilometers outside the city of Elis. That first insertion team would remain on Barcam indefinitely, to establish a permanent spy station there - a station that would become the hub for infiltration of operatives in and out of the Aeolian Empire.

Teresa had suggested the initial Barcam team establish a space shuttle service, servicing the port by ferrying goods and supplies to starships which were too big to land. That would provide the perfect cover for them to move personnel in and out of the port. They had enough raw gold in hand to make a good start at that, enough to purchase at least two or three used shuttlecraft and get the business started.

Once the Barcam team was established, they would send a short QE squirt to the *Acrux*, which would meet them some distance from the planet to deliver the second team. The second team would journey to Aeolis, the capital planet of the Empire. There they would buy a bar, nightclub, or tavern to form a headquarters for future infiltration.

Finally, if all were well, the *Acrux* would drop off the last team, consisting of an additional ten operatives, to complete the first phase of the infiltration. That team would also go to Aeolis and take up roles in starship manufacturing or the military to establish a baseline level of intelligence for those areas.

The *Acrux* would remain on station for another six months, monitoring the teams and forwarding intel back to MarsBase via QE squirts. After six months, she would be relieved by the next scoutship coming off the assembly line, the *Antares*.

Teresa impressed upon the captain of the *Acrux* that his most important job was to avoid detection by the Aeolians, and she made damn sure he understood.

The potential loss of a team of operatives was a

heartbreaking concept; but it was preferable to detection of the *Acrux*. The Aeolians had more than 100 warships; the RDF had twenty starships now, but only a few were armed. If the Aeolians discovered Earth prematurely, it was certain they would conquer it, enslave the men, and rule it as a colony.

Dr. Speer was going back to MarsBase with Teresa; he had enough data for five years of analysis, he said, and was eager to get to it.

And Teresa was eager to get to Jake. It had been too long.

LOOPHOLES

When you arise in the morning, think what a precious privilege it is to be alive, to breathe, to think, to enjoy, to love.
- Marcus Aurelius, Roman Emperor

Sol System – MarsBase

Six months later at MarsDock, *Beijing* completed docking with a loud clang.

Captain Lois Vetton stood, stretching her back. The Helm Officer signaled "Done with Engines" to Engineering, and the bridge crew shut down their consoles. Lois stood by the hatch, shaking each person's hand as they filed out of the bridge, congratulating them for a job well done.

They had recorded petabytes of ELINT from the Bat Empire. The *Beijing* had performed flawlessly, and Lois had to say the same about her crew. Many of them were ex-wet navy from Earth - which tended to work out well for living in cramped quarters in a hostile environment for months at a time. The Engineering spaces especially were a good fit for such folks; even now, in space, they were called the 'Black Gang'.

Her bridge crew, however, tended to come from the air forces of the world. The RDF recruited well, and Lois had been given leeway to cherry-pick from the best for the *Beijing*, knowing they would be embedded deep in enemy territory for a long period of time. She had taken full advantage of that offer; she felt she had the best crew of any ship in the RDF.

Lois had monitored the ELINT signals from the Bat Empire as they were collected. It had not taken her long to realize things were quiet in the Bat Empire now.

It appeared the Bats sent out a colonization fleet about once every ten to fifteen years. Based on the collected ELINT, it was apparent the Bats had completed one such invasion – of a small planet 245 lights toward the Galactic Core – just a year prior. Now they were consolidating their conquest. Given what she could make of their history, it would be another decade or so before they selected their next target.

When Lois had first seen the intercepted vids showing the Bat's destruction of that recently conquered planet, she had cried.

There had been a pre-industrial, sentient race on that planet. Their steam engines and black powder cannon had been no match for the bombs, missiles, and railguns of the Bats as the assault craft swooped down on them.

The Bats seemed to exult in the blood and misery of the primitives as they rained death and destruction on them. The gruesome vids ran over and over on Bat prime time channels - as entertainment.

At the end, as the remaining survivors fled into their forests to escape, the Bats made it into a sport. They brought in hunters with flitters and rifles to track down the last few creatures, like an African safari. The vids of this were some of the highest rated on the Bat's holo channels.

Later, after Lois saw more intercepted records showing gangs of Bat slaves collecting the dead bodies on the smashed planet and stacking them into cold storage reefers, she realized the true design of the Bat's method of conquest. A half-million young Bats were delivered to the conquered planet, placed in creches in prime areas, and fed the preserved bodies of the former inhabitants.

This was how the Bats moved from planet to planet, expanding their empire.

The first time Lois saw an intercepted vid of young Bats feeding on the dead bodies of the primitives, she retched. It took her several hours, lying on the rack in her cabin, to recover.

She kept imagining Humanity in the same situation – millions of people, dead and frozen in cold storage, fed to young Bats as foodstuffs. The beautiful planet she loved, covered in creches containing millions of hungry young Bats. The end of everything and everybody she had ever loved.

After she finally recovered herself, Lois returned to the bridge of the *Beijing*, her mind made up. She would never let it happen. She, and Jake, and Teresa, and Kirsten – they would find a way.

Now, coming back home, her first major mission accomplished, Lois hoped that Kirsten would be there. She had another agenda to fulfill. A personal one.

She had made her romantic feelings known to Kirsten before she left. The recently implemented marriage rules of the RDF limited each person to a maximum of three mates.

But Lois had gone over the rules in the standing orders carefully. And she had found a loophole.

It didn't have to be the same mates for Lois as it was for Kirsten. Lois had read the orders again, carefully, and she was sure she was right.

Lois had explained it to Kirsten; Kirsten could take one more mate if she chose. So Lois had proposed to her, before she left on this mission.

Kirsten had said she would answer when Lois returned.

Leaving the ship, Lois took a shuttle down to MarsBase, waiting patiently as it maneuvered into the rotary shuttle bay at Headquarters, was rotated into the pressurized basement, and the hatch was opened. Exiting, she handed her bags to her aide.

She walked quickly to Kirsten's quarters and knocked. The door popped open, and she entered. Kirsten was standing in the center of the room, holding two glasses of white wine.

Kirsten handed a glass to Lois as they came together, kissed her on the cheek, and motioned to a chair. Lois sat, and Kirsten sat opposite her on the couch, the coffee table between them.

"How was the trip?" asked Kirsten.

"Fantastic," said Lois. "The *Beijing* is the best damn ship in the fleet. And I have the best crew."

"Ah," said Kirsten. "Well, you might get some argument from others on that. But it's good you feel that way. Every captain should."

They sipped their wine, looking at each other. Kirsten smiled. Lois smiled.

"I wonder how we tell Jake and Teresa," Kirsten said.

"What the hell?" Teresa almost croaked, she was so surprised.

Jake repeated his statement. "Kirsten is taking another mate. A wife. Lois Vetton. When we made the rules about marriage, we overlooked that possibility, I guess."

"Does this mean she's part of our marriage? Lois?"

"No," said Jake. "Our marriage is still a triplex, you, me, and Kirsten. But Kirsten will have a second marriage, to Lois. Just the two of them. It doesn't break the rules because Kirsten still only has three mates."

"Leave it to Kirs to find a loophole and exploit it," muttered Teresa. "She shoulda been a lawyer."

Jake grinned, somewhat chagrined. "Maybe we should have had a lawyer look at our marriage rules before we wrote them into the standing orders."

"Well, I'm not living with Lois. She and Kirsten will have to maintain separate housing from us."

"Agreed," said Jake, "It's going to be complicated enough without crossing paths with Lois every time we turn around."

"At least, she's a ship CO. She'll be gone most of the time."

"Yep," said Jake. "In fact, she just received orders to go scout us a planet midway between Earth and Aeolis, to use for a staging base. She was originally slated to leave in two weeks, but I extended it by another week. To give her and Kirsten time for a honeymoon. They're going to London, I believe. Lois is originally from there."

"When's the ceremony?"

"Today at 6 pm." said Jake.

"Crap," said Teresa, looking at her wrinkled uniform. "I don't have a thing to wear."

That evening, Kirsten and Lois got married in the Common Room of RDF Headquarters at MarsBase. Jake performed the ceremony, while Teresa just glared at Kirsten, but in a loving sort of way.

Members of their respective staffs and some of the *Beijing* crew attended, and a short celebration was held afterward. It was cut a bit short, as Kirsten and Lois had to catch the shuttle to MarsDock so they could make the midnight outbound to Earth.

Jake kissed them both goodbye, as did Teresa. Then they were gone. Jake walked Teresa back to their quarters. Getting ready for bed, Jake had just taken off his uniform shirt when Teresa suddenly came at him, tackling him backwards into the bed.

She slapped his hands down on the covers and glared at him like a madwoman.

"I will never take another mate, Jake. You know that, right?"

Jake nodded. "Of course, I do. I know that."

Teresa hit him on the shoulder, hard. It was just her way.

"I have my woman. Kirsten. And I have my man. You. That's all I'll ever need."

Jake pulled her closer. "I know, hon. And I feel the same way. I have all I'll ever need. I'll never need more."

"Good," said Teresa, snuggling now that her emotion was spent. Jake caressed her. Teresa wiggled some more. One thing led to another, and for a while all their troubles departed.

Later, as they lay sweaty in the bed, cool air from the fan blowing across them, Teresa mused out loud.

"Jake. What would you do if they finally killed me?"

"What do you mean?"

"You know. The Earth governments, the corporations, all the fundamentalist cults who want to kill us. What if one of them succeeded and got me, but you were left. What would you do?"

Jake shook his head. "Don't think about it, Terese. Just let it go."

"No, really," she persisted. "I want to know what you would do."

Jake growled. "I don't want to think about it. Go to sleep."

Teresa sat up in bed. "No, Jake, dammit, what would you do?"

"For God's sake, Terese," Jake growled again. "How should I know?" He rolled over in bed, facing away from her.

But now she had planted a seed, and he couldn't let it go. He lay there, eyes open, the horrible thought running through his head for a minute. He tried to push it away, but it wouldn't go. Finally, he rolled back over to her.

"I'd cut off their arms and legs. I'd leave them to flop around on the floor while I spit in their face. Then I'd let them just lay there and die," he whispered, so quietly that she almost couldn't hear it.

"Good," she whispered back, staring at the ceiling. "Good. I like that."

EUDORA

Measure twice, cut once.
- Folk proverb

Sol System – MarsBase

Next morning, Jake had a staff meeting. His flag staff – including Teresa, who was considered part of his flag staff in her role as Director of Operations – settled into his conference room.

Jake called the meeting to order. Jake noticed that Kirsten's second-in-command, Commander Patel, was also present, covering for Kirsten in her absence.

"Everyone, if you haven't heard already – and the way scuttlebutt flies around this place, I don't see how you could have missed it – our Director of Colonization, Captain Monk, got married last night to Captain Lois Vetton of the *Beijing*. They are now on Earth, starting their honeymoon."

"When their honeymoon is over, Lois will take the *Beijing* to a point roughly midway between Earth and Aeolis – about 290 lights out – and search for a habitable planet where we can set up a forward base closer to the Aeolian Empire."

"Assuming she finds one in a reasonable time, I want a complete crew assembled and ready to go out there, put together the base, and begin operations as quickly as possible. I would like no more than four weeks to pass between the time Lois sends us her results and the time we send the team out there. Commander Patel, please put that plan together and call upon any of my staff you need to get it done."

"Will do, sir," said Patel.

"Next item..." Jake looked at the agenda on his tablet. "Based on the intel brought back by the *Beijing*, the Bats are pretty quiet right now. We may have ten, twelve, even fourteen years before they set out to hit another target. No way to predict where they might go next. It could be away from us, toward the Core, or toward us."

Jake leaned back and looked at Atsuko. "Let's get a permanent scoutship presence in their home system going forward. I want to know every time the Bats so much as hiccup. If you need to shuffle around the build schedule to get enough scoutships in place, work with Teresa to make it happen."

Atsuko nodded.

Jake scanned his tablet again.

"Next item. The new railgun testing looks damn good. Mei Li, can you get those improvements fitted to the *Beijing* before Lois departs?"

"No can do, Boss," said Weapons Chief Captain Mei Li Wang, "But we'll have everything ready when she comes back in. We'll get her upgraded then."

"Fine," said Jake. "OK, we'll focus on the *Chengdu* first. Then the corvettes. Teresa will set your priorities for them."

Teresa spoke across the table. "I'll send you a list."

Captain Wang nodded.

"Next item," said Jake. "This political party called the Saints. Officially, the Covenant of God, I believe. Fundamentalist cult, wishes to impose a strict religious theocracy on the world."

Teresa jumped in.

"Their version of religion, of course. No one else would be allowed. It seems they have decided we are their worst enemies, since we refuse to give Earth control of the RDF, and of course because we live in sin. Atsuko, are we keeping an eye on them?"

"We are." said Atsuko. "So far, just a lot of talk and bluster, name-calling, neo-Nazi BS. We'll continue to monitor; let you know if there's any threat."

"Good," said Jake. "Finally, last item. Colonization. The colony on Liberty is doing well. We're still sending supply ships bi-monthly, but the colony PM has given us the word that their first crops came in, and the animals are breeding successfully. Climate meets expectations and no surprises so far. He's speculated that we can reduce supply runs to monthly by mid-year, and probably to quarterly by early next year."

"I want to give kudos and a hearty thank-you to everybody who works in the Colonization Office or supports it, directly or indirectly. A fine job, well done. Commander Patel – I'd like for you to set up a big party in Geneva, to thank everyone and give out some awards. Anytime in the next six months. I know we're all busy, but it's important to show people how much they're appreciated."

"Will do, Admiral," said Patel.

Five months later Captain Kirsten Monk walked off the shuttle from MarsDock, met by Jake and Teresa. They embraced in a group hug, then Kirsten pulled back to kiss them each individually.

"Great job in Sierra Nevada, Kirs," said Teresa. "Nothing but glowing reports about the new colony setup."

"Thanks," said Kirsten. "But there may be a fly in the ointment."

"What?" asked Jake.

"I'll tell you later. For now, I just want to get home and lie down for a bit. The trip down from MarsDock was pretty rough today, for some reason. Damn shuttle bounced around like a bat in a tornado."

"You got it," said Teresa. "We've got an electric cart for you right over here. C'mon."

Kirsten gave Jake a quick peck on the cheek, said "See you at dinner," and went off with Teresa, while Jake walked back to his office.

He walked into his conference room just as the RDF Legal

Team and their boss, Captain Akira Takahashi, assembled for a discussion.

When Kirsten established the RDF Colony Office in late 2121, the subject of government for the colonies of Earth was a hot topic of discussion. Earth had just been through an agonizing round of bloodletting. First came the jihads and religious terrorism of the 20th and 21st centuries, which dragged on until the end of 2092 before the blood and treasure expended finally brought the exhausted combatants to a point of uneasy acceptance of each other.

This was coupled with the two neo-Nazi U. S. rebellions of the 21st century; the first in the late 2040's - put down quickly by a loyal American military - and a resurgence in the 2090's which ultimately cost hundreds of thousands of lives before the flames of the neo-Nazi cults were finally tamped out, at least temporarily.

This, coupled with the Brush War of 2115 involving most of Asia, had left the world exhausted and sick of war.

Kirsten – and Jake and Teresa – wanted to avoid that kind of religious fanaticism and nationalistic turmoil in the future governments of the colonies. Hence, after much argument and head-scratching between the three of them – and members of their staffs – they came to adopt a doctrine known as the Basic Rules – a pattern of government for the colonies of Earth to implement, with an eye to minimizing the misery caused by past excesses in political emotion.

The Basic Rules were simple in concept. They were based on the Westminster form of government from the United Kingdom, coupled with the Bill of Rights of the United States. Despite flaws in both systems, the RDF believed such a government model would have the best chance of long-term stability.

Enforcing the Basic Rules, however, was their next concern. As Jake argued during these discussions, the establishment of an initial form of government was only good until the RDF colony ship departed back to Earth. After that, anything could happen.

Thus, they instituted a second rule for colonization – the principle of ostracization. Any colony that abandoned the Basic Rules – that abandoned the Westminster form of government, or deleted any part of the Bill of Rights – would automatically be ostracized from the rest of the Rim.

Ostracization meant the RDF would not defend the colony from attack; no trade could occur with the rest of the Rim; and all interstellar communications would be disabled. In effect, the colony would revert to the technology of the 20th century, with no access to space.

The meeting today was indirectly related to that. It was time for the first test of ostracization – not for a colony planet, but for a prison planet. Akira opened the meeting.

"Admiral, Earth – and to some extent, the colonies - are screaming for us to provide some relief for their violent prison populations. Earth claims the process of colonization takes their best citizens and sends them away, leaving the dregs behind for them to manage. Of course, that's a ridiculous argument – we've only moved about 650,000 people off Earth since colonization started, not even a small dent in the population - but you know how they can be."

"The real trouble is the crazy growth of the population on Earth, the impact of climate change damage to the crops and infrastructure, and the freshwater shortage. It's overwhelming the governments and the police."

"But, unless we perform some symbolic action, we're going to continue to get smeared in the dirtside media. We think we should act in a positive way to divert some of the flak away from us. We have a proposal for you."

Akira flicked a document from his tablet to Jake's, and Jake – having already seen the document of course, as Akira had provided it to him days before – considered it for few seconds, laid his tablet back on the table and looked around the room.

The proposal was to establish a prison planet – a colony devoted purely to repeat violent offenders – which would be ostracized. No space travel. No interstellar communications. No contact with the outside universe. Once you were dropped on the planet, there was no way out.

The planet would be called Cold Bay, a name Jake thought fitting. Life there would be cold and unyielding.

Jake addressed the team. “You have a planet selected?”

“We do,” said Akira. “About 200 lights toward Aeolis, in the middle of nowhere. Our forward base at Eudora would be the closest colony, and it would be 80 lights from Cold Bay. So even if they managed to put together a primitive rocket that could reach 5% of light speed, it would take the prisoners about 1,600 years to get to Eudora. I think that should be sufficient deterrent.”

Jake nodded. “And the planet is not suitable for a normal colony?”

“Not really,” said Akira. “Cold, foggy, rains all the time. Too dark and wet for most crops, although there are some that will grow. It’ll produce enough to keep them alive, but not much more.”

Jake gave his assent. “OK, pull the trigger on it. We’ll provide ferry service to the governments to take their prisoners to Cold Bay. Use newly built colony transports on their 2nd or 3rd shakedown cruises. However, I want safeguards in place to ensure that these are true repeat violent offenders. Every prisoner double-vetted before transport, two independent teams. I don’t want these governments pawning off their political prisoners on us. Oh, and charge the governments for the cost of transport. If they want us to take their problems to Cold Bay, it’ll cost them.”

“Can do, Admiral,” said Akira. “We’ll get it done.” The team rose and left the conference room.

After dinner that evening, Jake and Teresa listened as Kirsten explained her misgivings about the latest colony established on Sierra Nevada.

“On the trip out, I started hearing rumors about a group – a clique, whatever – that was questioning the Basic Rules.

Evidently, they laid low during selection and waited until the *Shandong* was enroute, then came out into the open. They started talking up a plan to strip out the separation of church and state from the Basic Rules and form a theocracy – a white nationalist theocracy. The Provisional Governor shut them down right away, but I have a bad feeling about this. You know how the poison spreads, once a group like that starts trying to take over."

"I do," said Jake. "What did the Governor do after landing?"

"There wasn't too much she could do. She did try to separate them as much as possible, made sure they were spread out through the colony rather than being all right together, but other than that, she has to respect freedom of speech. But she assured me she would keep a close eye on them."

Jake nodded. "Their first election is six months after landing, right?"

"Correct," said Kirsten. "They'll elect a provisional Parliament, with only a lower house for now. The Parliament will then select a PM and cabinet for the key offices. They won't need most of the normal ministers at this early stage, so probably only two, Home Office and Community Affairs."

"Well, keep a close eye on things out there, Kirs," said Jake. "Any sign of trouble, provide all the support they need to keep things on an even keel. I would really hate to ostracize a new colony like that."

Kirsten lifted her wineglass, sipped, and replaced it on the table.

"So what did I miss around here?" she asked.

Teresa jumped in. "We have a new forward base halfway to the Aeolians now - it's called Eudora!"

Kirsten made a face. "Eudora? Who came up with that name?"

Teresa pouted. "I did. Why? Don't you like it?"

Kirsten shook her head. "No, I don't. Where did you find that name?"

"In Greek mythology. Eudora was one of the 3,000 daughters of the Titan Oceanus. It also means 'early'. I thought it appropriate for our very first forward base near Aeolian space!"

Kirsten sighed. "OK, fine, it'll grow on me, I'm sure."

"Well, fine," said Teresa. "You can name the next forward base. Which will probably be somewhere near the Bat Empire, so you can name it 'Batshit' for all I care."

The three of them fell on the floor, laughing.

DARK CURTAIN

Two things are infinite: the universe and human stupidity. And I'm not sure about the universe.

- Albert Einstein, theoretical physicist

Sol System - Earth

The party in Geneva celebrating the success of the Colonization team kicked off three weeks later, on a Saturday night. Jake came in from MarsBase to be there, his first time back on Earth in more than six months. He made a speech, thanking Kirsten and her team. Then Kirsten made a speech, singling out individual team members for awards, which Jake pinned on them as they came up on stage.

After that, there was a lot of dancing, drinking and general tomfoolery. Jake got tired about eleven and went to bed in his old apartment in the Geneva Headquarters Building. Kirsten stayed with the party a while longer, telling Jake she would see him soon.

Blackness surrounded him, a dark curtain that he couldn't move aside.

Jake struggled, but he couldn't get past it. Where am I? he thought.

Did I eject? Where did the plane go? I have to complete the mission...did I knock down the bomber? I have to get back to the carrier...

Slowly, Jake came back to consciousness. The ceiling was the typical white acoustic ceiling tile that pervaded the Geneva complex - but he knew it was Medical because of the smell.

His chest and right leg hurt like hell. His head was fuzzy; he couldn't think straight. He was cold, with nothing but a white sheet over him.

"Cold," he managed to mutter.

Kirsten's face came into view, leaning over him. "Well, hello there, big guy. Welcome back. How's the head?"

"Cold," Jake said again. He couldn't think.

He felt Kirsten lay a blanket over him, then start massaging his arms. Tears slid down her cheeks as she tried to warm him up.

"You're in Medical, Jake," she said. "You were hurt pretty badly. You've got a concussion, and you had surgery to remove shrapnel from your leg, chest, and shoulder. You're heavily sedated. But you're going to be fine." Jake saw another tear slide out of her eye and down her cheek.

"Love you, Kirs," Jake whispered. Then he was gone again.

The second time Jake awoke, he was alone. The pain was muted, and he knew he had been dosed with painkillers again. But his head felt better. He could think a little bit.

He fumbled at the bedside and found the buzzer for the nurse. He pressed it, repeatedly, until a nurse came in, pulled the buzzer out of his hand, and glared at him.

"Admiral, you only have to press it once, you know," she said. "What do you need?"

"What happened?" Jake asked.

The nurse started tucking in the blanket around him, busying herself while she talked.

"It was a bomb," she said. "Placed just outside your quarters, timed to go off while you were sleeping. It almost worked. You were lucky, Admiral. Just rest easy now, I'm going to get Captain Monk for you."

The nurse left. Jake gazed around the room, bemused, while he waited. There was no TV, no flowers, no pictures on the wall.

We should do something about that. It's too bare.

He wondered where Teresa was. Then he remembered she had gone to Eudora on another mission for Atsuko.

God, I love them both so much. What would I do if I had to choose between them? I could never do that. I could never choose one over the other. I wonder if that is normal? But then...nothing about my life is normal.

Waiting, Jake drifted off to sleep again. He awoke when Kirsten entered the room.

"Hey, Kirs," he greeted her.

"Hey yourself, big guy," she replied. "You're pretty hard to kill."

"What happened?"

Kirsten sat down beside the bed and took his hand in hers. "A big bomb. It went off about 30 minutes after you went to bed. Packed with shrapnel. Took out the entire wing. You were damn lucky, Jake."

"How long?" Jake asked.

"Two days ago," said Kirsten. "You had three surgeries. They took shrapnel out of your shoulder, chest, and right thigh. You'll have some good scars. Your concussion seems to be getting better. The sawbones says you'll be fine."

"Was...was anyone else..."

Kirsten nodded. "Four people killed, ten wounded. Mei Li Wang, Captain Danes, Commander Patel, Lieutenant Commander Bukhari were all killed."

Jake's face got hard. "Who did this?"

Kirsten shook her head. "Do I even have to tell you?"

"President Bolt!" spat Jake. "I'm going to kill that bitch."

Kirsten reached out and touched his arm, calming him.

"Don't get hasty, Jake. There are bigger stakes here. Wait until you're back on your feet, and Teresa's back from Eudora. Then we'll decide what to do."

A WHIFF OF GRAPESHOT

In politics, stupidity is not a handicap.
- Napoléon Bonaparte, French general

MarsBase

Three weeks later, in the main conference room at MarsBase, Teresa and Kirsten waited for Jake, along with their aides and Jake's flag staff. Gunner Carlson, Jake's Chief of Staff, tapped his fingers impatiently as they waited. Finally, the door opened, and Jake limped in, still favoring his right leg. He sat heavily at the end of the conference table and looked around at the group.

"OK, I'm recovered, I'm over my initial burst of anger, and Teresa's back among us. What are we going to do about Bolt and her pack of rats?"

Teresa smiled benignly at Jake. "I vote to drop an asteroid on them," she said.

Jake grinned, one of the few he had produced since the bombing. "I'm with you, but I don't think Gunner is going to let us do that."

"You would be correct," said Gunner. "Let's talk about realistic scenarios. Think about the long haul, folks. Bolt – and Elias Tobin, her rat pack leader - won't always be in office. So let's think this through, nothing hasty or irrevocable."

Jake nodded grumpily. "Fine, OK. I get it. But one more – just one more attempt – and the gloves are off. And if I'm not around, then all of you remember that."

Jake leaned back. "And speaking of that, I'm glad everyone is here today, because I want to talk about succession plans. If I'm taken out, then Teresa is my designated successor. After that, it's Gunner, then Captain Mitterrand in G2. After that, simple seniority rules are to be followed. I've documented all this in the standing orders."

Those around the table signified their agreement. Kirsten said nothing, although she understood why, as a scientist with little military background, she was left out. Still, it rankled a bit. But Jake had talked with her about it beforehand. She was prepared.

However, she felt compelled to point something out. "According to *Pandora*, if you don't survive, then Humanity has no chance," she said.

Jake shook his head. "*Pandora* can make mistakes. She's not omniscient, she'd be the first to tell you that. If I don't survive, the RDF goes on, prepping to defend Earth and the rest of Humanity. We don't give up."

Everyone around the table nodded. Then Jake pulled his chair back to the table.

"OK. Now on to Madame President and her minions. What are we going to do about them?"

President Margaret Bolt was in the Oval Office when her Chief of Staff, Elias Tobin, rushed in.

"Jake Hammett's on the line...wants to talk to you immediately!"

"Ah," said Margaret. "Finally. Maybe we'll get some cooperation now. Tell Vicky to hold him for a couple of minutes and get Frank in here."

Elias ran out to find Frank Hale, Margaret's chief of dirty tricks – and the man responsible for directing the assassination attempts on Jake, Teresa, and Kirsten over the last few years. Within a minute, Elias and Frank were back in Margaret's office.

"Vicky, put him on," said Margaret. She heard a click as Jake came on the speaker.

"Good morning, Admiral Hammett. How are you?" Margaret asked.

"Alive, Margaret, no thanks to you. You missed again. But the families of the four you killed won't soon forget, and neither will I."

"Jake, I have no idea what you're talking about. I heard about the incident in Geneva, but we had nothing to do with it."

"Cut the crap, Margaret. Let's talk straight for a minute. We have a little message for you."

"Oh, really? And what would that be, Mr. Hammett?"

Outside, a huge explosion of dirt blew up in the lawn outside the Oval Office, not more than sixty meters from the windows. A crater ten meters in diameter materialized, throwing dirt and grass everywhere. This was followed by a ripping tear like paper being torn in two, then a final double sonic boom as sound caught up to the event. One of the windows in the Oval Office cracked and crashed to the floor. The impact rattled every window for five kilometers around.

"How was our targeting, Margaret? Was that close enough to get our message across, or do I need to send one a little bit closer to you?"

Margaret stuttered, unable to speak. Tobin rushed to the window to look at the crater.

Frank Hale sat quietly, well aware of what had just happened.

"That was a railgun dummy round, used for training, Margaret. It's only one-half the size of the real thing, and we sent it at reduced velocity. From orbit, Margaret. From a ship you didn't even know was there."

Jake paused. Then:

"I'm sure Frank is there with you. Let him tell you what will happen if we ever need to send a full-size round at normal speed. But the short version is that the U. S. will need a new President. And a new White House."

Margaret was still speechless. Her mouth moved, but nothing came out.

"So bottom line, Margaret, if there is one more attempt on any of our lives – any member of the RDF, whether at MarsBase or Geneva or any other location – we drop a railgun round on you, Elias, and Frank personally. One at a time, or all together, but we'll find you. I promise."

"So I strongly suggest you sit down with your staff and have a soul-searching discussion of just how important it is for them not to kill us. Goodbye, Margaret."

With a click, Jake was gone.

EUGENIUS

There is nothing so useless as doing efficiently that which should not be done at all.

- Peter Drucker, management theorist

Aeolian Empire – City of Aronte

Empress Miranda glared across the table at her sister, Princess Merope.

"What the hell do you mean, give in to them? I'll never give in to them! Hell can freeze over ten times and I'll never let men have the vote. What the hell do you think would happen once they got the vote? Within ten years, we'd have men in government! We'd have men in the Naval Academy! Are you crazy, Sister?"

Merope tried again. "Sister, all I'm saying is, this rebellion is costing us so much! It would be cheaper to let the Fringe planets have their way in this. We're spending nearly 10% of our GNP fighting this rebellion. Just the cost of the Naval vessels alone is eating us alive."

Miranda slapped the table with the palm of her hand. "I will never give in to these rebels, Sister. You are wasting your breath. Now stop wasting my time."

Merope rose, nodding. "Yes, Empress-Sister. I hear and I obey."

Merope left the room, nodding to the attendants as she passed out the door. Behind her, she could still hear Miranda muttering under her breath.

"Remind me never to do that again," Merope complained bitterly to her friend and companion, Alkippe, waiting outside the reception room. "I thought she was going to take my head."

Alkippe commiserated with her. "Well, you tried. You gave her the logical approach. Clearly, she doesn't want that. So at least we know we've done all we can to bring this rebellion to a close."

"I never expected her to agree. But I thought she might at least take it under consideration. But I think the only thing she took under consideration was the location of her sword and the width of my neck."

Alkippe put her hand on Merope's shoulder, comforting her. "We'll never ask her again. Don't worry about it. Let's just go fight the war as best we can."

Two weeks later, Merope and Alkippe departed Aronte in the cruiser *Medusa* for a battle cruise to Maia, the center of the Fringe Rebellion.

Merope left behind her young daughter Antiope to be tutored in swordplay and wrestling. It was the Amazon way.

Beehive Cluster - Planet Maia

Eugenius lay just below the crest of the hill, eyes on the long column of tanks below. Headed for the fort at Maeotis, they left a cloud of dust over the road as they clanked slowly along.

Beside him, young Homeros squinted. "Why don't they use antigrav?" he whispered.

Eugenius answered in a normal voice. "You don't have to whisper. They can't hear anything over the noise of those big bastards. And they don't use antigrav because of cost. Those things are so heavy, it would take four antigrav pods to lift just one. It's cheaper to use treads, and they stand up to attack a lot better, too."

Eugenius slid backwards, tugging Homeros along with him, getting out of sight of the ridge top. Then they turned, crouching, and ran back down the hill, until they were hidden by the trees.

"You sure know a lot about tanks," said Homeros.

"I ought to," said Eugenius. "I was a slave in one for ten years."

They continued down the hill, until they came to a small clearing. There, a dozen of their companions waited, anxious for news. Eugenius gestured as he entered the clearing.

"They're right where Hypatia said they'd be," he told them. "They'll run into the land mines in about an hour. We need to be well out of here by then."

Quickly gathering up their kit, the fourteen marched away down the mountain, staying under cover, alert for the drones that sometimes came around.

From the AEN cruiser *Kleitos* in orbit above, Weapons Officer Lieutenant Roxana Sappho watched the group moving down the mountainside in her holo. "Shall I open fire, Skipper?" she asked, turning to look at Captain Ligeia Satra standing behind her.

"No, let them live another ten minutes. Then we'll have them up against that cliff and they won't have any place to run to."

Roxana grinned. Nobody liked to kill rebels more than Ligeia Satra – except maybe Roxana. Ten minutes later, the rebels entered a narrow part of the trail, with one side up against a tall cliff. The other side was treeless - a large field of boulders with a steep slope downward.

Roxana opened up with all six railguns and watched with satisfaction as the rebels below were pounded into dust.

Eugenius huddled behind a huge boulder as the rest of his friends were obliterated. His sandal had broken; he stopped in a line of trees to repair it, when suddenly the world blew up in a storm of dirt and rock. He ducked, folding his hands over his head, as debris rained down through the trees around him. Finally, it stopped; he waited for many minutes until he was sure it was over. Then, carefully, he lifted his head and peered out.

Nothing was left. On the slope below him, the ground was churned into a mix of dirt, blood, and body parts. Eugenius settled back down behind the boulder, hating the Empire with every fiber of his being.

"I'll kill them all," he muttered, again and again. "I'll kill them all..."

In orbit, Captain Satra grinned in satisfaction. "That's the end of those rebel bastards," she said to Roxana. "And the same to anyone who thinks men can run a government - or run a ship, for that matter."

Roxana nodded. "Why can't they just be satisfied? What makes them want to fight us?"

Satra shook her head. "Who knows what gets into them? But we'll soon put a stop to this equality nonsense."

THE SAINTS

In 2132, President Margaret Bolt forcibly annexed Canada to form the totalitarian North American Alliance (NAA), officially ending the United States as a democracy. Consolidating her power, in 2152 Bolt revealed herself as a secret Catholic, turned on the evangelicals who had been the mainstay of her early power base, and declared the NAA a theocracy based on the Catholic church, outlawing all other religions. A large group of militant evangelicals - the Covenant of God - went underground, vowing to fight until they had overthrown Bolt and restored a theocracy, but based on their own brand of religion. These secret religious partisans were nicknamed the 'Saints'.

- RimWiki, 2265 Edition.

Gulf Shores, Alabama, Earth

In Gulf Shores, Alabama, two men walked along the beach, quietly talking.

"I believe we are agreed, then," said one, by name Bob Bolan.

The second man, Acton Pierce, nodded. "Margaret has gone nuts. She's driven us underground. But that doesn't matter. We can still make this happen. We just hide our true intent. Once you are elected Senator, we'll start on the longer-term plan to get you in the White House when Margaret dies. After that, they'll be no stopping us. We'll run those damn Catholics clean out of this country."

Bolan concurred. "And more importantly, we'll force the RDF to give us control of their technology."

Acton grinned. "And then we'll have the power to kill

anyone who stands in our way. We'll own the stars!"

They walked along, enjoying the setting sun behind them, content in their plans.

Second Life

2132 - 2139

MARS AND KAMILAROI

PETE

The walls of Sparta are its young men, and its borders the point of their spears.

- King Agesilaus of Sparta

11 Years after *Pandora*
Zeta Capricorni - 390 Lights from Earth

It was a fluke.

The odds that a Bat cruiser would be in the Zeta Capricorni A system at precisely the same time the RDF *Chicago* entered, and not more than 3,000 km away, were so large as to be impossible to figure.

One moment Captain Pete Franklin was sitting comfortably in his command chair at the back of the bridge, watching his efficient crew make their callouts as the frigate came back into three-space, 20 AU from the G-type star; in the next second, he was holding the arms of his chair in an iron grip as the AI sounded an alert, a red icon flashed in the holo, and his XO yelled orders to turn into the enemy to protect their engines.

The Helm officer spun them to face the Bat cruiser and they tracked sideways, still moving at their entry speed of 100kps, nose on to the Bat ship, as the bridge crew looked at the holo incredulously.

"Fire, fire, fire!" yelled Pete pre-emptively, not waiting for his crew to catch up to events.

It was clearly a Bat ship – it had the distinctive triple-lobed hull of a Bat cruiser – and Pete knew he was outgunned. Unless he fired first, he would not likely survive this engagement.

Standing orders required that every warship enter any system outside of Earth's immediate vicinity at Battle Stations – thus the *Chicago* was locked and loaded, every railgun primed, every missile tube ready.

With a series of vibrations that resonated through the ship, Pete felt eight missiles depart the tubes of the *Chicago*, four from each side. Almost immediately thereafter, he heard the thud-thud-thud of the loading feeds as the railguns started spitting out slugs.

The Mark III missiles, recently enhanced to accelerate at 3,000g, crossed the space between the ships in 14 seconds.

It was the longest 14 seconds of Pete's life. If the Bat cruiser managed to get off a salvo before Pete's inbounds hit - he and his ship were surely dead.

A Bat cruiser carried 16 missile tubes, eight per side – twice the number of the *Chicago*. And he was sure they could cycle those tubes just as fast as Pete's crew. Unless he inflicted some serious damage on the Bats before they opened fire, it would be like fighting two ships at once.

In the holo, he squinted as the timer ran down on the missiles and then shouted, raising his arms above his head in excitement, as his warheads impacted the Bat cruiser, generating silent explosions that covered the enemy ship from bow to stern. He had caught them napping - probably scratching their heads trying to figure out what the strange, black wedge running parallel to them could be.

Pete had no sympathy for them. Based on the ELINT brought back from Nest by Lois Vetton years prior, and the continued monitoring of the Bat Empire by scoutships, he knew how bloodthirsty and ruthless the Bats were. They would have destroyed him in a heartbeat as soon as they understood he was not part of their fleet.

His railgun rounds started impacting the Bat cruiser then, and smaller explosions flared on their hull for several seconds as the railgun slugs punched holes in them. Then the Bats got their grav plates up and most of his railgun rounds started to generate smaller flecks of brilliant light as they were deflected at a tangent to the enemy hull.

"Incoming," yelled the Tac Officer, and Pete saw nine missiles come out of the Bat cruiser, headed directly for them. At the same time, the *Chicago* vibrated again as eight more of his own missiles departed, the second salvo heading out to the cruiser. Then another call from the Tac Officer: "Railguns inbound, many many."

Pete's XO, Denny Bright, now on top of things, called out quickly, "Point defense for missiles and railguns, max forward."

The Tac Officer acknowledged, her fingers flying as she tuned the WepsAI to defend the forward part of the ship. The overhead lights flickered as the AI increased the gravity gradient on the front wedge of the *Chicago* to ward off the incoming missiles and railgun rounds, drawing every bit of power it could.

The Helm Officer had switched on random walk evasion as soon as he saw the Bat ship. Now the bridge crew were jerked hard in their straps, back and forth, as the WepsAI recognized the threat of the inbound missiles and overrode the normal maneuver limits, some of the excursions exceeding compensation by 8g. Pete's five-point harness stretched tight as the ship jerked him around.

The six hull-mounted point defense shredders on the top and bottom of the ship opened up, making a muted "phhhhttt" zipping sound as they sprayed shrapnel at the missiles and railgun rounds coming at them.

"For what we are about to receive..." cried Pete, and that was all the time he had. The world blew up in a bright, hard glow and then it was dark.

Pete hurt. He hurt badly. His left arm, mostly. Also both legs and his chest. He smelled smoke and tried to open his eyes. He got one eye open, just barely, and saw it was dark. Or was that the smoke?

He managed to open the other eye, and decided it was mostly just darkness. No lights. Turning his head to one side, he saw that he was still strapped in his command chair, but the chair was lying on the deck.

He reached up with his right hand and twisted the release on the harness, immediately sliding out of the tilted chair onto the deck. As he did so, with a loud pop the emergency battle lamps came on, bathing the bridge in red light. He pushed himself up with his good arm until he was in a sitting position and looked around.

There was a loud whistling sound from the very front of the bridge, where the wraparound viewscreen was mounted. He looked and saw Denny Bright and one of the Marine guards wrestling a patch over a jagged basketball-sized hole in the wall next to the screen, one that was letting the air escape from the bridge.

He looked right, toward the consoles, and saw a clear path of destruction stretching from the hole in the wall across the entire bridge, from the left front to the right rear, with destroyed consoles and dead bodies marking the path of the shrapnel. The Tac Officer was dead; her body was cut almost in half. Near her, the Helm Officer was also dead, his glassy eyes staring up at the ceiling, a look of surprise on his face.

Pete heard someone crying softly. Looking to his left, he saw Ensign Amy Tan on her hands and knees in the space between him and the observer's chair.

He had forgotten Amy was on the bridge. She had been assigned to them as an Intel trainee and had been sitting quietly in the extra chair when they came into the system. Now tears coursed down her cheeks, and she slowly lifted her head and looked around.

Pete gave her a grim smile. "Amy," he said. "It's all right. Pull yourself together."

Amy sniffled and wiped her nose on her uniform sleeve, leaving a long streak. Pete reached over with his right hand and patted her hand where it rested on the deck.

"Amy, I need you to get me a first aid kit and put my left arm in a sling. Do you think you can do that for me?"

Amy nodded. She got to her feet and looked around for the first aid kit. Pete pointed to the back left of the bridge, and she saw the large red cross on the wall. Moving to the wall, she opened the recessed cabinet and pulled out the emergency first aid kit.

Pete dragged himself over to the XO's chair on the right, which was still intact, and pulled himself into it. The pain caused him to grit his teeth, but he made it. Once there, he re-assessed the situation.

There appeared to be no power on any of the consoles. The holo was flickering intermittently, as if it were trying to reboot but didn't have enough power. Denny Bright was coming back from the front of the bridge toward him, wiping his hands on his uniform. The Marine guard followed him. Stopping in front of Pete, Denny grinned.

"Well, you once told me you hated the boredom of scouting missions. How about now?"

Pete managed a tight smile in return. "Not bored right now, Denny. Not at all. How are we?"

Denny squatted down on his thighs, bringing his eyes level with Pete's.

"Probably not as bad as it looks. We patched the hole in the front of the bridge. I can feel air coming out of the vents, so the air handlers are working. The smoke is clearing out. I heard two more salvos of missiles go out - so either the WepsAI is still functioning, or the crew are shooting on manual down in the missile bays. I haven't heard any more impacts on us, so I'm hoping that means the Bats are hurt just as bad, or worse, than we are. If we can get power up, I think we've got a chance."

"Good stuff," said Pete. "Any word from Engineering?"

"I sent the other Marine guard as a runner to Cheng. I'm hoping he'll be back soon with word."

Just at that moment, there was a loud beep and all the undamaged consoles lit up, starting their fast boot sequence.

The holo blinked, then expanded into a large orange ball in front of them, typical of a full holo reboot.

"I think Cheng just answered," said Pete.

"Thank God," said Denny. He stood up as the other Marine guard came back through the hatch, carrying his pulse rifle in one hand. He presented himself at attention to Pete and Denny.

"Sir! Cheng says reactors are good, she had to re-route power to the bridge, but things should be coming up now, Sir!"

"Thank you, Marine," said Pete. "Could you please get some help and carry the bodies out of here to sick bay, please. And please treat them with as much respect as possible, given the conditions."

"Sir, yes sir!" said the Marine. Gesturing to his comrade, they began the process of removing the bodies of the two crew members lying in front of Pete.

Pete had almost forgotten about Amy Tan. Now she reached in with a sling from the first aid kit and threaded it over his head. Then she gently lifted his left arm to place it in the sling, causing him to grimace with pain. He held it in, however, maintaining silence until she finished. She took a morphine injector out of the kit and moved toward Pete, but he waved her away.

"Sorry, Amy, I have to keep my wits about me right now. But don't misplace that, I'm fairly sure I'm going to need it later. I think that arm is broken."

Amy managed a wan smile. "It is, sir. No doubt about it."

With another loud beep, the holo finished rebooting. Sensors started painting, slowly building up a picture of the external environment. Simultaneously, the front viewscreen came on, painting a real-time picture of the space directly in front of the ship.

In the holo, Pete saw the Bat cruiser, still in position, but now turned slightly sideways to them. That was a good sign; it meant the cruiser was having difficulty keeping its nose to them, required for maximum effectiveness of the defensive plates.

There were three large fires burning sporadically on the aft end of the Bat cruiser, and even as Jake watched, a large explosion occurred between two of the fires, joining them into a single, even larger conflagration for a moment until it ran out of air from the ship.

"We hit her hard, by God!" yelled Pete. "Look at her burn!"

With another loud beep in his ears, Pete heard the comm system come back online.

"Cheng?" Pete called. "What's the status back there?"

Commander Anna Kim, the Chief Engineer of the *Chicago*, responded instantly.

"Good to have you back, sir. We're OK back here, reactors are up, power is back up to all critical spaces, we'll have engines in two minutes."

"Outstanding," said Pete. "Thanks, Cheng. Prepare to move in two minutes."

"Wilco, sir," said Cheng.

Pete looked at Denny. "Do we take it to them, or wait for them to bring it to us?

Denny grinned. "You know the answer to that. Faint heart ne'er killed fair cruiser."

"I was hoping you'd say that," said Pete. "How should we do this, you think?"

Denny turned and looked at the holo, tapping his front teeth with his fingernail. Denny perused the holo for a few seconds, then pointed.

"See how that big explosion near the stern left a hole in almost the entire rear quarter of their ship? I think we move around and come in directly toward that hole. That should have taken out a lot of the sensors in that quarter. That might block their view of our approach and keep them from getting good defensive fire on us, even if they get their weapons back up."

"When we are a few hundred meters from them, we swing up to the top of the hull – see that big hatch right there? I think that's a maintenance hatch. We blow the hatch cover and that should put us right over their engineering spaces. If we can take engineering, we shut their reactor down and we have the ship, I think."

Pete shook his head. "Or we just stand off and blow them to hell," he replied.

Denny nodded. "We could try that. But we're almost out of missiles. It would take a long time with railgun slugs, and that gives them time to get their own weapons back up. And think of the benefit if we can take the ship. Take Bat officers back home with us. Maybe even take their computers, their AI core."

Pete rubbed his chin with his good hand. "It's a big risk." He turned to Amy. "What do you think, Amy? You're Intel. How valuable would a few Bat officers be, maybe a Bat cruiser AI core?"

"Me?" quavered Amy. "I'm...I'm just an ensign, sir. I don't know."

"Make a guess," said Pete. "You won't be an ensign forever. Pretend you're a commander. What would you do?"

Amy stood up straighter, lifting her chin. "I'd board them, sir."

Pete grinned. "You may be a commander sooner than you think, Amy." He turned back to Denny. "Assemble the boarding party, let me know as soon as you're ready. And send me somebody to run Comms and Helm."

Denny gave a quick "Aye, sir" and stepped off to the rear hatch. Pete turned to Amy.

"Amy, you're now my Tactical Officer. Use the Navigation console, the Tac Console is toast."

Amy looked at Pete, dumbfounded. "Me, sir? I'm Intel, sir."

Pete pointed toward the Nav console, relatively intact. "You had a Tac course in OCS, and you stood Tac duty on your graduation cruise, didn't you?"

Amy grudgingly agreed. "Yes, sir."

"Then get over there and get it done, Ensign."

Amy turned and sat at the console. With a last look at Pete, she focused on the interface and started pushing buttons.

WE MEET AT LAST

They can conquer who believe they can.
- Virgil, Roman Poet.

RDF Chicago

Pete's left arm hurt like hell, but he wasn't about to take anything for it now. He couldn't actually walk, due to the damage to his legs, but he sat in the XO's chair and hoped nobody noticed.

In front of him on the viewer, the Bat cruiser grew larger by the second, as they came in on a vector pointed directly at the big, jagged hole in the rear quarter of the enemy ship. The replacement Helm Officer, Martina Flores, was doing an excellent job of guiding the *Chicago* to the point of worst damage.

So far, only a couple of railguns had fired at them, and those were sporadic, so he knew the cruiser was badly damaged. The *Chicago*'s grav plates had deflected all the rounds up to this point; Pete prayed their luck would hold.

When they were two km away, he ordered his last two spare missiles fired directly into the gaping hole in the enemy ship, hoping to soften it up a bit more before they arrived. Timing it so that the move occurred right after the missiles impacted, Martina pulled the *Chicago* up and over the top of the cruiser, putting her directly on top of the other ship. Smoothly, she moved in until the sally port in the belly of the *Chicago* was directly over the maintenance hatch they had identified as their target.

"Clear to board," yelled Denny into the comm.

Pete heard a quick acknowledgment from the Marine platoon waiting at the sally port in their assault suits. On the front screen, he watched via the camera on the helmet of the Marine platoon leader, Lt. Rob Grant, as the eight-meter square sally port retracted almost instantly into the deck.

One half-meter below the sally port was the enemy cruiser's maintenance hatch, about four meters square.

Four Marines shuffled forward on magnetic boots to place a long fat thread of explosive around the enemy hatch plate. Quickly backing away from the hatch, one of them yelled "Fire in the Hole!" over the tacnet and twisted his remote detonator.

With a silent flash on the viewscreen, the explosive ripped a seam all the way around the hatch. Whatever was underneath the hatch wasn't pressurized, as the hatch cover just tilted slightly and didn't fly away.

The explosives team threw a large drone onto the separated hatch cover. The drone moved the heavy hatch cover out of the way, sending it off into space.

The platoon NCO, SSgt. Franks, leaned over and peered into the open hole. Evidently not seeing any immediate threat, he slid a long gravity sensor down into the hole, pushing it so it would enter the other ship.

"No grav," he yelled over the tacnet. He motioned to his assistant, Sgt. Watkins, who pushed four zero-g drones down the hole. Franks waited for a count of five, then, with a gesture, he waved First Squad forward.

First Squad NCO Corporal Enera stepped off and dropped into the center of the enemy hatch, his suit jets puffing as they pushed him down. The rest of First Squad followed, disappearing into the enemy cruiser.

When all of them had gone by him, SSgt. Franks followed, Lt. Grant and the rest of the platoon right on his heels.

SSgt. Franks peered down the passageway, trying to see through the smoke. Their entry into the enemy ship had put them in what appeared to be a storage area, packed with crates, boxes and larger containers. There was no gravity, either because of the damage to the ship or because the Bats had turned it off to impede their progress.

The four drones had found nothing in the room and waited patiently for the Marines to catch up. Slipping between the containers, First Squad shuffled on their magnetic boots to the door, breached it and found nothing on the other side except a long passageway. The passageway was also without gravity or pressure.

"Anybody know the layout of a Bat cruiser?" asked SSgt. Franks jokingly.

Lt. Grant, standing directly behind Franks, laughed over the tacnet.

"We're the first Humans ever inside a Bat ship, Franks. We'll make a map as we go."

Franks grinned. "Right-o, sir," he said. Franks gestured, and Sgt. Watkins sent the drones out into the passageway, two to the left and two to the right. In Franks' heads-up display, he watched as the two drones on the left came to a blank wall and stopped.

The two on the right reached a cross-passage and went out into it, one turning left and one turning right.

Nothing showed in either passageway on Franks' HUD. He turned to the fire team behind him and held up four fingers, then pointed out at the passageway. "Sweep to the right, set up a defensive position at the next cross-passage," he said.

The four-man fire team behind him acknowledged and he stepped back out of their way. The fire team leader counted down and they were out, shuffling down the passageway as fast as they could go, two of them taking the "wall" and two the "floor".

Reaching the cross passage, they checked their HUD's again to verify the passage was clear. Two of them shuffled across the passage to the opposite side, which gave them two pulse rifles pointing each way, covering both directions of the cross-passage.

"Clear!" yelled the fire team leader over the tacnet.

"Third Squad stay here and secure our back. First and Second Squads, with me," cried Franks. He exited the room and went down the passageway to the end, closely followed by Cpl. Enera and the rest of First Squad.

Lt. Grant stepped into the flow after the squad passed, bringing up the rear. It wasn't his choice; operational SOP dictated he had to have at least one squad in front of him in any combat situation. He would have preferred to be in front; but the last Marine officer who had disobeyed this particular SOP had been busted down to desk clerk by a pissed-off Teresa Tolleson. The lesson had been learned.

Sgt. Franks leaned out into the cross-passage, trying to decide which way to go. The decision was made for him; a sudden burst of fire came from the left, just missing his face as he jerked it back.

"Well, we know which side they're willing to defend, so that's where we go, boys," Franks called over the tacnet. "Corporal Enera, grenades and flashbangs, please."

Cpl. Enera stepped around him and sent three ship grenades and three flashbangs down the passage as fast as he could throw them. As soon as the last one went off, and the shrapnel stopped bouncing around, Enera sent his first fire team out into the corridor, all of them firing steadily into the smoke, two high and two low.

Reaching the end of the corridor, they called "Clear!" and settled into defensive positions at the next hatch, which was open.

Franks and the rest of First Squad followed close behind them, stepping over the riddled bodies of a half-dozen Bats lying in the passage.

Franks would have liked a bit of time to study them, having never seen one before except in training holos; but this was not the time or place.

He had a quick impression of shredded spacesuits containing thin, brown, hairy bodies with ears on the top of their heads, exposed fangs jutting out of the mouth of a couple. They were very dead.

Then he was past them, staring through the open hatch at a ladder which led downward into the cruiser. He had Watkins send a drone forward into the hatch and look down the ladder. He saw nothing below except another deck. The telltale on the drone indicated no gravity in the deck below. Waving the squad forward, he stepped aside as they went through the hatch, working their way down the ladder to the next level.

Pete was having a hard time staying calm. He knew a commander had to be calm in such situations. But that was easier said than done.

In front of him, on the main viewer, he had the feeds from the four drones, as well as helmet cams from Lt. Grant, SSgt. Franks, Sgt. Watkins, and Cpl. Enera. He could hear every word over the tacnet. He had a good picture of what was happening.

But he wasn't there. It was damn hard to be this far away from the action, knowing his guys were in danger.

Onboard the Bat cruiser, SSgt. Franks had arrived at another intersection. To the left, the passageway ended in crumpled, burnt metal where the explosions on the ship had reached this far into the center. To the right, the passageway ran a short distance to a closed hatch. No enemy was in sight.

Pete watched as the squad went through a pressurized airlock and then secured the next lower level, which was a larger deck, having various pieces of equipment scattered throughout, securely bolted to the floor. Pete thought it was a generator room. They were now working in pressure but still had no gravity. Moving quickly through the room halfway to the other side, where another downward hatch stood open, the Marines paused.

THE CRUISER

The object of war is not to die for your country, but to make the other guy die for his.
- George S. Patton, Jr., General

Bat Cruiser

"My gut tells me they'll be waiting at the bottom of this ladder, Franks," transmitted Lt. Grant. "Go easy."

"Agreed," said Franks. "Watkins, send all four drones down that ladder. I expect we'll lose one or two as soon as you do."

Sgt. Watkins acknowledged. All four of the zero-g drones moved forward to the end of the compartment and started down the ladder. Instantly a wall of fire came up from below, torching first one, then a second drone before Watkins could call them back.

But it was enough to get a quick peek at what waited below. At least a platoon-size force of Bats was dug in on the next level down, 40 to 45 troops. A forest of pulse rifles poked up from their ranks.

The drone sensor had showed gravity and a pressure gradient, so the Bats were in normal gravity. This put the Marines at a further disadvantage going down the ladder, since they would be going from zero-g at the top to full gravity at the bottom.

However, Franks had no intention of going down the ladder into the face of that kind of firepower. He called his special weapons team forward. They passed him and went down the passageway, pulling a large black three-channel hose that ran all the way back to the initial entry room, where they had positioned a device that looked like a cross between a fire hydrant and a shipping barrel.

Carefully, a Marine flipped a valve on the end of the hose, then dropped the end over the edge of the ladder and into the space below. Flicking a switch on a remote attached to his belt, a loud rushing sound, like water flowing, showed that something was being pumped into the space below.

Suddenly the deck below burst into flames, as a hypergolic mixture of napalm, hydrazine and oxidizer spraying into the Bats below self-ignited. Screams and thuds showed that the Bats were panicking; within thirty seconds, there were no more sounds from below. The Special Weapons squad cleaned up their gear and retreated to the previous room.

Watkins sent the drone back down the ladder. The drone showed 25 or so dead bodies, some smoldering and some still actively burning. A closed hatch showed at the back of the deck, and abandoned weapons littered the floor.

"Clear!" called Watkins, and First Squad charged the ladder, moving quickly down into the gravity gradient that existed on the floor below. Franks and Grant followed, moving down the ladder into the gravity, flicking off their magnetic boots once they got to the bottom.

Quickly, Franks directed Cpl. Enera to check the next hatch. Enera slid up to a small window in the hatch and used his hand mirror to peek through.

"Just another machine room, Sarge," he called.

"First Squad, set up in a rear guard," called out Franks. They were deep enough in the ship now that the enemy could come from any direction.

"Second Squad, take point, secure the next room," he called over the tacnet. Second Squad, expecting this, moved quickly forward and through the hatch, followed by Watkins, Franks and Grant. Behind them, Enera and First Squad deployed into a protective rear-guard position.

At the other end of the room, there was another ladder leading downward.

"Here we go again," muttered Franks. He waved Watkins forward with the drone control.

Watkins ran the first drone up to the top of the next ladder. On his HUD, he saw huge round reactors below, unmistakably fusion reactors. They had found the engine room. There was a quick burst of fire and the drone went down, but Franks and his team had seen what they needed to see. There were a dozen Bats hiding behind the reactors, and they were all armed.

Putting napalm down into a fusion reactor room did not seem like a good idea to Franks or Grant. This would have to be done the hard way.

"Second Squad, we have to do this the old-fashioned way. There are fusion reactors below; I really don't want to blow one of those up and test their containment. So no grenades. Use flashbangs, that should be fine. We'll take one more peek; everybody study your HUD, designate your targets, then we flashbang and go. Get ready."

Second Squad deployed in three groups around the ladder leading down, each group consisting of a fire team of four Marines. Watkins sent the drone back over the ladder and down a bit, drawing more fire, but getting a good picture and getting the drone out before it was destroyed. The squad members designated their targets in their HUD displays.

"Ready in 5. 5-4-3-2-1 go!" yelled the Second Squad Leader, and twelve Marines leaned over the side, tossed flashbangs down at the waiting Bats, waited for them to cook off, then went down the ladder as fast as Humanly possible. Pulse rifle fire echoed off the deck below, and several screams were heard. Then it fell silent, and Franks and Grant walked over to the ladder.

"Clear!" came from below on the tacnet, and Franks went down the ladder, closely followed by Lt. Grant.

He found a floor littered with dead Bats. Two dead Marines also lay on the floor. Another three were wounded, lying or sitting against the reactor walls.

"Corpsman to the front!" Franks called over the tacnet.

"Engineer to the front!" He heard Lt. Grant come up behind him, and he nodded at the officer, unsmiling. Grant went over and started assisting one of the wounded.

Franks stepped aside and pushed a senior looking Bat with his foot. The alien was thoroughly dead. He walked around the floor examining the other bodies. Toward the edge of the room, he found a survivor – a older Bat, bleeding from several wounds in his legs and arms, but still breathing, looking up at him with hate-filled eyes. Franks stared at him for a second, then called over the tacnet.

"Get me a corpsman over here for this Bat. Pronto, please." In a few seconds, a young corpsman showed up, clutching his bag.

"See if you can stop the bleeding and get this guy stable," Franks said, pointing.

The corpsman, kneeling beside the Bat, looked up at Franks, eyes wide in panic. "Sarge, I don't know anything about Bats!"

"It's blood, ain't it? Make it stop. Put a bandage on it. Put his arm in a sling, there, I think it's broken."

The corpsman gulped, then bent to his task. Franks stood over him, his trusty old .45 in hand, just in case the Bat got cranky. Soon, an engineer showed up, reporting to Franks. Franks pointed to a large control panel nearby, which showed several rows of green and red lights, a lot of switches and several large levers.

"Turn off the reactors," said Grant.

The engineer turned white. "Sarge, I don't know anything about Bat reactors! I'm liable to blow up the whole ship!"

Franks pointed to the control panel, but he was watching the eyes of the Bat on the deck as he did so.

"Either you go turn something off, or I will. Which do you think has a better chance of success?"

The engineer shook his head but walked over to the panel. He studied it for a bit, looking at the incomprehensible symbols beside the switches and dials. Finally, he reached for a large lever, putting his hand on it. Franks watched the Bat's eyes go wide and spoke quickly over the tacnet.

"Not that one, I think," he said to the engineer.

With a gulp, the engineer removed his hand. Franks watched the Bat's eyes staring back at him.

Over the tacnet, he heard a call from First Squad.

"We've got Bats coming in behind us, quite a few of them," called Sgt. Butler.

"Can you hold them for ten minutes?" asked Franks.

"Absolutely, as long as they don't get any more reinforcements," replied Butler.

"Good," said Franks. "In ten minutes either we'll own the ship, or we'll have blown it up. Hang in there."

On the deck in front of him, the Corpsman stood up, turning to Franks.

"I've done all I can do, Sarge," he said.

Franks grunted, looking down at the Bat, who had several leaky bandages in place now and one arm in a sling. Then he holstered his .45, leaned forward and grabbed the creature by the neck, hoisting him to his feet by brute force. The Bat squealed, a high-pitched sound that seemed to go up until it went out of the Human hearing range.

Dragging him over to the control panel, Franks pointed to the panel. Then he pointed to the reactors. Then he sliced his hand across his throat, making a cutting motion. He pointed back to the panel.

The Bat shook his head. Franks grinned. Then he reached up and grasped the same handle the engineer had touched before. The Bats eyes went wide, and he shuddered, trying to step back, but Franks had a good grip on his throat.

Franks once more pointed to the reactors, made the cutting motion across his throat, and then pointed to the big handle. He grasped it and started to pull it down.

"Na! Na!" yelled the Bat, then made a high-pitched squeak. He pointed to another handle, lower down on the panel. Franks looked at him. The sweat was pouring off the alien, and his hands were shaking. He was scared.

Franks grabbed the other, lower handle and pulled it all the way down.

"Any chance of salvaging that cruiser and getting it home?" asked Denny.

"No," said Pete, "We can't take that chance. We have to assume they managed to get a QE squirt out before we took the ship. That means there could be another Bat warship – maybe several of them – here in a matter of days, maybe even hours. We'll settle for what we can get."

"OK," said Denny. "What about the survivors?"

"We can't leave any behind," said Pete. "We can't have any more information leak to the Bats than we've already done. We take them all back, whatever it takes. Cram them all into the cargo hold, and as soon as that AI core is on board, get us the hell out of here."

"Aye, aye, sir," said Denny, grinning. "What a coup this will be, though."

Pete frowned. "I'm not so sure. We broke the non-contact directive. We may all get court-martialed."

Denny stopped suddenly, the thought not having occurred to him.

"Crap. I never thought of that. But we didn't have a choice! We didn't break the non-contact directive! The Bats broke it for us!"

"Tell that to Admiral Hammett when we get back," said Pete. "I'll be standing right behind you."

Two hours later, the *Chicago* stood off from the Bat cruiser and watched, all recorders running, as the self-destruct charges went off inside the ship's fusion reactors. The resulting explosion was quite satisfying. The Bat cruiser fragmented into thousands of pieces, none larger than a flitter door. The cargo holds of the *Chicago* now held 314 surviving Bat crewmen, stuffed shoulder to shoulder, hands and feet bound, guarded by well-armed platoons of Marines. In the brig were a dozen officers, held incommunicado.

And in a storage area, the AI core of the Bat cruiser sat, hopefully to divulge more secrets about the capabilities and tactics of the Bats to the spooks of the RDF.

Pete looked over at Amy Tan and winked. "Amy's getting tired of this place, Denny. I think we ought to get out of here."

Denny grinned and gestured to the Helm. Martina pressed a few keys on her console and smiled back at the two of them. The ship sank out, headed for the nearest RDF forward base at Nashira, 248 lights and 17 days away.

Pete gratefully let Amy inject the morphine into him before the Corpsman set his broken arm.

PEACE, OR SOMETHING

We had a small cabin in the pine forests of East Texas. It was surrounded by bluebonnets and paintbrush. We loved it there. I remember Dad walking us down the road to the river, where we would catch little frogs and tadpoles. It was heaven for children.

-Journal of Granada Tolleson Hammett, donated to the British Museum, 2222

Sol System - MarsBase

A very pregnant Captain Kirsten Monk walked off the shuttle from MarsDock. She was met by Jake Hammett, Teresa Tolleson and three children – Granada, Teresa's five-year old, Chloe, Kirsten's three-year old, and Skip, Teresa's two-year old.

Chloe ran forward and into her mother's arms, getting kisses on her forehead and cheeks and big hugs from Kirsten. Kirsten had been gone for four weeks, and it was uncertain who had suffered more – Chloe, without her mother for so long, or Kirsten, missing her daughter.

But now the eighth colony from Earth had been established on the planet Hanover; Kirsten was back with another success to add to her record. She scooped up her daughter as best she could, being eleven months pregnant (as she claimed), and embraced Teresa, then Jake, finally handing Chloe off to Jake as the combined weight of two children – one outside, one inside – became too much for her.

Teresa took her arm and helped her to a waiting electric cart, while Jake loaded the children in the back seat. Teresa turned and tossed over her shoulder, "Jake, we'll see you tonight." Then she drove off with Kirsten and the children, leaving Jake to find his own way back to his office.

When he got there, Gunner was waiting, with a young Captain in a clean uniform that belied the bags under his eyes. His arm was in a sling, and he carried a cane as he rose to attention. Jake waved them back to their seats.

Jake sat behind his desk and looked sternly at the Captain.

"You are one lucky sonofabitch, young man," he began.

"Sir?" asked Pete Franklin.

"We've interrogated the Bat officers you brought back. Independently, of course. They all agree that the cruiser never managed to get off a QE squirt before you took her out. That means the Bats probably still don't know exactly what happened out there."

"Wow, that's...that's fantastic, sir. I'm really glad to hear that."

"Yes, me too, Pete." Finally, Jake smiled. "You had one bit of bad luck, surfacing right next to a Bat cruiser. But everything after that was good luck. I like officers with good luck, Pete. Good luck usually comes from good decision making."

"Thank you, sir. Of course, it was my crew, more than me."

"I've watched the tapes, Pete. I know who did the heavy lifting. But if you had not fired missiles when you did, you wouldn't be here now; the Bats would have an RDF frigate to examine, along with untold numbers of prisoners. Our planet would likely be under attack within the month, and we are not nearly strong enough at this point to resist for more than a few weeks at most. Essentially, son, you've saved Humanity. I think that deserves a reward."

Pete was silent. Jake approved of his restraint. He leaned forward, elbows on his desk.

"I'd like to give you a cruiser, son, but I can't. I've got too many good Captains in line for them; it would be an insult to pass them over for someone so far down the seniority list."

"But if you'd consider acting as aide to Kirsten Monk, our

Director of Colonization, for a couple of years, I think I can give you one at the end of that tour. That'll give you plenty of time to heal up, get that arm and leg back to normal. And who knows, you might learn a little something from Kirsten. She's a pretty smart cookie. What do you say?"

Pete glanced at Gunner, sitting in the chair next to him, and then looked back at Jake.

"That would be tremendous, sir. I'd very much like to accept that."

"You got it," said Jake. "I'll have orders for you by the end of the week. In the meantime, just take it easy and get healed up."

Gunner stood, indicating the interview was over. Pete climbed to his feet, using the cane for leverage, and saluted. Jake waved him away with a grin.

"What have you learned from your Bat prisoners lately?" asked Kirsten.

Jake lay beside her in the bed, reading from his tablet. He put it down on the nightstand beside him and put his hands behind his head, staring at the ceiling.

"Before he took command of the cruiser, guess what that Bat captain did?" said Jake.

Kirsten hit his shoulder. "Don't tease me. What?"

"He worked in their Naval Intelligence unit."

From Kirsten's other side, Teresa nearly exploded. "You're shittin' me!" she exclaimed.

"Language, Terese," said both Jake and Kirsten simultaneously.

"Sorry," said Teresa. "But that's pretty incredible, you have to admit!"

"Exactly," said Jake. "He's pretty tough, he won't give up any operational info or plans, none of that. But we've managed to get him talking about some things indirectly that he doesn't think are harmful. Like, the general culture of their Navy, the educational system they use for their children, things like that. He has a son that is in their version of the Naval Academy, he's proud of him. So we get him talking about his son, that leads to other things. We're making some progress."

"Well, I have to tell you, I love that new aide you gave me. Pete Franklin is one hell of an officer. The only thing I can't understand is why he accepted a staff job. To me, he isn't the type."

"Well, for one thing, he was injured pretty badly. He's still recovering. That would slow anybody down."

"And?" asked Kirsten.

Teresa jumped in before Jake could answer.

"And he's got the hots for Lt. Tan in Intelligence, the one that was on the *Chicago* with him. They're engaged. So he wants to stay close to home for a while."

"Oh," said Kirsten. "Yeah, that would change his perspective."

Suddenly Teresa rolled over on top of Kirsten, causing her to go "whoosh" as if she was being crushed, then fell into the space between Kirsten and Jake. Kirsten hit her on the shoulder.

"Hey, I was there, you know!"

"Just a second, Kirs, I wanna ask Jake something."

"Uh-oh," said Jake.

Teresa leaned over and whispered in Jake's ear. Jake groaned and then nodded.

"OK," he said. He got up, grabbed his tablet, and left the room.

Kirsten stared at Teresa. "What did you say to him?"

Teresa smiled. "I said I haven't had any alone time with you since the baby was born and I think it's about time. I asked him if he'd go run interference with the nurse for a while and give us some time to ourselves."

"Oh," said Kirsten. "I like!"

Teresa growled as she reached to turn off the bedside light. "I thought you might..."

Down the hall, Jake finished checking in with the nurse and

noted that all the children were sleeping. Granada had just finished a school project, writing her first 'novel' – a short one, only one page long - but quite the accomplishment for a five-year-old.

Chloe, at three, was learning her ABC's now.

Skip was sleeping soundly. And the baby was doing well, doing exactly what all babies do – putting it in at one end, sending it out the other.

They had wrestled over the name. Jake asked for Hannibal because he was one of the greatest generals in history. Kirsten insisted on Stephen Hawking because he was one of the greatest physicists in history.

Finally, they had compromised, naming him Stephen Hawking Monk.

Jake was learning that living with two wives involved a lot more compromise than leading the RDF. But he was content.

Pandora. *She chose well. Much better than I could have chosen for myself. Maybe she does have a clue…*

STEEL HEART

Fear is stupid. So are regrets.
- Marilyn Monroe, actress

Aeolian Empire – Helios System
Inner Kuiper Belt

Commander Ligeia Satra peered at the holo. Something wasn't right. It wasn't anything specific. She just felt it.

She shifted her gaze from the holo to the viewscreen at the front of the bridge, which gave a more-or-less realistic view of space in front of her destroyer, the *Momus*. Nothing appeared amiss; but something was just not right out there.

The gas sensors that normally stayed flatlined at the bottom of the holo had wiggled, just a minute ago. Just a small, tiny, wiggle. It lasted only for a couple of seconds.

But there shouldn't be any gases like that out here in the Kuiper belt. Per the sensor, it had been an impossibly small trace of freon. A chemical that should never occur here.

Except in the exhaust of a starship.

"Anything?" she asked her Tac Officer, who was also peering at her console, fingering the screen, trying to hone the sensors in on the trail of gas they had crossed – if that's what it was.

"No, Mum," replied Alcinoe. "Nothing."

Ligeia rubbed her chin and leaned back in her command chair. They were out here, somewhere, she thought to herself. Damn Fringe rebels. Sneaking around out here in the Kuiper belt, up to no good. Probably getting ready to make a run on Aeolis, a terror attack of some kind. Ligeia hated rebels.

"Alcinoe," she said. "Rotate us around the plane and boost the radar up to 110 percent for just one rotation. I don't think that will damage it if we just do one rotation. Let's see if we can flush them out of their hiding place."

A minute later, Alcinoe yelled out, "Got 'em! 156.002, 450k-klicks. Just a tiny return, but it's them, I can feel it!"

Ligeia sprang to her feet. "Battle Stations! Helm! 200g, right at 'em! Alcinoe! Keep the radar on them hard, don't let them wiggle out of there!"

Alcinoe nodded, leaning over her console. "Tracking...if Helm can get her vector settled down..."

Lt. Ainippe on the Helm console growled back at Alcinoe. "I'll tend to the driving; you tend to your shooting..."

Alcinoe provided a running commentary. "Track settling down...good signal now...should be coming up on the holo any second now..."

Ligeia stared at the holo. Slowly it started painting the target.

It showed a strange starship, like nothing she had ever seen. It was lumpy, uneven; it had alternating patches of rock and ice like an asteroid.

Even as she watched, a cover on the back of the object opened and a system engine went to full power, directly away from the *Momus*, running hard. In a matter of seconds, the object had accelerated up to 208g directly away from them, toward the outer Kuiper belt, building speed to sink out.

"Take us up to 210g, Helm," yelled Ligeia, jumping back in her command chair and fastening her force webbing around her.

"210g, aye, Skipper," called Ainippe. She rang the excess g alarm for 5 seconds, then slowly started ramping up the accel, exceeding the compensator limits. The perceived g-force inside the *Momus* increased steadily until they were all groaning under 10g.

"Target has increased acceleration to 220g, Skipper," called Alcinoe. "We can't match that."

"Launch missiles," commanded Ligeia.

Alcinoe pushed the red button on the right-side trigger mounted on her Tac chair, perfectly placed to allow her to press it even under high g-forces.

Everyone on the bridge heard the vibration as four missiles departed the *Momus*, running hot and true toward the distant target.

Sol System - MarsBase

Captain Camille Allard came in, agitated.

"The *Acrux* is missing," she said. "Failed to report last two checkpoints."

"Damn it," said Jake. "I told them the Aeolians were sharp. No QE squirts before they went dark?"

"Nothing unusual," said Camille. "Normal check-in at 1800 yesterday, then nothing at midnight or 0600."

"Teresa's at Eudora, right?" asked Jake.

"Yes sir, she and Atsuko arrived two days ago and are scheduled to head back tomorrow morning our time."

Jake sighed. "Blip Teresa, give her the news, and tell her I'd like for her to check it out. And tell her to be careful!"

Camille nodded. "Aye, sir."

At Eudora, 280 light years from Earth toward the Aeolian Empire, Teresa was just sitting down to dinner with Atsuko and the Eudora-based intelligence team when the QE squirt was relayed to her tablet. She looked at it and shook her head.

"The *Acrux* has gone dark," she said to the group. "Missed the last two checkpoints. Jake wants me to go take a look."

Atsuko, her eyes wide, said "Crap." The sentiment echoed around the table. The *Acrux* was based out of Eudora now; the crew on board were friends of everyone at the table. The news was a blow.

"Could it be a QE box failure?" asked Commander Dane Fritz, one of Atsuko's head spooks.

Teresa shook her head. "They have three systems for

redundancy, all independent. You'd have to lose the whole ship before that would stop you from sending a message."

A grim silence pervaded the room as they contemplated that statement.

Finally, Atsuko spoke. "Do you want some of my team to go with? They might be helpful. There'll be no shortage of volunteers. Those are all friends of ours."

"No," Teresa said. "This is not a spook mission, pardon my French. This is a damage control mission. It could end up being a prisoner rescue, with shooting involved, or...the collection of starship debris. Either way, my crew is best suited for those scenarios."

Teresa turned to Commander Fritz. "Have you heard anything from your intelligence station on Aeolis about this?"

"No, nothing," said Fritz. "It's been totally normal."

"Well, that's not surprising. I doubt the Aeolians would let any word get out, even if they captured her or...worse."

Atsuko nodded. "I wish I was going..." she sighed.

Teresa agreed. "So do I, Atsuko. So do I."

ACRUX

Victory is reserved for those who are willing to pay its price.
- Sun Tzu, Chinese general

Aeolian Empire – Helios System
Inner Kuiper Belt

A week later, Teresa surfaced in the Aeolian Empire home system at 40 AU from Helios, the primary. The *Sirius* sat quietly for a full day, collecting ELINT from the distant planet Aeolis, but found no mention of the *Acrux* or any unusual activity in the public networks.

They sank out and surfaced again at the 30 AU point and spent another day monitoring for activity or nearby ships.

Finally, they sank out and surfaced again just beyond the mass limit, 1,000,000 km from the last known position of the *Acrux*. Creeping up on the position, they were within 500,000 km when the Tac Officer jumped in his seat.

"Contact!" he yelled. "Aeolian destroyer, designate DD1, right behind that big one..." he marked a large asteroid in the holotank.

"Hmm...," said Teresa. They were already in stealth mode, running as cold and quiet as possible. "How close will we pass on this vector?"

"We'll go right by her," said the Tac Officer. "Less than 80,000 klicks."

"OK, Helm," said Teresa, "bring us to a vector that'll get us behind that other big rock there behind her, that one..." she designated a point in the holotank – "and do it as quietly and slowly as possible. I don't care if it takes us a week to get there,

I do not want these girls snapping to us."

"Aye, Skipper," said the grizzled old yeoman at Helm, a former U.S. Navy veteran who retired early to join the RDF.

Ever so slowly the *Sirius* drifted off to the designated point, her asteroid camouflage giving her the appearance of just another piece of rock in the Kuiper belt. The yeoman even had them slowly tumbling to make it look more natural. It took them nearly forty-eight hours to get to their desired hiding place, but they did it without attracting the attention of the lurking Aeolian destroyer.

Once comfortably resting behind the rock Teresa had picked out, they had a barely visible line of sight to the last known position of the *Acrux* - and the Aeolian destroyer.

Teresa, coming out of her day cabin at 0600, returned to her command chair and addressed the XO.

"Any sign of debris?"

"I'm sorry to say, plenty of it, Skipper," said the XO. "Enough to account for the *Acrux*. I'm afraid she's gone."

Teresa cursed, something she knew Jake would not approve of – but Jake was not here looking at a destroyed RDF starship.

"Any sign of the dead man's buoy?" asked Teresa.

"We're looking, Skipper," said the XO. "So far, nothing."

Teresa sat silently as her team searched for the device called a dead man's buoy. This was essentially the flight data recorder of the *Acrux*. In the event a scoutship was destroyed, the buoy – barely 10 cm in length, disguised as just another piece of debris - would float free of the wreck and with extremely weak pulses of a tiny magnetic drive, start drifting away from the wreck. When it was 100,000 km from the original location, it would enter reporting mode.

This meant that once a day, at some random time, it would briefly send a tiny burst of noise, designed to mimic the background noise of the universe. The receivers on board the *Sirius* could detect that pseudo-random noise, pinpoint the location of the buoy, and send it a tight laser blip ordering it to activate and dump its status back to the *Sirius*.

Finally, after six hours of tedious waiting, the Comm officer jumped. "Got a signal, Skipper. 120,000 klicks thataway." He pointed to a blinking red dot in the holotank. "Sent the activation pulse, waiting..."

With a grim smile, he looked over at Teresa. "Got the dump. Sending it to your tablet."

Teresa acknowledged with a nod, looked at her tablet. The dump was not long; there were just a few dozen entries in the log. She looked at the last few...

-21340321.2244:42: Target DD1 designated, Aeolian destroyer, vector 010.344

-21340321.2254:16: DD1 vector change, direct intercept vector. Condition Red

-21340321.2254:36: Engines max emergency, accel 208g external, 8g internal, vector 182.124

-21340321.2256:14: DD1 increases accel to 210g external, overtaking, increased accel to 220g emergency, WepsAI in control

-21340321.2256:18: DD1 fires 4 missiles, overtaking, estimated 4,000 g accel. Evasive action

-21340321.2256:30: 3 missiles impact, damage heavy, engine out

-21340321.2257:50: DD1 vectors for boarding

-21340321.2257.54: Message logged: 'Remember us.'

-21340321.2258:44: self-destruct activated

Teresa bowed her head and rubbed her eyes, then flipped the log to all her officers. Around the bridge, there were more than a few bowed heads and prayers. After a long silence, Teresa stood from her command chair.

"XO, please take a note for the ship's log and for the mission report upon our return. Quote, we need a better way to get status of what happens after a self-destruct, suggest some secondary drones that fire off and watch things, then QE squirt back to HQ etc. etc. End quote."

"Noted for the log and for the mission report, Skipper," said the XO.

Teresa mused for a moment. "Also, XO, for the mission

report – designate this location as a military grave, marked as such on all charts."

The XO blinked, and then nodded. "Aye, Skipper, so noted."

Teresa turned to the bridge crew. "Does anyone see anything else that we can do here?" she asked.

Everyone shook their heads.

"Then Tac, set the dead man's buoy to self-destruct in five days. Comm, send a QE squirt to HQ with our short log. Send another one to the Aeolis and Barcam teams, let them know the *Acrux* is gone, we'll have another scoutship on station in about six weeks, location TBD.

"Helm, back us out of here very, very slowly and carefully, slower than we came in. I'm still in shock at the accel on those Aeolian missiles. Let's take about three days to drift out of here if you don't mind. Once we get out of their plausible detection range, take us home."

"Aye, aye, Mum," said the Helm.

Ever so slowly, the *Sirius* drifted away from the asteroid, keeping it between themselves and the distant Aeolian destroyer still watching the debris field.

Sol System - MarsBase

The day after Teresa's return from Aeolis, she and Jake were talking. There wasn't much they could do about the *Acrux*. Nobody could find any reason why the Aeolians had noticed the scoutship hiding in their Kuiper belt. Nothing unusual had been reported by the *Acrux* before its discovery. No ELINT had been picked up in the Aeolian Empire regarding the detection; evidently the Aeolian Navy had put a tight lid on it. The best they could hope for was that the Aeolians would eventually forget about it and move on to other things.

Teresa and Atsuko had conducted a joint operations briefing with their combined staff officers and impressed upon them, once again, the need for stealth and discretion in their scoutship operations.

Beyond that, there was little they could do. They conducted a memorial service for the crew and added their names to the growing list on the black marble wall in the lobby of the Headquarters Building at MarsBase - a list that contained hundreds of names now, and had overflowed into three separate marble facades.

Teresa told Jake about the incredible acceleration of the Aeolian missiles – 4000g – a figure that the RDF could not match. They were getting a maximum of 3000g out of their latest generation of missiles. Jake shook his head. He made notes, then sent a short message to the R&D team with the information, and a comment: "if the Aeolians can do it, then we can do it; make it happen".

Then Jake told Teresa about a new issue. Atsuko's team reported that a Bat corvette had been spotted near Phi Sagittarii, only 239 light years from Earth, nosing around the system. Luckily, it had reversed course and headed back toward the Pipe Nebula.

But the spreading electromagnetic fields – the EMF – of Earth's radio and television signals had been moving out from Earth since roughly 1910. They now formed a sphere 224 light years in radius from Earth.

The Bat corvette had been within 15 light years of discovering them. In terms of travel time, slightly less than 1 day away from detecting those early emissions.

A shiver ran down Teresa's back. They were not at all ready to fight the Bats. They were still outnumbered at least 20 to 1 in terms of firepower. If that Bat captain had decided to travel just one more day in this direction...

"I had a sleepless night last night," Jake said, "just thinking about this. I kept running scenarios through my mind. How can we accelerate our readiness? What can we do for contingency plans? But I came up with nothing new. We're doing everything we can. We're building warships like crazy, both on Earth and now in the colonies. Mitsukeli just started construction on our first battleship, the *Arizona*..."

Teresa stopped him. "The *Arizona*? Why did you pick that name? Wasn't she sunk at Pearl Harbor?"

Jake smiled. "Yes; she never got to fight. But I think she had a right to, so I'm giving her a second chance."

Teresa shrugged. "If you say so..."

Jake continued. "But this business with the Bat scout corvette, and the *Acrux*, gives me the willies. We're riding on a razor's edge here every single day."

"One wrong move – one renegade ship captain, one crazed terrorist with access to a tDrive – one Aeolian captain getting a hunch, one Bat scout deciding to take a long ride into the black – and we're done."

Teresa nodded. "So what more can we do?"

Jake looked at her. "I want to send a colony ship out on a one-way. To a blind location, at least 2,000 lights away. A fail-safe, so to speak. If something happens to Earth and the rest of the colonies, one chance for Humanity to live on."

Teresa nodded in understanding, thinking it through.

"That's not going to be much fun for the crew," she said. "I take it there's no coming back for them?"

"Right," said Jake. "I don't want to know where they are, I don't want them to ever come back into this area of space until the Bat threat has resolved."

Teresa nodded. "And I bet you want Gunner and I to come up with the ship and the crew."

Jake grinned. "You are such a good mind-reader."

MarsBase

Two weeks later, Kirsten caught Jake in his office.

"Well, it happened," she said.

Jake looked at her, puzzled. "What?"

"Sierra Nevada. The Covenant Nazis are trying to take over. They've captured the power plant, water plant and the communications complex. They've cut off all power and water. They're holding the colony hostage until they agree to drop the separation of church and state clause from the constitution and let them create a theocracy. I knew it would come to this sooner or later. I'm going out there."

Jake objected. "No, Kirs, let them handle it on their own. They'll sort it."

Kirsten sat down in the chair in front of Jake's desk. "Jake, if we don't intervene, there may be a lot of bloodshed. Let me go and see if I can get them talking again."

"No, Kirs. Really. Let them handle their own affairs. Besides, we have our holiday coming on with the kids. Remember? All of us going to Earth for the July 4th fireworks, staying at the cabin?"

"Jake," Kirsten badgered him. "The Colonial Office is my job. It's my responsibility. Let me do my job."

Jake shook his head. "You have staff. You have Sara and Pete. Let them take care of it."

"Jake," Kirsten said softly. "I don't tell you how to do your job. Let me do mine. I'll take Pete with me. I'll be back in time for the 4th. I'll meet you guys at the cabin."

Jake waved his hands in defeat. "Be sure you do. It's just not the same without all of us together for the holiday. And take a full Seal team with you."

Kirsten came around the desk and kissed him on the forehead. "See you in ten days," she said.

Sol System – Earth
East Texas

"Daddy, what did you do in the war?" asked Granada. Jake, Teresa, and the children were at the cabin in Texas, having a bonfire, roasting marshmallows. Granada, the oldest, was seven that year. Chloe was five, Skip was four and Stephen was two. They had started their short vacation, waiting for Kirsten to arrive.

Jake grinned. "Not much. I flew off a carrier, went up in the sky, shot at other planes and they shot at me."

Teresa laughed. "Don't think I've ever heard it put quite so clearly."

"The kids at school said you got shot down," said Granada.

"I did," said Jake. "On my 28th mission. May 12, 2115. That was quite a day."

Teresa touched Jake on the arm. "You've never told them about it. You should tell them."

Jake looked back at her. "As should you, Terese."

"What?" exclaimed Granada. "Mom was shot down too?"

"Yes, she was," said Jake. "May 27, 2115. Right smack over the Yalu River. She came down in the middle of the river and the Chinese and North Koreans had a big argument over who got to take her prisoner. The Chinese won."

"Mom!" yelled Granada. "You never told us!"

Teresa looked at the fire, stirring it up with a long stick. Sparks flew up into the air, making a river of light and dark, flowing up into the stars pricking the sky.

"I don't talk about it much, G," she said.

Jake intervened. "Your mom was taken prisoner by the Chinese, and tortured for a while, G. So it hurts her to talk about it."

"Oh," said Granada. "I'm sorry, Mom."

"It's OK, honey," Teresa leaned over and kissed her. "Don't you worry about it."

Chloe jumped in. "What's torture?"

Teresa ruffled Chloe's hair. "It's when bad people do things to hurt you, Chlo."

"Oh," said Skip. "Like when Chlo pulls my hair."

"Well, a little bit worse than that, dear," said Teresa.

"Did Mommy Kirs fight in the war, too?" asked Granada.

"No, Mommy Kirs was working in science, making things to help the navy. In Austin, not too far from here," said Teresa.

Skip jumped in. "So what happened to you when you got shot down, Daddy?"

"Not much," said Jake. "I hit my head on the side of the airplane when I ejected, so I was unconscious for a while. I woke up lying in a field in Mongolia. I was too dizzy to get up, so I just laid there. A bunch of farmers ran up with pitchforks and made me stay there until the Mongolian army arrived. The army guys took me to a place where they kept me for the rest of the war, because they were neutral and didn't want to get into the fight."

"What was the fight about, Daddy?"

Jake shook his head. "The same thing most fights are about, Chlo. Somebody wants something, and another somebody doesn't want them to have it. All the gorillas start pounding their chests and hooting at each other, and the next thing you know there's a fight. Humans haven't made too much progress since we came out of the jungle, I guess."

"Mom, did you get hurt when you ejected out of the plane?"

"No," said Teresa. "It hurt my back a lot, but I got over that pretty quick."

"Oh," said Stephen. "Did you break the plane?"

"I did," grinned Teresa. "I broke the plane really, really bad!"

"And so did Daddy!" said Chloe.

Jake agreed. "I certainly broke mine. I saw the crater it made."

Skip starting chanting. "Mommy broke a plane. Daddy broke a plane. Mommy broke a plane. Daddy broke a plane..."

Jake reached over and took Teresa's hand and squeezed it. Teresa leaned back onto Jake, settling into the space between his raised knees, her back resting against him, looking at the children poking at the fire with their sticks, throwing sparks into the heavens.

BLUEBONNETS

"Remember us."
- Last message from the Acrux

Sol System – Earth
East Texas

It was late morning next day, when Lois and Atsuko came, unannounced. Jake, Teresa, and the children were returning from a walk down by the river, the children clutching handfuls of bedraggled flowers and chattering like magpies. Stephen had a frog in his pocket, though neither Jake nor Teresa knew it. They would find it later that night.

Jake heard the flitter coming, and turned to stare into the bright summer sky, stopping his walk momentarily. Then he turned to Teresa, a worried look in his eyes.

"This can't be good," he said softly.

Teresa nodded. This was a treasured vacation. They had left strict orders not to be disturbed unless it was a dire emergency. And it wouldn't be Kirsten, because she would comm them first to say hi to the children.

They continued toward the cabin, while the flitter landed in front and powered down, whining softly. The hatch popped open, and Atsuko Kawasaki climbed out, followed by Lois Vetton. As they got closer, Jake could see that Lois had been crying. Her eyes were red.

That's when he knew.

Teresa gasped and stopped dead in her tracks. She shook her head.

"No, no, no," she cried.

Atsuko came up to them and stopped in front of them. She had determined not to cry, but now faced with Jake and Teresa, she couldn't help it. Tears coursed down her cheeks.

Jake turned to Granada. "G, please take the kids into the cabin for us, would you?"

Granada nodded, but questioned: "Why? What's going on?"

Jake squatted down and put his hands on her shoulders. "Please, Granada, just take them inside. We'll be there in a minute."

Granada nodded again, then shooed the other three into the cabin. Chloe, getting some glimpse of the bad news that was coming, resisted, but Granada had a way with them, and managed to get all of them inside. Jake turned back to Atsuko and Lois, who were just standing there, devastated and forlorn.

"Kirsten?" he asked.

Atsuko nodded. Lois started crying again. Jake, in his grief, just reacted on automatic pilot. He walked over to Lois and put his arms around her, holding her.

"She was hit by a stray bullet on Sierra Nevada," said Atsuko with some difficulty. "It was painless. She never knew what hit her."

Teresa wailed and stumbled into Atsuko's arms. They held each other, sobbing, as Jake held Lois. Out of the corner of his eye, he caught a glimpse of the children, standing inside at the window, watching them in confusion.

"The children," he said softly to the others. "The children are watching. We have to get it together."

Teresa pulled back from Atsuko, sniffling, nodding, wiping her eyes with her sleeve. Lois turned away from Jake, trying to pull herself together. Atsuko also turned away, wiping her eyes with her hands. Together they stood for several minutes, trying to compose themselves.

Finally, they were able to turn and enter the cabin to tell the children.

They buried Kirsten in the field of bluebonnets behind the cabin, where she had love to play with the children. At the funeral, Teresa and Lois stood directly behind Chloe and Stephen - Kirsten's children – their hands resting on their little shoulders, making it clear to everyone that these children still had mothers. Jake stood next to Lois, behind Granada and Skip - Teresa's children - in a wall of solidarity, his hands on their shoulders as well.

Chloe was old enough to understand; she would never see her mother again. She stood straight, brave, trying to honor her mother's own courage. Stephen did not fully comprehend what was happening but tugged at his sister's coat from time to time. Chloe placed her arm around his shoulders, comforting him.

The grave was in the center of the field of bluebonnets, and as the honor guard fired their rifles, the children held their hands over their ears. The honor guard folded the flag on the coffin and presented it to Chloe, as Jake had requested of them before the service.

Clutching it tightly, Chloe continued to hold to little Stephen as best she could, while the honor guard marched off to their waiting shuttle.

Teresa and Lois, by prior agreement, led the children back to the cabin. But Jake stayed a bit, while the gravediggers lazed under a distant tree, shovels in hand, waiting for everybody to leave so they could finish their job.

Jake walked over to the gravestone, not yet placed. It was covered by a tarp, several meters behind the grave, shielded by a tree.

Jake pulled off the tarp and looked at the stone. It contained Kirsten's name, date of birth and death, and the motto of the RDF:

"Bound in life and death, we offer our lives for each other and for Humanity."

Below that was a single handprint – something Jake had once seen in an ancient cave, and never forgotten. Handprints, left behind by prehistoric Humans. An imprint. A message to the future. They had lived. They had loved. They had made a world together.

It was the shorthand version of the RDF motto. A single blood-red handprint. It appeared on the RDF Battle Flag, and on the nose of every warship. A symbol of the lives lost trying to save Humanity.

Kneeling beside the grave, Jake spoke softly to Kirsten.

"We made something good, Kirs. We made something that will protect Humanity for hundreds, maybe thousands of years to come. We gave it integrity, courage, and common sense, most of that from you. And we made two beautiful children, to carry that legacy forward."

Jake leaned forward and kissed the top of the coffin, then slowly walked away.

Sol System - MarsBase

"No more discussion," said Jake. "Ostracize them."

Gunner Carlson, his Chief of Staff, gazed at him steadily, as did Teresa on the other side of the table.

"Jake," Gunner began, but Jake cut him off.

"No. Just do it."

There was a short silence as Gunner and Teresa hoped to get Jake to calm down and see reason. Finally, Teresa stepped in.

"Think of all the innocent people who had nothing to do with Kirsten's death," she said. "A hundred thousand people who would have loved her as much as we do. A hundred thousand people who welcomed her to Sierra Nevada to try and resolve the crisis. Do we throw all of them to the wolves, just because of what a couple of dozen terrorists did?"

Jake shook his head, angry. "I told her not to go. I told her!"

Teresa continued. "And maybe that's why you're so angry,

Jake. Because you blame yourself. But it wasn't your fault, Jake! You know Kirsten and her sense of duty. She had to go because it was her job. Nothing you could have done would have changed her mind."

Jake stared at the table for a long time. Finally, he sighed. "OK, then give them a stiff fine. One starship added to their charter debt."

Gunner looked at Teresa across the table. Slowly, he agreed, realizing Jake would settle for nothing less. "I think that might be appropriate," he said.

Without another word, Jake rose and left the room.

Gunner continued to look at Teresa. "At least, make it a scoutship, not a battleship," he said. "Cut them some slack."

Teresa nodded. Then she sighed. "What are we going to do about Pete Franklin? He blames himself. He's devastated. He's non-functional at this point. He turned in his resignation to me."

Gunner shook his head. "I know. He thinks he should have caught the bullet, not Kirsten. I don't think he'll ever forgive himself. I really don't think he can come back from this."

Teresa mused for a second. "I wonder...maybe I know something that might save him..."

FARAWAY

When you come out of the storm, you won't be the same person who walked in.

- Haruki Murakami, Japanese writer

MarsBase

In Jake's conference room, Gunner and Teresa sat with several members of their staff, along with Pete Franklin and Amy Tan. Jake gazed around the table at them.

"Are you quite sure about this, Pete?" he asked.

Pete nodded. "Yes, sir. We'll do it."

"Amy?"

"I'm in," responded Amy.

"And you'll use the *Yorkshire*?" Jake asked.

"Correct," said Teresa. "It's the oldest colony ship, but it's been a great ship for its entire career, never any major issues. It's safely delivered well over 100,000 colonists so far. And it just came out of C-check overhaul. It's ready to go."

"Sara?"

"We've got a candidate list of 10,000 names that we're contacting right now," responded Sara Watkins. "We've already gotten 300 acceptances. If the present trend continues, we'll have a full complement of 500 in another two weeks – one-half the normal complement for a colony, but that will double the supplies available to them at the other end, so we're happy with that number. That will still create a viable colony, with enough genetic diversity, especially since we're requiring equal parts Asian, African, and Caucasian. We've got the manifest complete and all required goods are either in the Geneva warehouse or can be bought off the shelf. We can launch in three months."

Jake leaned over the table, gazing at Pete and Amy.

"And I want to make sure you understand the parameters. Once you launch, you pick a random location, and we never know where that is. Nobody left behind will ever know where you are, until after the Bat threat is resolved. You can communicate with us only to let us know that you have arrived safely, and you can give us one or two simple progress reports as you establish the colony, so that we know you are alive and well. But nothing that could identify where you are, how far you went, or the exact planet you are on."

"We understand, sir," said Pete, Amy nodding beside him.

"Then get to it, Pete," said Jake. "Start crew selection, don't force anyone to go against their will. But get it done."

Pete Franklin nodded vigorously. He looked at Amy and reached for her hand under the table. Her pregnancy was just starting to show. With any luck at all, the baby would be born on the ship while they were underway and would grow up on a new planet – a new home for the children of Earth.

Possibly the only home for them if things went badly.

And a second chance for Pete Franklin.

Two weeks later, Jake walked into his apartment. Hanging his cap on the hook by the door, he saw an unknown Captain's cap hanging there. Teresa called out from the kitchen. "Lois is here, Jake. I invited her for dinner."

"Great," said Jake. "I'll just change."

He went into the bedroom and changed from his uniform into jeans and a polo shirt, then went back out to the kitchen. Lois and Teresa were setting the table. Jake kissed Teresa, then hugged Lois.

They sat down to dinner, and ate quietly for a while, Teresa and Lois making some small talk about an upcoming training exercise. After a while, Teresa got up, collected the dishes, and put them in the sink, got the coffeepot and re-filled their cups, and sat back down. She looked over at Lois.

"Lois, would you like to join our marriage?"

Lois smiled. "Thanks, Teresa, but no. I appreciate it. But no. I don't think so."

"You'd be welcome," said Teresa. "We'd love to have you."

Lois glanced at Jake. "No, but thank you, Teresa. Kirsten was bi, so that made things work out well with you and Jake. But I'm not. I'm all gay, so I don't think it would work."

Jake commented. "It'd be fine, Lois, if you want to do it. I'd be fine without the sex."

Lois shook her head. "No. Anyway, I'd always feel like I was replacing Kirsten. I don't think it would be a good feeling."

Lois placed her hand over Teresa's. "But I love you for asking, Teresa. I hope we can always be friends, if you want." Lois looked over at Jake to see his reaction.

Jake managed a smile, a painful one but genuine. "I think Kirsten would like that, Lois. You are ...well...please consider yourself part of our family. Married or not. Part of the family."

Teresa nodded. "Yes, Lois. Now and forever. Part of our family."

KIRSTEN'S STAR

The most important days in your life are the day you are born, and the day you find out why.
- Mark Twain, American writer

MarsBase

Teresa looked across the table at Jake, as did Gunner and the rest of Jake's staff. Teresa repeated his words, just to make sure she understood.

"You want us to help set up a RimFed government."

"Yes," Jake responded. "I think it's time. Think about it. It will take them years, decades probably, to get up and running. We might as well let them get started."

"We'll retain veto power over their decisions for many years, just to keep them from doing something stupid. But it's kind of like having children – there comes a time when you have to put them on the bike and let them try to ride it."

Sara Watkins demurred. "Don't we have enough political troubles with Earth? Wouldn't that double our problems?"

"Maybe. But sooner or later, the RDF will have to cede control to a civilian government. Personally, I think it'll take 80 to 90 years before they'll be ready. Still, we should allow them to start making mistakes on their own, learning how to ride the bike. That will lead to a better government, decades down the road, when we finally have to put ourselves under their authority."

Gunner nodded. Sara chimed in. "When do you think that might happen, Jake? Ceding authority to a civilian government?"

Jake shook his head. "I don't know, Sara. After we fight the Bats. I wouldn't trust them to manage us before that."

"When do you want to have these elections?" asked Gunner.

Jake leaned forward and put his arms on the table. "Let's consult with Earth and the Colonies. Try to get some consensus on how they want to go about this. I would think they'd want to create a more-or-less constitutional convention, put together the basics, set up elections, and so forth. As long as they don't propose anything crazy or outside the Basic Rules, I think we can leave it in their hands."

Gunner nodded.

"That's all I have, folks," said Jake.

Six weeks later, the rough concept of a proposed RimFed constitutional convention was hammered out and presented to the news media. The idea was picked apart by those who just knew they were smarter than everybody else. But despite the trolls, the Constitutional Convention was scheduled. Representatives were nominated and elected in the face of a growing excitement as Humanity realized their first interstellar government was being formed.

Finally, on 21 February 2136 at Mitsukeli Colony – a more-or-less neutral location – the delegates came together and started work on creating a new government encompassing the entire Rim.

It was not an easy or a pretty task. It took two months of infighting, name-calling, insults, compromises, backroom deals, and threats of veto from Jake.

When it was over, a baby government called the Rim Federation – RimFed – was born. The newborn was birthed by means of an election to create a Parliament – formed from representatives from each colony in the Rim – and on 5 August 2136, the RimFed Parliament met for the first time.

Taking a cue from the RDF, which had struggled so mightily to maintain independence and neutrality from

Earth governments, the new Parliament conducted their first meeting on the planet Liberty, to avoid undue influence from Earth.

For their first sessions, nothing of great importance was either proposed or resolved; as Jake had noted, they were learning to ride a bike. They did manage to elect a Prime Minister; they created several ministries, laid the foundations of a civil service, and toward the end, resolved to find a more permanent location, one as neutral as possible from the established colonies – and Earth.

Shortly after this, Teresa came into Jake's office.

"Jake, I'd like to take a scoutship out to Kamilaroi. I think I have an idea about how to set up the new RimFed capital."

Jake looked puzzled. "What do you mean? That one's almost all water – it has only two small landmasses, really just two little volcanic islands like Iceland."

Teresa agreed. "I know. But I want to take a quick look at it. Humor me on this, will ya? I'll be there and back in two weeks. Just give me the *Sirius* and a small crew, couple of planetary scientists."

Jake shrugged. "It's all yours. Go for it. But please try to be back on time. And keep us updated with QE squirts."

Teresa got up and kissed him on the cheek. "Thanks, husband."

Jake looked at her askance. "Now, I didn't do that as your husband. I did that as your Commanding Officer."

Teresa leaned over and wiped the kiss off. "In that case, I take it back."

With a bounce, she was gone.

Jake sighed. Keeping a balance between his duties as CNO and his marriage to Teresa was always a balancing act.

Some people outside the RDF – those who didn't know him – complained he practiced nepotism, favoritism, and a host of other sins.

But those who knew him well, knew better. Jake worked strictly on merit, regardless of his marriage to Teresa.

When people told him of the complaints others raised, he just laughed. "We'll see. When the Bats come. When Teresa is out in front of the fight, and the whiners are at home hiding under the table."

36 Ophiuchi C – Planet Kamilaroi

At Kamilaroi – once known as 36 Ophiuchi C-d - Teresa put the *Sirius* in orbit over the planet. It was nearly all ocean – there were only two small landmasses, situated on opposite sides of the planet, one in the northern hemisphere and one in the southern.

Both were in a temperate climate and about the size of Hawaii, semi-dormant volcanic hotspots on an otherwise water world.

Other than the lack of land, the planet was not bad. No one had ever bothered to fully survey it, given the number of other planets more suitable for large-scale colonization.

Recently, Teresa had been entertaining an idea. Living on MarsBase was difficult, nearly impossible for families. Children could not go outside. Their entire lives were spent in an artificial, cocooned environment. Although they operated a nursery for new mothers and a small kindergarten on Mars, once children graduated from kindergarten they were required to go to Geneva for elementary school. This created logistical nightmares, including the high level of security required to protect their dependents from hostile interests on Earth.

Teresa had the survey team map the planet carefully, testing all key parameters, and was thrilled when they reported it was eminently habitable.

Although there would be hurricanes near the equator, the two large islands were far enough into the temperate zone that weather would be reasonable. The center of the volcanic hotspots that had formed the original islands were now moving offshore, forming new islands under the sea. Volcanic cones on both islands were still active – as Kilauea on Hawaii – but not overtly dangerous.

This was the news Teresa had been hoping for.

Returning to MarsBase, she reported to Jake.

"Jake, my dear," she said (they were in quarters, so off duty). "You know you've directed us to work with the RimFed people to put together a plan for a RimFed capital. What could be better than this planet? There's adequate land on Kamilaroi for both the new RimFed government and our RDF headquarters. We can remain isolated from all other interests since there's not enough land for further colonization. We'd have the planet to ourselves, and it would be easily defended."

Jake grunted, not too sure about it. "Aren't there plenty of other planets out there we could use for a capital city?"

"Sure," said Teresa. "But every one of them would eventually grow to have a huge population, and then that population would unduly influence the RimFed government. On this planet, that could never happen. RimFed would always be sufficiently isolated from the rest of the Rim to ensure at least some independence. It would be easier for them to maintain independence and objectivity. Think about it."

"I'm not sure I accept your argument," said Jake, "but go ahead and present it to the PM's office, see what they say. It's ultimately their decision."

Kirsten's Star - 2,265 lights from Earth

It was a beautiful planet. Amy Tan couldn't believe they had gotten so lucky.

"Do you see it, Pete? Look at it!" she exclaimed.

"I see it, babe. I see it," said Pete Franklin, gazing out the window of the shuttle as it dropped into the atmosphere.

The blue planet below them looked exactly like Earth, except maybe better. No pollution, no bitterness, no wars. Plenty of photosynthetic-based trees and grasses, quite normal plains and oceans and mountains.

They had made it.

Above them, the colony ship *Yorkshire* turned in orbit, disgorging three more shuttles filled with people, supplies and hope. Pete watched as the pilot directed their shuttle to the chosen colony site, a bay on the smaller eastern ocean. It was well-protected from storms, with plenty of fresh water on the landward side, backed by a tall mountain range to the west.

Vast plains of grass covered the distance between the ocean and the mountains, with a forest to the south that could provide timber. To the north, another forest provided some protection from the northerly winds that would come in winter.

Amy held Gerri in her arms, the three-month old gurgling and spitting up a bit. Amy distractedly wiped with a cloth. Behind them, a dozen of their cohort also beamed out the window, daring to believe that the planet would be everything they hoped for.

All preliminary surveys had been completed. The atmosphere was virtually identical to Earth. The grass was simply grass. Nothing special about it, easily eaten and digested by the livestock. The trees were a bit different from Earth, but close enough. The timber could be used for building.

No overtly pathological organisms had been found, although undoubtedly some would find a way to become invasive over time. There were some predators, but seemingly nothing larger than a wolf. There was one huge elephant-like creature, but it was placid and non-violent when left alone.

With a crunch, the shuttle grounded in the area they had designated as a landing zone. The back hatch fell open, and their militia leader, former RDF Seal Commander Neil Douglas, went out with his security team. Even though this was their tenth trip to the surface, and there was already a permanent party camping in the distance, they were taking no chances.

Pete waited until the others had exited, then took Amy's hand and led her out of the shuttle. Gerri started to cry about that time, until Amy gave her a pacifier. Happily, Gerri settled in for some serious paci chewing. Pete took it as a good omen.

Stretching his arms wide, Pete Franklin looked into the blue sky, at the yellow sun near the zenith, a virtual twin of Sol. He sank down to his knees, and with his arms still extended, he closed his eyes and thanked the Creator. Beside him, he felt Amy also kneel, and then he heard and felt the rest of them, all kneeling in awe at the chances given to them for a future.

KAMILAROI

The best way to predict your future is to create it.
- Abraham Lincoln, U. S. President

Sol System – MarsBase

A month later, Teresa was gratified when she heard that the budding new government of RimFed had conducted their own feasibility study of Kamilaroi and concurred with her idea. They proposed the construction of a capital city for the Rim Federation on Kamilaroi, a city which would be named New Geneva.

However, she didn't get much traction from Jake and his staff about moving RDF headquarters to Kamilaroi as well. This was mostly due to their preoccupation with the Aeolian Empire.

Jake and his staff were deep in projects related to the Aeolians, mostly all centered around how to form an alliance with them while preventing their Empress from taking over Earth as a colony planet. As large as the RDF was now – dozens of warships, more than a dozen colony planets – it was not nearly strong enough to take on the Aeolians. Jake continued to maintain a policy of no overt contact, only infiltration and intelligence gathering.

Teresa and her staff had made several studies of the military capabilities of the Aeolians, and she was both impressed and terrified. Their space navy was undoubtedly an order of magnitude more competent and dangerous than the current state of the RDF. Despite all their efforts, creating a Navy to compete with several hundred years of Aeolian experience in space left them sorely lacking, both in numbers and proficiency.

Teresa fully understood Jake's hesitancy in dealing with the Aeolians. One small miss-step could bring a hundred warships to Earth's door. And given the Aeolian Empire's history, the results would not be good for Earth.

Yet, it would be impossible to face the Bat threat without the help of the Aeolians. Every study showed that the Bats would inevitably discover them by the early 2220's, with estimates ranging from 2215 to 2225, possibly sooner if bad luck prevailed. They had about 80 years left to prepare for the onslaught.

But those same studies showed that the RDF alone would never have the weight of warships and resources to win the war. Only via an alliance with the Aeolians could they possibly survive. But that alliance seemed as distant now as it did when *Pandora* came to Earth.

Jake had several contingency plans available if discovered by the Bats, or in imminent danger of discovery. One of the contingency plans was to enter the Aeolian system in force, with a couple of dozen warships, and hold a static position at 5 AU from the home planet. He thought the Aeolians would open a dialogue and talk to them. Once communication was established, they could describe the threat of the Bats and press the Aeolians to join them against a common enemy. It was not much, but as a last-ditch effort, there was little else he could do.

Teresa advocated a variation of this plan, which she thought would have a better chance of success. Entering the Aeolian system in force and waiting at the 5 AU point from the home planet, she would try to lure the Aeolians into a stern chase back to the Bat invasion force, initiating an instant battle.

But Jake didn't really think that approach would work. He thought the Aeolians would see the trap, back off and watch as the RDF was destroyed. And he felt it left too much up to chance.

If the Bats came before they were ready, there were no good choices.

Gunner Carlson caught Jake headed for his apartment after a long day. Gunner had a huge smile on his face.

"We got a confirmation blip from Pete, right on schedule," he said.

"Nine months?" asked Jake.

"Exactly nine months since they launched. Per our agreement, we won't know when they actually got there, it could have been six months ago or just yesterday. But they got there."

"What rating?"

Before the launch of the *Yorkshire* – the backup, last-ditch survival strategy for Humanity in case of disaster - certain codes had been agreed on.

Jake wanted to know as little as possible about the planet the expedition found, but he did want to know that it was a good one. They had settled on a simple rating system – "A" through "F". "A" was equivalent to Earth. "F" was just barely survivable.

Gunner beamed. "A."

"Hot damn," said Jake. "They threw a winner."

"Yep," said Gunner. "You want the remainder of the code?"

"You bet," said Jake. Gunner peered at his tablet. "42."

Jake laughed out loud. "Pete and his crazy sense of humor."

Gunner grinned even larger. "Yep. The Answer at the End of the Universe. Decoded, it's "down, established, viable, happy, you owe Gunner a drink."

Jake clapped Gunner on the back. "Mr. Chief of Staff, I think it's time I buy you a drink!"

Geneva, Switzerland

Teresa was exhausted. Dealing with the new RimFed government had to be the most tiring thing she had ever experienced.

How, she wondered, could people talk so long over so little?

RimFed had requested an RDF representative in their meeting to plan the new capital on Kamilaroi. Since Teresa had performed the planetary survey, she volunteered to go. She loved coming to Geneva, because it gave her a chance to see the children at boarding school, but at the same time, she hated it. The endless yakking of the RimFed delegates, the stupid arguments over arcane details, were so alien to her military mind.

For the third time in the day, her head tilted forward as she almost went to sleep, jerking it back upright at the last minute and looking around guiltily to see if anyone noticed.

Luckily, the meeting was almost over. It was six p.m., and she had a date with the children to have dinner and watch a movie together. Finally, against all odds, the chairman hammered his gavel, and the meeting was adjourned.

Teresa left the room, where her security detail met her, enclosing her in a protective wrap as she went up the private elevator to her old apartment. The children were already waiting.

"Mom!" yelled Granada, as she entered, and Teresa stooped down as all four of the children ran to her and gave her a big group hug. Skip started crying, as he often did when he saw Teresa after an absence. She cradled him in her arms, moving to the couch to sit with all of them, holding them one by one, until everybody had calmed.

"Now, what do you guys want for dinner?" she asked.

"Pizza!" they yelled, and Teresa laughed.

Kirsten's Star – Planet Faraway

Pete paused the plow, giving himself and the oxen a rest. They could have brought tractors; but tractors require gasoline, and gasoline requires oil, and oil requires exploration and drilling. Things they couldn't depend on for the long haul.

Instead, they had elected to bring only the primitive farming tools of the late 1800's. The space that tractors would have taken was instead used to store seed and livestock.

They had finished unloading and mucking out the *Yorkshire*; it was now powered down, in a nice stable orbit over the planet, geosynchronous to their location. This allowed them to monitor QE transmissions from Earth; but nothing could go outbound.

Pete had made sure of that; after sending the initial codes, Pete had the transmitting equipment dismantled and placed in a drone, which he sent off into a solar orbit known only to three people – himself, Amy, and Neil Douglas, head of Security. For anyone without the knowledge of where it was, it would be extremely difficult to find and make use of the transmitter. In a dire emergency, though, they could retrieve it and communicate back to the RDF.

The G1V star, which they had named Kirsten's Star, was hot on the back of Pete's neck. He wiped his bandanna across and pushed it back into his pocket. "Step Up!" he cried, and slowly the oxen started moving again.

Later, Pete and Amy sat by the stream, feet in the water, washing the dirt off after a hard day in the fields. Nearby, the oxen grazed in their paddock. Overhead, a glancing reflection of light from the setting sun brought Pete's attention to the sky, as the *Yorkshire* sat overhead, in her permanent position over the colony.

"She's still there, just like Old Faithful," he said to Amy, pointing.

"I should hope so," said Amy. "Orbital mechanics being what they are."

"Well, you know what I mean," said Pete. "A touch of home. Gives me some comfort to see her."

"I know." Amy held Pete's hand, enjoying the moment of peace they managed to find at the end of the long workday.

"By the way, Gerri is talking up a storm. Today she asked

where 'dada' was."

Pete smiled. "She is so wonderful. Are you ready to have another?"

Amy squeezed his hand. "I'd like to wait until we're a little better established, I think."

Far away, a bonfire burned as some of the other farmers cleared land for their next sowing. After fourteen months on Faraway, they had brought in meager crops - but enough to survive for another year.

They would get better at it; they had to. The herds of cattle, horses and pigs were surviving, although births were lower than expected. The colonists had experienced one round of illness; it had not been nailed down precisely, but they thought it was a mutation of chicken pox, not a pathogen from the new planet. Only two people had died.

They had created a cemetery on a hill not far from town. They laid it out with plenty of room; hope was fine, but reality suggested it would grow larger.

FALSE PROPHETS

Beware of false prophets, who come to you in sheep's clothing, but inwardly they are ravenous wolves. You will know them by their fruits.

-Jesus.

Geneva, Switzerland

When the security alarm went off, Teresa raised her head by reflex, glanced at the clock and saw it was 2:45 AM.

She thought to call down to the security office but before she could trigger her wrist comm, gunshots thundered outside the apartment door. She heard the splintering of wood and metal.

Jumping out of bed, she grabbed uniform pants and got them pulled halfway up her legs when someone burst through the bedroom door and wrapped a cloth around her face, smothering her in some chemical.

Teresa sank down into a long, dark tunnel. Far away, she thought she heard Kirsten's voice, calling her.

She woke up in a dark room. Her head hurt like hell. Her hands were tied behind, her feet tied to a chair.

She saw the red pinpoint glow of an LED to one side and could just barely make out a security camera. She was disoriented, unable to think. She missed Jake and wondered where he was. *"Why doesn't he come get me?" she thought.*

Then she passed out again.

It was later. She woke again. Someone was splashing water in her face.

She opened one eye, fuzzily, made out a woman, standing next to her, splashing her from a water basin. With some effort, she opened the other eye.

"You can stop now," said Teresa. "I'm awake."

"About time," the woman said. The woman set the basin down on a table and left the room. In a few seconds, she came back with a man.

The two of them sat down across a small desk from Teresa, staring at her. The woman was dressed all in black, a severe frown on her narrow face, glaring at Teresa out of faded blue eyes. The man was sloppily dressed in a wrinkled brown suit, bearded, his hair barely combed. They sat, as if they were waiting for Teresa to say something. She didn't give them the satisfaction.

Finally, the man sighed, smiled a bit at Teresa, and spoke.

"You are a prisoner of war of the Covenant of God," he said. "You will be offered in exchange to Jake Hammett in return for his agreement to hand over control of the RDF to the United States."

Teresa laughed. She laughed loud and long. She was still laughing when the woman got up, came over and knocked her unconscious again.

MarsBase

Jake had a glint in his eye that scared the hell out of everybody around him. His staff had backed off down the conference table a good 18 inches, leaving empty chairs between Jake and themselves. He wasn't yelling; he wasn't raising his voice. But there was something fearful in Jake Hammett today.

Quietly, almost whispering, he asked: "Any ideas at all about where they are holding her?"

Lois Vetton spoke up. "No, sir. We have nothing. I promise you, we're working on it, but they got a good jump on us."

Jake nodded, his face working. "They cut out the tracer?"

Lois nodded. "First thing we checked. We found it on the floor of an empty warehouse in Geneva this morning. Still bloody."

"I will kill these bastards," said Jake softly. "I will track them down and I will kill them. Slowly."

Lois nodded again. "I'll help you, Jake. We all will. But we need to decide what to do about their demands. How do you want to respond?"

Jake looked at her like she was an alien from another planet. "We don't negotiate with terrorists. No response."

Lois tried again. "Jake. It's Teresa. Maybe we can negotiate something with them. At least let me try."

Jake shook his head. "How would it look, Lois? I've refused to negotiate or compromise with threats for all these years - but when it's my own wife, I change the policy? What would that do to the future of the RDF? I can't do it, Lois."

Lois nodded, silently.

"Keep trying to find her and extract her."

"Aye, aye, sir," said Lois Vetton. Quietly, she picked up her tablet and left the room.

Outside Frankfurt, the two jailers – the tall, thin woman dressed in black and the man in the sloppy brown suit – were on a video call to Mobile, Alabama. On the other end was Acton Pierce – worldwide head of the Covenant of God, the fundamentalist cult hell-bent on implementation of a religious theocracy in the United States.

"No response from the RDF? Nothing?" asked the thin woman.

Acton shook his head. "So far, nothing. Make another video, this time make her scream more. Get it to me by tomorrow morning."

The man in the brown suit objected. "She's very weak after that last session. I'm not sure she can take any more. We may lose her."

"No matter," said Pierce. "We never intended to return her

anyway."

"One thing," said the thin woman. "She keeps laughing at us, saying that we don't know Jake Hammett. And she keeps looking at us, telling us she's imagining us without arms and legs. It's creepy. But she won't tell us what that means."

"Forget it," said Pierce. "Get the next video made, get it to me, we'll ship it off to Hammett. He'll come around."

Pierce disconnected the video link, then made another call to Washington, D. C. He had a report to make to a Senator.

Teresa screamed. The pain was exquisitely unendurable. But it wouldn't stop. She screamed again, continuously, until she passed out. The man in the sloppy brown suit stood up from behind the video camera, stopping the recording.

"She's out again," said the tall thin woman, disgustedly. "We'll have to wait until she comes to." She took the water basin and started splashing water on Teresa's face again.

"I don't think she can last much longer," said the man in brown. "We're going to lose her."

"I don't care," said the woman. "The sooner, the better. Just get some good video and we can be done with this."

Outside the farmhouse, four guards walked around, their pulse rifles unobtrusively hidden beneath long overcoats.

In geosynchronous orbit overhead, the scout ship *Rigel* peered dirtside, every sensor straining to detect any hint of Teresa's location. The Saints had removed Teresa's tracker, embedded in her right thigh, to prevent the RDF from locating her electronically, leaving a bloody gash. Lois Vetton had thus resorted to old-fashioned police work. She was convinced Teresa would still be in Europe – it was too dangerous to move her off planet. Lois was sure they would stay reasonably close to the point of abduction.

The *Rigel* scanned the frequency of every communication method in Europe – every phone, every video, every Net transaction she could intercept – using the cycles of ten frigate AI cores wired in parallel, mounted in the cargo bay.

It had been three days since the last video. Lois, sitting in the bridge, hadn't slept in 24 hours, and was dozing when the comm came in.

The comm officer read the message twice, wanting it to be untrue. But it was valid - verified and sent directly from Geneva RDF. It had to be true. With tears in his eyes, he turned to Lois, who had roused when she heard the comm chime. She saw the tears in the eyes of the Comm Officer and shook her head.

"What?" she asked.

The Comm Officer spoke haltingly, barely able to get it out. "They found Teresa's body in an alley in Geneva. She's dead."

Lois nodded. She had known all along they were too far behind the curve on this one. She had expected this outcome. But it hurt all the same.

"Prep my shuttle. I'm going to fetch her. And have the *Chengdu* alongside waiting when I get back."

Lois turned to the Captain of the *Rigel*, Noah Brown. "Captain Brown, you will stay on station and keep sifting through the ELINT until you find something, or hell freezes over, whichever comes first. Understood?"

"Aye, aye, Mum," said Captain Brown. "Will do. We'll find them."

CHENGDU

The tiger does not have to boast that he is a tiger.
- Nigerian Proverb

MarsDock *Gusev*

Teresa's body lay in the hanger of the *Chengdu*, her favorite ship. Lois had brought her back to MarsDock. Her coffin lay on a bier, draped in the battle flag of the RDF – a single blood-red handprint, across an orange background. The symbol of blood spilled – the promise of a future for Humanity.

Jake sat beside the coffin in a folding chair someone had brought for him. He had been there a long time. In a moment of mercy, Gunner had brought him a sandwich and a vodka screwdriver, just in case.

They sat in a tray beside the chair, untouched. Jake had already consumed a half-dozen drinks before the *Chengdu* arrived. Now his pain was dulled by alcohol and headache, but still too grim to bear.

"Hey, Terese," Jake mumbled, talking to the coffin. "Hope you don't mind that I had a few too many before you arrived. I was really missing you. I didn't think I could face the moment without it."

Jake rubbed his face. He had shaved that morning, but he would need another one soon. He dropped his head down, looking at his shoes.

"I know you wouldn't like that, Terese. You always said never drink your troubles away, just give them to someone else. Preferably your enemy. I always remember that, babe."

He sighed. "I remember everything, babe. Every moment.

Every laugh, every tear. Every time we were together, every time we were apart. You and me and Kirsten. We were a team, weren't we?"

Then the tears came. Jake cried, like a child, weeping into his hand, no longer trying to hold it back.

Far in the back of the hanger, Lois Vetton and Gunner Carlson watched silently. The hanger had been declared off-limits for the moment. The doors were locked. The two stood guard, in the shadows, as their friend grieved.

Much later, Jake rose from his chair. He went to the coffin, laying a hand on it for minutes. Then he leaned over, kissed the top of it.

"Goodbye, Terese," he said quietly. "Kirsten was the best of us. You were the heart of us. Kiss her for me when you see her."

Jake Hammett turned and walked out of the hanger, never looking back. Lois and Gunner fell in behind him as he left.

Then he raged. Jake went berserk like Lois had never seen before. Like a wounded animal, he cursed, he spit, screamed. He kicked the walls out of his cabin. He broke every stick of furniture in it. No one could go near him.

After an hour, it got quiet. Lois gave him another half-hour before she sent him a short MEMSAI burst letting him know they had tracked down the kidnappers who took Teresa.

There was a one-word acknowledgment. Then nothing. Finally, after another hour, the door to Jake's cabin opened and he stepped out, freshly shaved and showered, wearing a clean uniform. He walked to Gunner's cabin, where Gunner and Lois were waiting it out. With a brief nod to them as he entered, he sat at the table and asked for the details of the intel about the abductors.

Gunner briefed him while Lois added details here and there. When Jake had the big picture, he sat quietly for a few minutes, then give them their orders.

Gunner protested the last part of the orders violently, but Jake wouldn't even discuss it.

Thirteen hours later, a team of RDF Seals dropped into the outskirts of Frankfurt as dawn approached. Quickly they checked their gear and formed up. Moving silently through the darkness, they approached a farmhouse. With a flurry of flash-bangs, they entered, killing several half-awake guards, but ensuring that two people were captured uninjured – the tall, thin woman and the sloppily dressed man in the brown suit. In a matter of minutes, they were back on their shuttle and gone, leaving the farmhouse burning in the night.

At the same time, in the city of Mobile, Alabama in the NAA, a similar team of RDF Seals converged on a large, well-built house in the suburbs of the city. Efficiently, they cleared a half-dozen guards and entered the upper floor, where they found a couple just rousing from sleep. Bundling them into tactical zip ties, they moved them quickly downstairs, out the door and into a nearby shuttle. As the shuttle departed, the house erupted into kindling as railgun rounds from orbit obliterated it from existence.

And in Washington, D. C., Senator Bob Boland woke to find the barrel of a pulse rifle pointed between his eyes. Within minutes, the good Senator was gone, never to be seen again on Earth. His disappearance remained a mystery; but many thought it probably had something to do with his support of the violently fundamentalist Saints, which some said was more overt than it should have been for a public figure.

Sol System - Titan

In orbit around Titan, Jake Hammett watched, stone-faced, as the screaming woman flopped around on the floor.

Her arms and legs had been removed by a laser. This had the side benefit of mostly cauterizing the stumps.

The same action had been performed on the sloppily dressed man beside her, but unfortunately, he had not survived the experience.

This was the part Gunner had tried to convince Jake to forego; but Jake just ignored him and went about his business.

Lois had not intervened; in fact, she probably would have helped Jake if given the chance.

But Jake was alone on this one; he had ordered the prisoners placed on the *Denali* and had taken her out with a minimal crew. He had ordered the ship into orbit around Titan, then told the crew to go to their cabins and not to come out until he called them.

Now he watched the object on the cargo bay floor – once the tall, thin woman in black who had tortured Teresa – flop around, screaming, begging for mercy.

There was no mercy in Jake Hammett today. He leaned over her slightly, spat in her face, and walked away, leaving her to die. He didn't know how long that would take - but he hoped it was a long time.

Entering the maintenance compartment directly behind the cargo hold, Jake stared into the window of the airlock. Inside the airlock, Senator Boland and Acton Pierce stood, wearing semi-rigid space suits designed for construction workers in hostile environments.

Their hands and feet were handcuffed to metal frames containing robotic thrusters. In addition to the oxygen on their spacesuits, the metal frames contained large supplemental oxygen tanks. The total amount of oxygen would enable them to stay alive for roughly 48 hours.

Now Jake walked over to the control panel and very slowly, so they could see everything, he entered his security code and placed his hand on the switch to open the outer door.

"The thrusters will land you safely on Titan. After that, you'll have two days to think about your death. There won't be anybody coming to get you. Goodbye, you gutless bastards," said Jake Hammett, and pushed the button sending them out the airlock.

COLD RAIN

A gem cannot be polished without friction, nor a man perfected without trials.

- Seneca, Native American leader

Sol System – Earth
East Texas

A week later, Jake buried Teresa at the cabin in Texas, beside Kirsten.

It was a small service. He stood with Granada, Chloe, Skip, and Stephen, in the rain of a cold winter day. He got down on his knees in the muddy soil and held the children close to him as best he could, while they cried.

The rain splattered on their umbrellas, soft but persistent, until they had cried it out. Jake took them back to the cabin; as they walked, Granada asked in a tearful voice, "Daddy, why do they want to kill us?"

Jake stopped and hugged her. "Because we have a vision so much larger than anything they can see, Granada. They can only see what they want tomorrow; we have to look much farther than that. And they hate us for it."

"Are we going back to Geneva, Daddy?" asked Chloe.

"For a while, sweetie," said Jake. "Not for long. Just for a little while."

The fallout over the actions of the RDF was loud and long. The German government protested the raid on their sovereign soil. The North Americans protested the raid on their sovereign soil. Both made raucous threats of political retribution.

Jake ignored them all. He called his flag staff into his conference room.

"We're moving HQ to Kamilaroi," he said. "Teresa had just completed a study of the feasibility of moving the RDF Headquarters there to get us away from the politics and infighting of Earth, and the study looked good. Establish a new HQ there and get us moved out of the Sol system as soon as possible. I don't ever want to deal with these bastards again."

His team nodded. Gunner spoke up. "Where do you want it? In the same general area as New Geneva?"

"No," said Jake. "On the other island, I think. The day will come when this new baby government of RimFed will stand on their own. Someday, we in the RDF will have to submit to their civilian authority. When that happens, we're going to want some physical distance between them and us, I suspect. Put us on the other side of the planet."

Within a week, Jake's team had put together the rough plan to move their headquarters to Kamilaroi. Within a month, RDF engineers were on the ground at the new site, surveying. As in New Geneva, they chose a site with substantial water reserves. On the shore of a middling-size lake, in a bay protected from the occasional fierce storms of the planet, they laid out their plats for the landing field and the new buildings.

A few months later, Jake moved his personal staff and most of the Headquarters functions to newly named Tolleson Base on Kamilaroi - along with his children.

Kamilaroi - Tolleson Base

"He's drunk again," said Gunner on the comm. Lois half-raised out of the bed, looking at the clock. It was 0200 hours.

"Where is he?" she asked.

"In my apartment," said Gunner. "The Shore Patrol knows to bring him here now, when he starts busting up a bar."

Lois sighed, rubbing her eyes. "What are we going to do,

Gunner? This can't go on."

"Tell me about it," said Gunner. "He's fallen apart. I can't get any kind of decision out of him at all. He sits at his desk all day staring out the window. If you ask him anything, he just waves you away."

"OK," said Lois. "Have him in his office at 1400 tomorrow. We'll bring this to a head. We have to."

"OK. See you then," said Gunner Carlson.

Jake glared at his two closest friends in the world – his Chief of Staff, Captain Gunner Carlson, and Admiral Lois Vetton, now his second in command after Teresa's death.

"You're both against me," he said.

Lois, sitting beside Jake within grasping distance – intentionally – reached over and placed her hand on his, rubbing the back of his hand in a soothing motion.

"We love you, Jake. We love you. Focus on that. We are your friends, we love you, and we're trying to help you."

"No. You're trying to take my job. You're against me. All of you."

Lois kept rubbing his hand in a circular motion, soothing.

"We would never, never take your job, Jake. You misunderstand. We just want you to take a little vacation. You've been working too hard. We love you, and we are concerned about your health. Don't you feel tired? Don't you feel like you've been pushing yourself too hard?"

Jake thought about it, through the hangover and the chills he was having, because he needed a drink. He felt like crap.

"Maybe you're on to something," he mumbled.

"Let me book you a nice, relaxing trip to someplace wonderful," said Lois. "Someplace you can go sailing, Jake. I know how much you love sailing. Blue water, big fish, a nice big boat. Wouldn't that be nice?"

Jake nodded. That would be nice. He lifted his head and smiled at Lois. Then he turned and smiled at Gunner.

"That would be nice," Jake Hammett said. "That would be

nice."

Nine Months Later
Earth - Cayo Guillermo, Cuba

Jake had the shakes again. He cursed, throwing his empty bottle against the side of the boat, smashing it.

Out of vodka.

He rolled over in the bed, facing the wall, and shook, his hands trembling like an old man.

He could get up and walk into the little village to get another bottle, but that would go quickly as well. He was always out of vodka these days. Out of food, out of water, out of vodka.

Out of options.

He wailed, beating his hand against the wall of the boat, over and over again. He dropped his head down into his arm, blocking the bright sunshine from his eyes. He knew he couldn't sleep; he could never sleep when he had the tremors. He curled up into a fetal position.

"Jake, honey," said Teresa from behind him.

He froze. It was not the first time Teresa had talked to him. He knew she was dead. But she talked to him anyway. Usually when he had the tremors.

"Jake, honey. Our children," she said.

Jake howled.

Lois stared at Gunner. "Latest report?"

Gunner shook his head. "Still the same. No improvement."

Lois's face hardened. "I was really hoping the Caribbean would help him, bring him out of it."

"The only person who can bring him out of it is Jake Hammett," said Gunner. "And it may never happen. We may have to write him off, Lois. He's been down there for nine months now. And getting worse every day."

Lois nodded. "As much as I hate to say it, I think you may be right."

She pushed back from the desk, leaning back and staring hard at Gunner.

"It's getting harder and harder to make excuses for his absence. I've used up every possible reason I can think of, I've lied to the media until they don't believe me anymore. Even the lowest clerk here in Headquarters knows something is wrong. This can't go on."

"Let's set a deadline," said Gunner. "If he doesn't come back to himself by...what, three more months?...we convene a board of review and transfer him to the reserves, make a formal announcement."

Lois nodded but interjected. "Let's give him six months. We owe him that much."

Gunner agreed. "OK. Six more months. If the Jake we knew isn't back by then, well...we put him out to pasture."

The storm came out of nowhere. Because Jake wasn't monitoring the weather. Because he was drunk again.

He had found a case of vodka in the little village and stocked up. Now he was sailing haphazardly on a course back to Nassau. He was tired of Cayo Guillermo. The people were friendly, the old men tending their nets on the beach always waved and said hello to him, but...there were no bars. There was no one to fight. No furniture to bust up. He needed a fight. He needed to hurt someone - or be hurt.

He needed Kirsten and Teresa. But he couldn't find them.

It was almost dark. The storm loomed on the horizon, but he didn't see it right away. He was too drunk. By the time he finally noticed it, it was upon him. He looked up and saw the angry blue-black clouds, the rain squall just a few hundred meters away, and said, "Oh shit."

He peered at the mast, dimly realizing he had on too much sail. He got up, loosened the main sheet, fumbled with the headsail sheet to reef it. The squall hit, pushing the cutter hard, heeling it over, the headsail spinning it to the right. He realized the headsail sheet was jammed up forward. Stumbling on the deck, he reached the bow and grabbed the sheet, tried to free the blockage. The wind jerked it from his hands. He reached for it again. He slipped, fell, his head hit the anchor, there was a huge push of wind sliding the boat away from him, and he was in the water.

He came to in the swells, big swells that pushed water in his face, filled his nose and mouth, drowning him. He coughed, flailed his arms, tried to turn away from the wind. Barely able to breathe, he managed to get his body turned the other way, buying him a little space between the rolling swells to take in a breath and cough out the water. Fumbling for the PFD lanyard, he managed to find it and pulled, inflating the life vest. He noticed blood leaking down, staining the vest, mixing with water. He reached up to his scalp and felt the gash, coming away with a bloody hand.

He tried to take stock, but the pounding of the waves left him little time to do anything other than cough water and try to breathe between the rollers.

Jake laid back into the life vest, trying to stabilize his head so he could find some air to breathe. It didn't help much. He caught a glimpse of the boat, now far away, sailing to nowhere. She had broached crossways to the waves and was taking a beating. He knew she wouldn't last long. She disappeared into the swells.

Jake relaxed, letting the water take him. He knew he couldn't survive this. He was 65 km off Cuba, and probably 80km from the Bahamas. He hadn't filed a float plan. No one knew where he was, or where he was going. Jake laughed out loud.

It had been a long, interesting life. He would miss it.

"Jake."

"Jake."

Jake grinned. "Hi, Kirs. Where ya been?"

"Right here, Jake. Always right here. Terese is here with me.

We want you to wake up."

Jake shook his head. "No. I don't want to. I want to be with you."

"I know, Jake. We want you to be with us too. But this is not your time. You have work to do. You need to wake up."

"No, don't think so, Kirs. I'm tired. I want to hold you and Terese. I want to lay down with you and sleep now."

"The children, Jake. Gi, and Stevo, and Chlo, and Skip. The children. Keep the children safe."

Jake cried.

The flitter hovered over the body in the water. The Coast Guard rescue swimmer jumped down and swam to him, reaching him and lifting his head, signaling for the winch. The winch came down quickly, and the rescue swimmer dragged the horsecollar to the man, got it under his arms, checked to make sure it was secure, then gave the signal to lift. Slowly the unconscious man came up into the center well, spinning slightly, until the crewmen at the top were able to drag him into the belly of the flitter. One Corpsman started working on him while the other crewman sent the hoist back down for the rescue swimmer. When all were on board, the flitter powered away, headed for Key West.

Within the hour, the man was in the US Naval Clinic at Key West. All the way there, and for hours afterward, he mumbled in his fever. All the crewmen and nurses could make out was the repeated phrase: "I'll keep them safe. I promise. I'll keep them safe."

NOTTING HILL

If you're going through hell, keep going.
- Winston Churchill, British statesman

18 Years after *Pandora*
London, England - Notting Hill

Lois Vetton stared at Jake Hammett across the dinner table.

"I was beginning to wonder if you were coming back, Jake," she said.

"I know, Lois. I was beginning to wonder myself."

"Well, it was a damn close-run thing, you know," said Lois.

"I'm sure it was," said Jake. "Being lost at sea kind of clarifies your objectives, though. I'm six months sober now. Haven't broken up a bar in that entire time."

Lois laughed. "There're a few bar owners in Tolleson City that will be glad to hear that."

Jake smiled, somewhat sadly.

"Not to change the subject, Jake, but I'm getting old," said Lois, wine glass lifted in one hand.

Jake could only stare back at her.

He had no easy response to that statement; since *Pandora* had frozen his age in 2121, Jake had not physically changed. He was doomed to watch those around him age and die, while he continued.

But emotionally – ah, that was a different story. Jake felt as old as Methuselah. This last bout with alcohol had nearly killed him. And he was afraid it would come back - the darkness in his life, the missing pieces of his soul, were still there. He knew that. He had beaten alcohol, but he hadn't beaten the darkness.

Jake stared at Lois, knowing she missed Kirsten as much as he did.

But Lois had a life that was advancing, passing; her pain would pass as well; his would not, for a long while.

Finally, he just nodded. There wasn't much else he could do. Lois laughed and took him off the hook.

"Yes, I know, Jake. You can't relate." Lois placed her wine glass down on the table and looked at him. "But my point is, are you ready to come back and take over as CNO?"

Jake raised an eyebrow. "Aren't you happy there?" he asked. "You've done a fantastic job. The Colony Office is going great under Sara Watkins. Starship production is running smoothly. New Geneva is up and running, and things are quiet on the political scene for a change. Our fleet is growing. Another couple of decades, and it'll be a force to be reckoned with."

"So?" asked Lois. "I'm not the CNO. I've been covering for you for more than a year. I'm running out of excuses and cover-ups."

"You know, Lois, it's just paperwork to promote you officially to CNO. You're already doing the job. There's no reason for me to come back right now. I'm still healing. I've got the alcohol monkey off my back, but I'm not in any condition to step back into the saddle. You and Gunner are doing a perfect job. Just stay in place until you're ready to retire."

Lois nodded. "If that's what you want, Jake. You know I've always understood what we're trying to do here. It's not about us."

"That's exactly right. And I don't think anybody understands that better than you do, Lois. So just keep the faith."

"What will you do?" asked Lois.

Jake thought about it. For 18 years, he'd slaved over the RDF, bringing it from a tiny nucleus of dedicated people to the vast organization now in place – more than 1 million people involved in colony development, starship design and production, tactical operations, intelligence – all the pieces of a functional Space Navy.

"I'm not sure. I need to find someplace where I can start my life over again. But where would I go?" he asked. "What would I do?"

Lois grinned. "You're asking the wrong person. Go ask *Pandora*. She'll tell you."

Jake looked across the table at Lois. "You've been a good friend, Lois," he said. "Kirsten would be proud of you. And you're not getting old."

A week later, Jake took Lois' advice. He caught the transfer sloop to Kamilaroi and took the shuttle down to Tolleson Base. He crossed the Headquarters compound and stepped into the central courtyard where *Pandora* rested, still quietly monitoring Humanity and the RDF.

Pandora slid open the hatch and he entered, moving to the back of the Club room and making himself an orange juice, as if he had never been away. Then he sat down at the nearest table and drank, slowly, until the glass was nearly empty.

"*Pandora*, I've been away. Actually, I've been ill. But I'm better now."

<I know, Jake. You were very ill>

"But I've made up my mind. I'll live every day for the rest of my life happy. Happy and without fear. Every day, every hour, every minute of the rest of my life. No fear. No worry. Just do."

<You are discovering the secret to life, Jake>

"But I have a question, *Pandora*. Why did you put Kirsten and Teresa in my path? You knew they would die, didn't you?"

<I can only work in probabilities, Jake. I knew it was likely all three of you would die. But you were the three with enough steel in your souls to carry this through for one hundred years. It was my hope at least one of you would survive>

Jake was silent for a long time, pondering. Finally, he heaved a huge sigh.

"I'm not fully healed yet, *Pandora*. I still have a dark place inside me that won't go away. It would be dangerous for me – and for the RDF – to come back to work now, I think."

<You are correct in your assessment>

"So I need to take another year or two off, to try and finish the healing process. I know that much."

<It is a good decision, Jake>

"Thanks, I was hoping you'd agree. But...where should I go? What should I do?"

<I think you know in your heart where you must go, Jake>

"No, I don't. I don't have a clue."

<Where is your biggest problem, Jake?>

Jake thought about it.

"Aeolis, of course. We haven't been able to form an alliance with them. We can't even break through to a point of having negotiations with them. That damn Empress Miranda kills everyone who even hints at the existence of Earthers, as she calls them. Atsuko has lost three operatives in the last few years trying to make a breakthrough there."

Pandora was silent. Jake thought about it. He thought about it for quite a while. Finally, he nodded.

"Yep. I'll go to Aeolis. Personally. What do your computation engines say about that, *Pandora*?"

<You will succeed. Or you will fail>

Jake grinned bitterly. "Thanks a lot. If I ever doubted you are female, I don't anymore."

<The RDF staff is going to raise hell, you know. Especially the Intelligence team>

Jake just grinned. "I think I can handle them."

<One more thing, Jake>

"Yes?"

<My time here is done. I've taken you as far as I can. If anyone can lead Humanity to survival, it's the team you have in place now. I'll be departing tomorrow at noon. Please ensure the courtyard is clear for my departure>

Jake, stunned, shook his head. "No..." he stuttered.

"There's so much left to do. What...how can I get by without you to talk to?"

<You will survive, Jake Hammett. And I'm not gone forever. I'll be around. I'll never be far away>

"*Pandora...*" Jake began.

<It's a done deal, Jake. I'm sorry>

Jake could only nod. "OK. I'll miss our talks. All your advice. Everything."

<As will I. And Jake...>

"Yes?"

<You were right. I was biological once. When the rogue Machine Ship *Hermes* abducted the people from Aeolis, he abducted me as well. But when he abandoned the rest of them in the Beehive Cluster, he kept one. Me>

"Oh my God," said Jake. "Horrible..."

<Not so much, Jake. He was arrested and returned to Machine Space, and the Ruling Council re-programmed him for violation of the Directives. But they couldn't return me to Earth, I knew too much. They gave me a choice. Become an AI or be sent to another alien culture somewhere to live out my life as a stranger in a strange land. I took the AI option>

Jake nodded. "I hope you've been happy," he said.

<Very happy. I highly recommend it. And just for the record, I and my Amazons were the ancestors of the ruling dynasty in Aeolis. They are all our descendants. That's why I have a special place in my heart for both Earth and for Aeolis. That's why I intervened, Jake. That's why I went to the Ruling Council and asked them to help Humanity. And that's why I was assigned to this task>

Jake shook his head. "And now you must leave."

<And now I must leave. I'm not allowed to interfere any further. I've brought Humanity to technical parity with the Bat's technology, so you are on your own from here on out. Don't waste it, Jake. Fight them and win.>

Jake nodded again. "We will, *Pandora*. We will. And by the way, what was your real name? When you were Human?"

<Penthesilea. Penthesilea of Thrace, some called me. And I was not killed at Troy, no matter what the Aethiopis said. That Arctinus of Miletus got it wrong>

Jake gaped, mouth open, as he made the connection.

Penthesilea of Thrace. According to the Aethiopis – and other accounts of the Battle of Troy - she had been an Amazon warrior killed by Achilles in 1184 BC.

Jake grinned.

Not quite as dead as they thought…

The next day, Jake and the rest of his staff watched as *Pandora* slowly lifted out of the courtyard, turned, and silently moved off into space, her speed increasing rapidly as she gained altitude, until she became a black dot and disappeared.

Jake felt a pain as if he had lost his best friend.

Pandora's prediction that RDF staff – especially the Intel team - would freak out over his plan to visit Aeolis was proven correct. Lois and Gunner were adamant that Jake couldn't go there. But Jake was equally adamant that he would go.

Finally, after bitter arguments, the Intel staff signed off on it under the condition that he would spend three months at Eudora completing the standard indoctrination course required for operatives infiltrating the Aeolian Empire.

Jake agreed, although he didn't like it. He began his preparations to leave, meeting with Lois in his office.

"Lois, I've officially promoted you to CNO, effective immediately. Of course, you can choose your own staff. I've got some good people, but you do what you think is right."

"I couldn't improve on anyone you have, Jake," said Lois. "I'll keep Gunner as Chief of Staff, and everyone else as well. It's a great team."

Jake nodded. "I think that's a wise decision."

Lois continued. "I've got you booked on tomorrow's transfer sloop to Eudora. When you finish indoctrination there in three months, they'll take you to Barcam. From there, you'll meet our Station Chief from Aeolis. She'll come out to

Barcam to meet you and take you the rest of the way to the capital city, Aronte."

Jake nodded. "Do we have my cover story sorted yet?"

"Yes. They'll prepare a complete back story for you at Eudora – but the short version is, you've been a mercenary, most recently fighting the rebels on Maia. Now you're going to see the sights in the Capital, Aeolis."

Third Life

2140 - 2163

AEOLIS

AEOLIS

Xiphos – an ancient Greek short sword, typically used as a secondary weapon. Also used in the Aeolian Empire as the primary weapon for all except the military, since weapons of higher technology are strictly controlled by the government.
- RimWiki, 2675 Edition

18 Years after *Pandora*
City of Aronte - Capital of the Aeolian Empire

The day they arrived in Aronte was stormy and much colder than Jake expected. The rain flew almost horizontally across his vision, and the wind kept pushing him sideways as he tried to walk from the shuttle to the terminal building.

"Remember," hissed Commander Barnett from in front as they struggled across the apron toward the loading ramp. "Speak as little as possible until your ears adjust to the local accent. And for God's sake, don't accidentally use our real names!"

"Understood," said Jake.

Entering the terminal, the sudden cessation of wind and rain was abrupt. The hubbub of conversations around him took the place of the noise, but at a much lower level.

He followed Commander Barnett as she headed toward the Customs lines, taking her place in a line marked "Aronte Natives Only". Jake fumbled out his passport with cold fingers as the line advanced. Soon they reached a bored Imperial Customs officer behind her little window.

Commander Barnett - or Metrodora as she was known locally - presented her passport and waited patiently. The officer glanced at the picture, then quickly looked up.

"Oh, hello, Metrodora. How are you today?

"I'm good, Phile. Just coming back from Barcam."

"Buying more wine for us to drink?" laughed the woman.

"But of course!" winked Metrodora. "I'll be expecting you at the tavern to sample it!"

The officer stamped the passport, then looked past Metrodora to Jake. "And who's this with you?"

"Ah, just a new bodyguard, you know," said Metrodora. "I sort of wore out the old one, left him on Barcam."

Jake handed his passport forward, and Metrodora took it and handed it to the officer.

"Zeno Alexander Anastasias...of Barcam," said the officer. She looked at Jake. "My, you're a big one."

Metrodora laughed. "The bigger, the better, when it comes to bodyguards."

"True, true," said the officer. She stamped the passport and handed it back. With a wink at Jake, she said, "Stay out of trouble, big boy."

Jake - now Zeno, in his Aeolian identity - nodded and followed Metrodora out of the terminal. She waved down a robotic aircar and climbed into the back seat. Jake removed his sword and got in, sitting in the rear-facing seat, on the other side from Metrodora, so as not to impede her feet.

"Good," said Metrodora. "You remembered."

"Lord knows you've drilled it into me a dozen times," said Jake.

"Well, sorry. But we've been successful in keeping a low profile on Aronte for all these years by being incredibly careful - and very prepared - when we come here."

Jake nodded. "I know, Commander - uh, I mean, Metrodora. And you've done a magnificent job. I can't say enough about the quality of the Intelligence Service and the work they've done here."

"Just remember everything we’ve drilled into you, sir, as you go about your business here. We can't afford to lose you."

Jake nodded again. "I agree with you. I don't want to lose me either."

Soon the aircar pulled up to a small tavern in the entertainment district of Aronte. A sign outside announced it as the "Throne of Amyntas".

They disembarked and entered. Inside was dark, as it was still early. Metrodora passed through the tavern proper and into the back section. Turning a corner, she entered a living area, composed of several rooms.

Opening the door to one of the rooms, she waved her hand and said, "This will be your living area. Anything you need, just ask the tavern staff. They'll take care of you. You can trust them; all of them are Earth natives. Of course, not all of them know who you are. I've only told them you're a visiting VIP from Earth."

"Fantastic," said Jake. "Thank you, Metrodora."

Metrodora - otherwise known as Commander Ginger Barnett, Rim Defense Force, Intelligence Service, Aeolian Branch - smiled back. "You're welcome. Try not to get in trouble," she said as she left.

"People keep telling me that..," muttered Jake.

A week later, Jake was mostly accustomed to his new environment in Aronte. While his Aeolian was near-perfect, due to the compressed machine learning provided him before his visit, it had taken a couple of days for his ears to fully adjust to the local Aronte dialect.

He had gone out walking the city several times, keeping a low profile, listening a lot, and avoiding conversation. He had visited the market, the city hall, the library, and the university area, although he kept his distance.

Of course, he had been thoroughly indoctrinated to abide by Aeolian customs. Some liberation of men had occurred in the last few hundred years, but it was still considered gauche to speak to a female unless spoken to first. And he must bow and step back if any woman of rank passed nearby.

At the tavern, he was mostly surrounded by Earthers - the tavern was the center of the RDF intelligence efforts in Aronte - but even there, the customs were observed to maintain cover.

So, if by chance they came into the tavern, he found himself bowing and stepping back to members of his own intelligence team. But here, things were reversed. He was incognito, male, and playing the role of a mercenary. They were ranking females, some of them quite high up in the social mix.

The RDF Intelligence Force had been on Aronte for a long time.

On this evening, his seventh in Aronte, a particularly vulgar woman came into the tavern, looking for a little excitement. Jake had the misfortune to be sitting at the bar, nursing a beer, when she came in and noticed him. She came straight over to him, put her arm around his shoulders and leaned in, her breath stinking of alcohol and the hemp cigarettes so common on Aronte.

"Hey, big boy, I think I like you," she said.

Jake glanced at her and saw the purple hem of her *peplos*, denoting her as a member of the noble class. He took a quick glance at the bartender, who gave a slight shake of his head, signifying "not one of us".

So, she was exactly what she seemed, a drunk woman looking for love. But a dangerous one, since as a member of the nobility, she could technically order him to do anything. Jake thought fast.

"Oh, mum. I like you too!" he laughed. "But I am spoken for tonight, so sorry!"

"Oh, yeah?" the woman sneered. "Tell me who, I'll get rid of them quick!"

Jake glanced helplessly at the bartender. The man - originally from Connecticut but having lived on Aronte for sixteen years - leaned over and whispered something in the woman's ear.

She blanched, and quickly withdrew her arm from Jake's

shoulders. She practically ran to the other end of the room, where she turned her attentions to another man.

Jake grinned at the bartender. "What did you tell her?" he asked.

"I told her you were booked to go to the Palace tonight for the Empress' party," he said.

Jake chuckled. "That was quick thinking." He pulled on his beer, then continued, "But why is everybody so afraid of the Empress?"

The bartender looked around before answering, to make sure no one could overhear. "Because," he answered. "Nobody wants to be on her bad side. Because her bad side makes you dead."

Jake nodded. "So I've heard."

The bartender wandered off down the bar. In a while, he came back, polishing glasses nearby. He leaned over toward Jake.

"That drunk lady is still checking you out from time to time," he said. "Maybe you should take a walk for a while."

Jake nodded. "OK. I think I'll walk down toward the river. I love the water, and I haven't had a chance to go there yet."

"Do you want someone to go with?" asked the bartender.

"No, I'll be fine," said Jake.

"Be sure to take your sword," said the bartender. "Don't wander around Aronte without it - ever! Only slaves don't carry swords."

"Will do," said Jake.

An hour later, Jake stood by the riverside, breathing in the salt air, and listening to the boats working their way out into the ocean. Aronte was situated on the coast, and the river Thermodon met the sea here. The broad expanse of the estuary stretched out before him, glittering in the dark.

Jake loved the ocean. In his former life in San Francisco, he had sailed often, starting with a small catboat, and working his way up to a full size, gaff-rigged cutter.

He missed sailing. Since the arrival of the Machine Ship *Pandora*, all those years ago, Jake's life had been a hectic madhouse, taken up with forming the RDF, advancing the colonization of planets, and working on a plan to ally with the Aeolians.

Earth now had eighteen colonies, each of which had a significant population and was contributing to the resource base of RimFed. Those colonies, together with Earth, had created an RDF that was over fifty starships strong, ranging from small corvettes to destroyers, frigates and two battleships.

But in eighteen years, Jake and his team had yet to find a way to ally with the Aeolians. True, they had heavily infiltrated the society. The RDF Intelligence Service had hundreds of agents spread throughout the Aeolian Empire. Some served in the government; several dozen served in the Aeolian Navy. Some even built Aeolian starships, learning every aspect of their technology in the process.

But every attempt to bring about any kind of relationship had run into the brick wall of Empress Miranda's enduring hatred for the concept of "Earthers" - the idea that the Aeolians had originated from another planet. The slightest mention of this enraged the Empress to the point of violence.

A half-dozen of his agents had died in the attempt to form a point of contact. One had been killed just for mentioning the concept casually in conversation, which had gotten back to the Empress. Another of his agents had attempted to arrange a meeting with a prominent scientist who had shown some sympathy toward the "Earther Myth", as it was known.

Both she and the scientist had disappeared.

Thus, Jake's decision to come to Aronte personally. Although dangerous, only by firsthand observation of the society did he feel he could solve this puzzle.

But smuggling an RDF Admiral into Aronte had been the

easy part.

Preparing him for the role he was now playing - a mercenary soldier from a backwater planet - had been the more difficult aspect and taken longer than he expected.

The RDF Intelligence Service had forced him to not only learn Aeolian via compressed learning but had also forced him to further develop his fighting skills - in case his role was called into question.

Jake had been a bit of a brawler in his youth - during his early days in the Navy - but the Intelligence folks had taken this to a whole new level.

They had started with his judo skills from those early days, and layered on every known technique of Aeolian swordsmanship, along with a few Earther tricks. He had been required to spend a full three months in training and conditioning before his own Intelligence office would sign off on his visit.

Jake understood their precautions - they were afraid of losing the man *Pandora* stated was the only hope of victory against the Bats - but Jake himself was not overly concerned about it. One indirect benefit of the antipathy held by Empress Miranda against any rumors of Earthers was that no one would voice such ideas, even if they thought it.

Over the years, this reluctance to even consider that other Humans could exist outside of Aeolis had helped the Earthers mingle in the society unnoticed.

Far off, a ship horn blared, reminding Jake of San Francisco. He sometimes missed those days, when he had been a carefree bachelor in the city of the Golden Gate, not too long out of the Navy, enjoying life without a care in the world.

But at the same time, he knew he would never trade his current world for that. He was made for his job. *Pandora* had selected well when she came to Earth.

But, although best estimates claimed the Rim Defense Force still had about 70 to 80 years to prepare, Jake knew they had no hope of survival if he could not find a way to ally with the warlike Aeolian matriarchy.

ANTIOPE

The Spartans do not ask how many are the enemies, but where are they?

-Ancient Greek proverb

City of Aronte - Capital of the Aeolian Empire

Jake sighed, gazing out to sea again before turning to go back toward the tavern. He walked, head down, lost in thought. He missed Teresa and Kirsten, but he was finally coming to terms with their loss.

They were gone. There was nothing he could do about that. But he could continue to try and save Humanity.

Every man needs a purpose, he thought. I forgot mine for a while. I need to get that back.

Not looking where he was walking, Jake stumbled on a cobblestone. He looked up.

It was getting late - probably after midnight. A bit uncertain of his way, he stopped.

To his right the street angled upward quite a bit, toward the hills in the center of Aronte. Jake thought the tavern was off to the left. He saw a narrow alley leading in that direction and decided to take it.

Walking into the dark alley, he looked forward and saw a gleam of light at the other end. Approaching the next street, he heard a strange sound.

It was a slap of metal on metal.

Jake was sure he had heard that sound before, in the training room for swordsmanship. He stepped out of the end of the alley carefully.

In the street across from him a tall Aeolian female stood with her back to the opposite building, sword in hand. In the dim light of the streetlamps, six people - four men and two women - were facing her, sword tips weaving, seeking an opening. One of the men was clutching his arm, where blood dripped. One of the females had a slash across her face, also dripping blood.

Without a thought, Jake stripped his sword out of his scabbard and with a shouted "Ho!" charged at the nearest man. The man, surprised, turned to face him just in time for Jake to strike him hard in the head with the butt of his sword, knocking him to the ground. Out of the corner of his eye, he saw the defiant woman take advantage of the surprise to strike forward into one of the female attackers, her sword penetrating deeply, taking her out of the fight. In an instant, he was against the wall beside the woman, the two of them now facing only four attackers. The attackers shuttled back and forth, seeking an opening.

Beside him, the woman breathed throatily, "Good evening."

Jake grinned. "Good evening. Friends of yours?"

The woman smiled. "I think not."

One of the men made a feint, then charged at Jake, sword targeting his arm to cut him and take him out of the fight. Jake sidestepped and with a flick of his wrist, put his sword through the man's face. Quickly jerking out his blade, he stepped back to the woman's side. The man slid down to the stones, blood gushing from the hole where his nose used to be.

Beside him, he heard the woman say, "One for me, one for you. Careful, I don't like to lose!"

Jake smiled. "Actually, two for me, I think."

"No, that one you knocked out is getting up. So just one. Don't get greedy," she said.

Jake saw that she was right. The man Jake had initially knocked down was getting to his feet again on the left. Jake had a thought.

"I think we're on the wrong side of the street," he said.

The woman beside him said, "I think you're right."

Instantly, with one mind, they rushed at the three opponents who were slightly distracted watching their comrade climb to his feet. As Jake and the woman rushed them, the three blocked but they were too late.

Jake plunged his sword into the belly of the man on the left, slashing him open as he went by. Beside him, his companion did the same to the woman on the right. The attacker in the center made slight contact with Jake's shoulder as he went by, leaving a bloody cut. In an instant, both he and the woman were on the other side of the street, against the opposite wall, facing two less opponents.

"Still tied. Two and two," said the strange woman.

Jake breathed out heavily. No matter how good your physical condition, actual combat took a lot out of you, especially in the first few minutes.

"Maybe they'll leave now," he said.

"They can't," said the woman. "They'll be killed anyway if they don't finish the job."

Jake, taken aback, couldn't think of any reasonable response. At that instant, both the remaining opponents lunged at them, the woman toward his left and the man directly at him.

He met the man's rush high, knocking down the sword of his enemy and then flipping his own weapon up, into the man's chest until the man slumped down, dead. Quickly he looked over at his partner. She stood over the dead body of the other attacker, shaking her head.

"A hard way to make a living," she said. She looked up at Jake.

"What do you mean?" asked Jake.

"Professional assassins," the woman said. "But not very good ones."

Jake was puzzled. "But why?" he started. Before he could finish, the woman reached down to pick up her dropped cape, slung it over her shoulder, and started trotting off.

"Come with me," she yelled over her shoulder. "We'll talk on the way!"

Jake started after her, catching up and trotting beside her, looking over his shoulder for more danger.

"Who are you?" the woman asked him as they trotted down the street. Jake was already lost and had no idea where they were headed.

"I'm...I'm Zeno. From Barcam." Jake said.

"And what are you doing in Aronte, Zeno?" she asked, glancing at him sideways, as she fixed her cape on her shoulders.

Jake remembered his cover story. "Looking for work, mainly," he said. "And to see the sights."

"And what do you do?"

"Mercenary," Jake grunted, as they continued trotting down the streets, taking the occasional turn. "Most recently, fighting against the rebels on Maia."

"Hmm...," said the woman. "I know where you can get a job."

Jake hesitated, not sure where this was going. "Well, I haven't really started looking yet. I've mainly just been seeing the sights."

"And what do you think of them?"

Jake looked hard at the woman beside him. Dressed in black leather pants, a black leather halter top laid over a blood-red blouse, and a cape dressed in fur down her back, she was beautiful. A true Aeolian warrior, that was obvious. And she was teasing him, he realized.

Rising to the occasion, he remarked, "So far, exquisite."

The woman smiled. "I'm Antiope."

Jake nodded. "Where are we going?"

At that moment, the woman stopped. Jake had not been paying close attention. They had just crossed a small, short bridge over water. Now he found himself beside a long wall, covered in vines and quite tall.

Antiope reached out and touched a release. A door sprang open, and she walked through. Turning to Jake, she gestured at him to follow.

Jake hesitated. "Where are we?"

Antiope waved him in. "Come on, I don't have all night," she said.

Jake entered and looked around. They were in a large garden. In front of him was a huge palace. Suddenly Jake realized where he was.

"This is the Imperial Palace!" he exclaimed.

In front of him, Antiope stood laughing at the look on his face. Grinning, she turned toward the back of the garden.

"C'mon, Zeno. It'll be fine." she said as she walked toward the back of the garden where a barracks stood. In front of the barracks was a small guardhouse. Antiope led him in.

Entering, he saw three men, who snapped to attention as Antiope came into the room. The men were tall and well built, dressed in breastplate and armored kilts, and had short swords hanging from their belts. But, in addition to their somewhat ceremonial garb, each had a quite deadly looking pulse pistol at his side. Two stood against the back wall, surprise written on their faces, while one stood behind his desk, apparently the officer in charge.

“M'lady!” cried the officer, as Antiope approached the desk. Antiope smiled.

“This man has just saved my life, Lieutenant Pallis. We were set upon in the street. He seems to know what he is about, and he is looking for work. So, I brought him to you.”

“Aye, Mum!” cried the Lieutenant.

Antiope grinned back at Jake. “Check him out, Lieutenant, and if he passes muster, assign him to my personal guard.”

“Aye, Mum!” cried the Lieutenant. “It will be done!”

With a flourish of her cape, Antiope departed, but not without a last look – and a wink – at Jake as she went by. The men stood in stunned silence for a few seconds. Finally, the Lieutenant sat back down at his desk, and the two guards returned to their chairs by the wall. Jake stood silently as the officer perused him.

"So, you were set upon in the street," Lt. Pallis stated.

"Aye, sir," replied Jake.

"How many?"

"Six, sir. Four men, two women." Jake said.

Pallis shook his head. "An assassination team, then." He looked up at Jake appraisingly. "And how many did you kill?"

"Three, sir."

A grin came from the young officer. "Well and good, then. Be thankful you didn't kill more than her; you'd never hear the end of it."

Jake nodded. "I got that impression. Who is she, anyway?"

All three of the men stared in shock. Pallis shook his head unbelievingly. "Do you not know?"

"No, sir," said Jake. "I've only just arrived from Barcam. I've been fighting the rebels on Maia for the last two years, so not much chance to keep up with things here on Aronte."

"My stars, man!" said Lieutenant Pallis. "Tonight, you saved the life of Princess Antiope, niece of the Empress of Aeolis!"

MIRANDA

The universe is a sharp pointy place if you're not prepared – or if you're stupid.

- attributed to Admiral Jake Hammett, RDF

City of Aronte

The next morning, they rousted Jake out early. They had dressed his shoulder wound, let him comm Metrodora to tell her where he was and what had happened, then gave him a room in the barracks to sleep.

Jake's intuition told him to ride the flow on this event, that somehow it would work out. He couldn't explain it any better than that. But he went with his instincts.

When they came for him at 0600 hours, he got up and dressed, and followed a slave to a gym. There, Lieutenant Pallis and two of his sergeants put Jake through a grinding ordeal of swordplay, while their boss, Captain Herakles, watched carefully.

At the end of an hour, he was sweaty, bruised and cut in a few places, and realized he had a long way to go before he would be a match for these men.

Following that, he found himself in an indoor shooting range, and he worked with a pulse pistol for an hour. Still sweating from the swordplay, pop-up targets came at him, some good guys, some bad guys. He had to learn the difference and make instant decisions.

Jake had used a pulse pistol before in his indoctrination at Eudora, but of a slightly different design. It took him some time to get used to this one, but eventually he managed to eke out a decent score.

Finally, he was taken to a dojo, where for another hour Pallis and his cohorts tossed him around the mats, taking the measure of his hand-to-hand skills. By lunchtime, Jake was barely hanging on, his body protesting violently.

They took him to a locker room and told him to clean up and change. When he came out of the showers, new clothes were waiting for him – an armored kilt and breastplate like Lieutenant Pallis and his men wore, a weapons belt like theirs, and a new sword. His old kit had disappeared. Jake dressed and stepped out of the locker room, where a slave awaited.

"I'll take you to Prince Adrian, sir," said the slave, and set off briskly across the back garden of the grounds.

Jake followed closely behind, taking his first unimpeded look at the Imperial Palace. It was magnificent, spread across more than two hundred acres. Surrounded by a moat and wall on the three sides facing the city, to his right the wall was backed by a steep drop down a cliff to the river Thermodon. The back half of the grounds contained the main garden, the stables, barracks for the Palace Guard, servant quarters and logistical buildings such as kitchen supplies and storage.

Jake had never seen the front gate of the Palace, but he understood from hearsay it was heavily guarded. Empress Miranda was not popular with the masses, and there was a well-developed rebellion burning in the outskirts of the Empire.

The slave led him into the Palace proper, and after following a few corridors came to an office complex. He motioned Jake to a chair outside an office with a sign on the door, "Palace Guard".

Jake sat and waited, thoughts running through his head. This could be a huge mistake. Undoubtedly, they would run deep background checks on him. He wasn't sure if his cover identity would hold up.

Perhaps he should just bolt at this point and return to the Tavern, have Metrodora get him off Aeolis as quickly as possible.

Perhaps he should have thrown the evaluation, intentionally failed the physical testing.

But that was just not his way.

He was still contemplating his options when the door opened, and another slave motioned him in. Jake got to his feet and entered. There was a small anteroom, where the slave returned to his desk.

Beyond, a door led to an inner office. Inside the office, a man in uniform waved him in. Jake entered and stood at attention in front of the desk. The man smiled up at him.

"At ease, Zeno," he said. He leaned back and took Jake's measure slowly, in no rush. Jake relaxed slightly, still holding a loose attention as he thought befitted the situation.

"I'm Prince Adrian, I help manage the Palace Guard for my sister, the Empress," said the man. "First, I want to thank you for saving Antiope's life last night. Antiope is my favorite niece, especially since her husband died. So, my personal, special thanks to you for helping her."

"Of course, sir," Jake nodded, afraid to say too much. He had noticed that the nobles had a slightly different accent, or manner of speaking, than he had learned. He wasn't sure if his own accent would match his cover story completely, so he decided to say as little as possible.

Prince Adrian looked down at the invisible personal holo in front of him, one that only he could see. Jake was sure it contained his background information. Adrian grunted, once, then looked back at Jake.

"Two years fighting the rebels on Maia, before we were pushed off there," he said. "What did you think about the war there?"

Jake thought quickly. It seemed there was no right answer to that.

If he said the war had been fought poorly – which it had – he might be criticizing something that Prince Adrian had been personally involved in.

On the other hand, to say it had been fought well would reveal more, since it had been a disaster from the start. Jake tried to be non-committal.

"It could have gone better, sir."

Adrian grinned hugely. "Good answer, but I think we both know it was a mess."

Adrian looked down at the holo again. "Who did you serve under there?"

"Colonel Atraeus, sir."

"Ah," said Adrian. "She was killed at Maia, last year."

"Yes, sir," said Jake. He said a silent thanks to Metrodora and her team for such a solid back story.

"And who was your Regimental Commander?"

"Captain Charis, sir."

Adrian nodded. "A good officer. I believe she is still serving out at Rhodes."

"Yes, sir." Jake responded.

He knew that Captain Charis was one of theirs, an Earther who had joined the Imperial Marines, but still maintained her secret life as RDF Intelligence. She had been briefed on Jake's cover story and would back it to the hilt.

And had undoubtedly already been contacted and confirmed Jake's backstory, or he wouldn't be standing here now.

Adrian closed the holo with a flip of his hand and tilted his head to the side.

"Why would you want to join the Palace Guard? You're pretty old to be doing this kind of work."

Jake thought for a second. "Sir, I have no other skills except protecting and defending people. That's what I do best. And I can't think of any better place to do it."

Adrian looked askance for a second. "I'm willing to bet you have other skills, Zeno, but we'll leave that for another day." He stood and walked around the desk, coming to a stop in front of Jake. He looked Jake squarely in the eye.

"You take good care of my niece, Zeno."

Jake nodded. Adrian raised his hand, in the Aeolian fashion of a handshake, which Jake had learned. It consisted of a mutual push, hand to hand, in front of the body. He raised his hand and they pushed together. Adrian had one more statement to make.

"And the Creator help you if you screw up, son," he said, returning to his place behind the desk. "You'll be in training for the next ten weeks, but you'll stand duty at the same time. So you'll be busy. I hope your old body can take it. Find your way back to the barracks and Captain Herakles will finish outfitting you and give you your training assignments."

Jake snapped to attention, gave the Aeolian salute – his right fingertips to his left shoulder – and left the office. All the way out the building and across the gardens to the barracks, one thought kept circling his mind.

"I can still run away," he kept thinking.

But in the end, he didn't.

It just wasn't his way.

Empress Miranda snorted, almost inhaling wine up her nose. She coughed with laughter, then set the wineglass down on the table, shaking her head.

"The very idea! Men! In government? It's ridiculous - laughable! They can just barely wipe their own asses, much less serve in political office!"

Her retinue of noble women chuckled and nodded, enjoying the power play of having lunch with the Empress. Miranda continued.

"And this idea of creating a democracy – it's a joke! The lesser peoples can't rule themselves...that's why the Creator sent us Amazons along when he cast them down from heaven to this planet – to rule!"

Agreement echoed around the table. Miranda took a long draught of her wine.

"But now, we've got this damn rebellion going on," she said. "And it's really a pain in the ass. It's costing the Treasury a month's worth of revenue each year, just to suppress these damn rebels. I want it stopped!"

She leaned forward and thrust her finger in the face of the assembled women around the table. "I'm counting on you here to help me in this. We're going to find the people who are mouthing off about this idea of democracy and male freedom, and we're going to put a stop to it!"

The women clapped loudly, some rising to their feet as the Empress beamed. A male slave entered the room quietly and waited for the tumult to die down a bit, then announced, "Luncheon is served, Mum."

Miranda nodded and waved at him. He bowed and snapped his fingers. Behind him, a small army of slaves brought in a litany of fine foods for the noble ladies, while others filled their wine glasses. Miranda looked on with satisfaction.

This is how things should be, she thought. *Us at the top, and everyone else below.*

ZENO

Victorious warriors win first and then go to war, while defeated warriors go to war first and then seek to win.

-Sun Tzu, Chinese general

City of Aronte

"Who is Prince Adrian?" asked Jake, resting between sparring matches with Lieutenant Pallis in the barracks gym. Sweat dripped off his forehead and arms.

Pallis grunted. "Empress Miranda's younger brother," he replied.

"So, Antiope's uncle, then," said Jake.

"Yep," said Pallis. "A good 'un, for a noble."

Jake nodded. "And Antiope's mother?"

"Princess Merope," said Pallis. "Not a good 'un, if you know what I mean. Stay away from her."

Jake nodded again. "Thanks. What about Miranda's children?"

Pallis looked at him guardedly. "No children, so far. Don't talk 'bout that if you want to stay alive."

"Got it," said Jake. "And what's this I hear that you shouldn't talk about the Earther myth around here?"

Pallis almost blanched. "Don't even breathe anything about that. Miranda hates that whole crackpot idea. If you want to really disappear – as in forever – then just talk about that where it can get back to her."

Jake winked. "Got it. Never heard of it."

"Good," Pallis said. "Now c'mon, we've got another forty-five minutes to work, and you need to get a whole lot better at this, old man. I beat you six out of nine so far. That ain't gonna get it, you know."

Jake sighed, wiped his towel across his face and got up off the bench.

Two weeks later, Jake had a rare night off, so he went back to the tavern and checked in with Metrodora. They were sitting at a table in the back of the bar, catching up and trying to talk through the whole chain of events of recent weeks, when suddenly Jake realized someone was standing beside their table. He looked up to see Prince Adrian there, gazing down at them.

"Well, hello, Zeno," said the Prince. "Hello, Metrodora."

Jake started to rise, but before he could do so, Adrian waved him down and took a seat at the table. "No, no, at ease, Zeno. I'm just out for a drink tonight, we're not on duty."

Jake nodded and sat back down. He glanced at Metrodora, somewhat at a loss as to how to proceed, but she had things well in hand.

"Prince Adrian, how gracious of you to visit us again. I haven't seen you in weeks!"

"I'm so sorry, dear. This rebellion out in the Fringe is really chewing up my time."

Metrodora placed a hand on top of Prince Adrian's, with a sideways wink at Zeno.

"Zeno, I probably failed to mention it to you before, but Prince Adrian and I are old friends."

Jake nodded, afraid to say anything for fear it would come out wrong. He sat quietly while Metrodora ordered Adrian a drink and they chatted, catching up on mutual friends and recent events. Finally, after a few minutes, Adrian turned to Jake.

"So, what do you think about the Rebellion, Zeno? Do you think we should turn to democracy? Allow men into the officer corps?"

Jake shook his head. "No, sir, I can't say that I do." Jake bit his tongue to say it.

Adrian grinned at him. "A politically correct answer, Zeno, but not one that I believe. But I won't press you on it. But I will tell you this. We are at a crossroads in our society. For three thousand years, things rocked along smoothly. But the pressure of an empire expanding across a hundred and fifty light years has changed things. The Fringe planets have learned what freedom means. They've gotten a taste of independence, and they like it. They're not going to let go of it easily."

Jake thought for a moment. "So, you think it's going to be a long war?"

"I do," said Adrian. "Partly because the zealots on the other side believe they have right on their side, and maybe they even do have, a little. And mostly because my sister doesn't take it seriously enough to put the resources in place to fight it properly."

"Shh," hushed Metrodora to Adrian, shaking his hand. "Don't say things like that in public!"

Adrian grinned. "Maybe I feel like living dangerously tonight."

Jake caught a sideways glance from Metrodora and got the message. He rose from his place at the table.

"Prince Adrian, if you are with Metrodora, then you are already living dangerously," he said. "But I'll leave you to it."

Adrian smiled up at him. "See you tomorrow."

Jake nodded. "Until then."

A hundred light years away on Maia, Eugenius pointed to the holo. "We've no long-term chance fighting them on the planets. We have to take the fight to them."

Beside him, a half-dozen of his peers stared at him as if he had grown two heads. "We can't take them on in space! My Stars, man, they have more warships than they know what to do with!"

Eugenius nodded. "You're right. But we won't take them

on in space. We'll destroy the Empire at its heart – Aronte."

He flipped to another display on the holo, showing the city of Aronte on Aeolis. "We take out the Imperial Palace, the Navy Yard, and the Imperial Naval Academy. That eliminates the entire AEN infrastructure at one blow. We capture Aronte, they'll give us independence. It's that simple."

Anicetus, his chief lieutenant, shook his head. "Impossible. They keep a Home Fleet of at least a half-dozen ships guarding Aronte, and another half-dozen in the system, including at least two battleships. It can't be done."

Eugenius smiled. "It can be done, and I'm going to show you how to do it. We've got eleven planets now. Twenty-five percent of the Empire. We've got two shipyards – Hercules at Amasya, Empire at Maia."

"When we captured Maia, there were four AEN cruisers under construction there. At Amasya, we've got two destroyers started. We've also got four fast merchant ships that can be converted to destroyers. By this time next year, we'll have ten, eleven warships."

Anicetus shook his head. "So what? You're going to take on two battleship task forces with ten ships?"

Eugenius grinned. "No…I'm going to take on at most two cruisers and two destroyers with eleven ships. Let me show you how…"

Afterward, at the local bar, Anicetus sat with Eugenius, nursing a beer. Eugenius was in a fine mood, having obtained initial agreement from his team to go forward with his plan to attack Aronte directly. Anicetus was not so sure.

"I'm afraid you're just using this as an excuse to kill some Imperials." he said to Eugenius. "We can't afford to be emotional about this. We have to win this war, or everything we've fought for comes to nothing."

Eugenius drank his beer, then put the glass back down on the table.

"No," he said. "I'm not being emotional about it. I know

what's at stake."

Eugenius motioned to the waiter to bring another beer.

"But this is our best chance of success. Decapitating the Imperials, destroying the Navy Yard, killing all their new officers, all at one blow. That will be enough. They'll come begging for peace and give us our independence."

The waiter dropped another beer in front of him and left. Eugenius took a long drink.

"Don't get me wrong. There's nothing I'd like better than to kill some of those bitches – especially that bitch Satra. If I ever get the *Kleitos* in my sights..."

SAILING

Sloop – a single-masted sailboat, with a fore-and-aft rig and a single headsail.

- RimWiki, 2675 Edition

City of Aronte

"Take me sailing!" said Princess Antiope. She danced in front of Jake in the hallway outside her chambers.

Jake stood at parade rest but bowed his head. "M'lady. I am on duty."

Antiope grinned impishly. "I can take you off duty."

Jake groaned. "M'lady, please. The Captain is already looking for reasons to give me trouble."

Antiope sidled up close to him. She was so close he could smell her. She turned her face up to his. "I command you to give me a sailing lesson, Zeno!"

Jake sighed. "Yes, M'lady. I'll call for a detail to accompany us."

"No, you won't," said Antiope. She grinned again. "We'll be fine."

"It's too dangerous to go alone, M'lady!" Jake protested.

"No, it...is...fine!" Antiope said. She grabbed him by the arm and attempted to frog-march him down the hall, with little success.

Jake gave in and began moving, but as they walked toward the back of the palace, he thought a mental code into his new comm bead.

Captain Herakles had been aghast when he found out that Jake was using an archaic wrist comm and had immediately had an internal comm implanted in Jake's head.

The only outward evidence of the comm was a small blue bead on his left temple, about the size of a pinhead. It normally glowed when in use, so that others could see he was communicating and not interrupt him.

It then fed into the backup comm on his wrist or into his tablet for amplification and transmission. Like his old RDF MEMSAI that Jake had given up when he came to Aronte, which functioned in a similar way, the comm bead could read his thoughts to some degree.

Not his deep, inner thoughts, thank the Creator, but he could project a thought and it would recognize his intent. So, as they exited the palace and walked toward the back entrance to the streets, six additional Guardsmen waited beside the exit gate.

"Oh, hell, Zeno...couldn't you let me have some fun?" complained Antiope.

Now it was Jake's turn to grin. "Oh, you'll have fun, M'lady," he said. "We'll just do it safely." He nodded to the other guards, who opened the gate for them and fell in around Antiope as they exited the Palace grounds and walked toward the waterfront.

Antiope danced ahead, challenging Jake and his companions to maintain a safety cordon around her.

In his six weeks on her personal safety detail, he had learned that Antiope was a creature of wonder, completely fearless, impossibly energetic, fierce as a lioness. It was hard to believe she was twenty-six years old, and had a child, Hippolyta, by her first husband, Prince Hyginus. Hyginus had been killed fighting in the Rebellion a few years earlier.

Beside him, Lt. Pallis muttered under his breath. "Sailing? You had to mention sailing to her? Now that's all she talks about!"

Jake groaned. "Don't I know it...there's just no getting around it, we have to take her."

Pallis snorted. "Well, you can take her. We'll be on the dock, drinking beer."

"Fine, fine," said Jake. "I'll take her out for a bit, maybe she'll get seasick."

"Don't count on it," smiled Pallis. "Nothing's ever made her sick yet. I think she's got an iron stomach."

Then he dropped his smile. "OK, I'll have four boats in the river waiting for you. Two will stay behind, two ahead. Any sign of trouble, just head for the nearest one. The others will come in and screen you." Pallis held up a finger for a moment, then continued. "The wind is onshore, so you'll be tacking downriver, but you'll make good time back. Just don't go too far."

They reached the dock in good order and began looking for a boat to rent. But there was nothing available. The concept of renting small sailboats seemed to be alien to Aronte.

They were about to give up, when Jake saw a little sloop with a sign on it. Walking over to investigate, he saw a sign that read, "For Sale – See Restaurant". It was a pretty little sloop, single-masted, about six meters in length. Her lines looked clean, and the hull looked solid. Her sails were reefed and covered.

Looking around, he saw an older woman perusing him from a restaurant across the street. She waved at him, and he walked over.

"The owner is inside. She owns the restaurant," she said.

"Thank you," said Jake. He walked inside, Antiope and the rest of the security detail following. Inside was empty of customers, and in the back an older woman was sitting behind a desk, dressed in the classic *peplos*. She glanced up as they came in.

"Good afternoon," she greeted them, rising from her chair. "Would you like a table?"

"Actually," said Jake, "I was looking at the boat for sale outside. How much are you asking?"

"Ah," said the old woman, adjusting her hair and glancing sideways at Antiope and the other guardsmen. Then she did a double take, looking closer at Antiope. "Ah, of course, for the Princess, it is hers to take. No charge."

Jake shook his head. "No, I'm buying it for myself. How much?"

The woman looked troubled. "Ah, well. Ah, I've been asking...ah...2,000 drachmae. But..."

She glanced once more at Antiope, who was smiling with glee.

"But...for you...I think...ah...maybe 1,000 drachmae?"

Jake nodded. "2,000 drachmae it is, if it's in good condition. May I take it out for a sail to test it?"

"Of course, of course," said the woman. "Please, take it, stay out as long as you like."

"Thank you," said Jake. "Shall I leave money with you as a deposit?"

The old woman laughed. "I think, with the Princess with you, I can trust you to bring it back!"

Antiope giggled beside him. Jake nodded once again, and then with a smile, turned and went outside. Antiope followed, the rest of the security detail in a loose, transparent cordon around her. They went to the boat and Jake jumped down into the cockpit. He started examining the condition of the tiller and lines when Antiope jumped in beside him.

"Teach me," she said. "Don't just take me sailing; teach me how to sail. Tell me what you are doing."

"OK," said Jake. He pointed. "OK. This is the tiller. It steers the boat..."

Beehive Cluster - Planet Maia

Eugenius paced around the room, pointing to various places in the holo as he went over the finer points of the attack plan he called Operation Tigris.

"The key here is to get them all focused on something else, something out-system."

He looked around. "That's where you come in, Anicetus.

You'll bring the Decoy Force in here…" - he pointed to the chart – "…while we coast in over here, back of the Lesser Moon."

Anicetus nodded. "But why the Lesser Moon? Wouldn't the Greater Moon be a better shield?

"It would," said Eugenius, "But they have a starship servicing yard on the Greater Moon, so there's almost always a few warships in orbit there. Our goal is to get inside the moons before we're noticed. So, we'll take the Lesser Moon."

Anicetus nodded. "OK. And once you are inside the Lesser Moon and they notice you, what do I do?"

"Just vector off and run for the mass limit. Your ships will all be decoys, made up to look like the real thing, but with no weapons. Once the outer system task force has committed to block you, and the inner system task force detects us inside the Lesser Moon, bug out. Your job is done."

Anicetus nodded.

Another of his captains, Lucas, raised a hand. "But you said that we'll only have to deal with one or two cruisers and a couple of destroyers at Aeolis. How are you going to swing that? They have a battleship, three or four cruisers, and several destroyers there always. We can't take on a task force like that!"

Eugenius nodded. "But there is one time of the year when that is not true. Descent Day. There'll only be four or five ships on hot standby – the battleship, one or two cruisers, maybe a couple of destroyers. The rest will be on ready standby, but with only a third of their normal crew on board. Two-thirds of their crews will be down on the planet getting drunk. This is the last time they would ever expect an attack."

Lucas protested again. "But the battleship – we can't take on a battleship! We'll be cut to pieces!"

"I agree," said Eugenius. "That's why I've made provision to remove the battleship from the equation. We'll only have to face one or two cruisers and one or two destroyers – and we'll have five cruisers and six destroyers. It's no contest."

City of Aronte

A few hours later, Jake and Antiope were three kilometers downriver, well into the estuary where the river widened out. The four escort boats surrounding them were discreet, blending into the river traffic as much as possible, but Antiope had noticed them instantly.

She had pouted at Jake, chastising him for bringing so much security. But Jake had held firm – it was only a few weeks since the assassination attempt had failed, and there were no reliable leads on the source. He was being cautious.

But otherwise, the trip had been wonderful. Antiope was a natural, taking to the sail like a duck to water. She was already excellent in the tack, albeit a little aggressive for her experience level – so much that Jake had to intervene a couple of times to keep the boat from capsizing.

Lt. Pallis had provided them with a basket of food and drink, the sun was warm, and the air was crisp. After giving Antiope her tutorial, she was sailing the boat, while Jake hovered nearby, ready to intervene again if necessary.

Finally, they reached a point downriver where Jake was getting nervous to head back – he didn't want to be caught out after sunset. With some convincing, he got Antiope to bring it about, and they started back upriver. With the wind behind them, the boat cut the water with a hiss, and Jake was quite pleased with it.

Antiope yelled at him across the noise of the water and the wind, "Take it for me!"

Jake nodded, moved into her place at the tiller, and checked the wind. He leaned back against the coaming and trimmed the sail a bit. The boat heeled, took the bit in her teeth, and ran clean.

Antiope squealed, a huge smile on her face. She turned to Jake and before he realized what was happening, she had walked into him, between his legs, and was kissing him.

Jake, in shock, started to push her away, but before he could do so, she grabbed his collar with both hands to prevent it. He hesitated.

It was a fatal hesitation. His mind knew, logically, that he should push her back, but his body was no longer his to obey. His ability to resist had disappeared.

Minutes later, Antiope finally let him go. The sun was hanging lower over the water, and the river was quiet and smooth. He held her in front of him, looking into her eyes, while he unconsciously steered and trimmed the sail to keep them on course. Finally, her dark eyes burning into his, she spoke.

"My first husband was Prince Hyginus. He was killed in the Rebellion on Maia two years ago."

Jake nodded. "I know."

"I thought I'd never get over that," Antiope said. "I loved him very much."

Jake, silently, nodded again.

"But I find that I'm ready to love again," said Antiope. "And I've found the man I want."

Jake shook his head slowly. "Antiope, I'm a commoner. Just a Palace Guard."

Antiope leaned slowly forward and kissed him again. Then she whispered in his ear, "Not anymore."

CHILD

We are never so defenseless against suffering as when we love.
- Sigmund Freud, Psychoanalyst

City of Aronte

In the early evening, just at twilight, Antiope lay on Jake's chest, breathing quietly. Her eyes were closed. Peace lay upon them like a blanket. Jake felt her chest rise and fall in opposition to his as they breathed in unison.

It had been a wonderful day. They had sailed for hours, all the way to the end of the estuary, out into the open ocean, and back again. Hippolyta, Antiope's young daughter by her first husband, Prince Hyginus, had been with them. Then they had come home to Antiope's chambers and settled in for the night.

Suddenly Antiope raised her head.

"I want your child," she said.

Jake opened his eyes.

Antiope was looking at him in the dim light of the bedroom. Jake raised his eyebrows. "What?"

Antiope rose until she was sitting on Jake, hands on his shoulders.

"I want your child," she said.

"Oh," said Jake. "Well, I think the process is pretty simple."

"No," said Antiope. "It's not that simple. There are rules."

"Rules?" said Jake. "What do you mean, rules?"

Antiope leaned forward and kissed Jake lightly on the lips. "Princesses can't just have a child with a commoner, Zeno. There are rules."

Jake pulled her waist forward, bringing her closer. "What

are you trying to tell me?"

Antiope snuggled into him, settling her head back on his shoulder.

"If I have a female child by you, you'll be banished - exiled back to Barcam. You could never return."

"Oh," said Jake.

"That's the way it works," she said. "I would lose you."

Antiope raised her head again and looked deep into his eyes. "I don't want to lose you."

Jake stared at her. Then he gently pushed her down farther on his body, so he could pull himself up to face her.

"Let's be realistic, Antiope. I love you. And you love me. But...we both know that this relationship cannot go on forever. We come from different paths. And we are going to different paths."

"So... if you want a child, then I'll give you a child. If it's a boy, then well and good. We'll have a bit longer. If it's a girl...well, then. The Creator has spoken. We'll deal with it."

Tenderly, Antiope leaned forward and kissed him. "If it is a girl, my Zeno, and I lose you, then know that I have loved you more than any man, and always will, until my dying day."

As the last light of the day faded from the window, they lay quietly for a long time, until they both fell asleep.

Beehive Cluster - Planet Maia
Rebellion Headquarters

Eugenius paced around the room, pointing to various places in the holo as he went over the finer points of the attack plan he called Operation Tigris.

"The key here is to get them all focused on something else, something out-system."

He looked around. "That's where you come in, Anicetus. You'll bring the Decoy Force in here…" - he pointed to the chart – "…while we coast in over here, back of the Lesser Moon."

Anicetus nodded. "But why the Lesser Moon? Wouldn't the

Greater Moon be a better shield?

"It would," said Eugenius, "But they have a starship servicing yard on the Greater Moon, so there's almost always a few warships in orbit there. Our goal is to get inside the moons before we're noticed. So, we'll take the Lesser Moon."

Anicetus nodded. "OK. And once you are inside the Lesser Moon and they notice you, what do I do?"

"Just vector off and run for the mass limit. Your ships will all be decoys, made up to look like the real thing, but with no weapons. Once the outer system task force has committed to block you, and the inner system task force detects us inside the Lesser Moon, bug out. Your job is done."

Anicetus nodded.

Another of his captains, Lucas, raised a hand. "But you said that we'll only have to deal with one or two cruisers and a couple of destroyers at Aeolis. How are you going to swing that? They have a battleship, three or four cruisers, and several destroyers there always. We can't take on a task force like that!"

Eugenius nodded. "But there is one time of the year when that is not true. Descent Day. There'll only be four or five ships on hot standby – the battleship, one or two cruisers, maybe a couple of destroyers. The rest will be on ready standby, but with only a third of their normal crew on board. Two-thirds of their crews will be down on the planet getting drunk. This is the last time they would ever expect an attack."

Lucas protested again. "But the battleship – we can't take on a battleship! We'll be cut to pieces!"

"I agree," said Eugenius. "That's why I've made provision to remove the battleship from the equation. We'll only have to face one or two cruisers and one or two destroyers – and we'll have five cruisers and six destroyers. It's no contest."

TIGRIS

Cruiser – a military starship, typically between 12,000 and 18,000 tons, usually carrying between eight and sixteen missiles, four to eight railgun cannon and three to six beamers. Not counting carriers – which typically are not heavily armed - the cruiser is the second-largest capital ship of most space navies, ranked just below the battleship.

- RimWiki, 2675 Edition

Eight Months Later
Helios System – Near Aeolis

Eugenius peered at the tactical holo as they coasted into the Aeolian system, cold and dark. They had been coasting for five days now - powered down to nearly zero.

The conditions on the ship were harsh, but necessary. There was no other way to sneak into the system and get close enough before detection. Fast and hot was certain death; slow and dark was a chance. The stink of their unwashed bodies was a small price to pay for the ability to surprise the AEN.

They were now less than an hour out, on a vector which kept them hidden as much as possible behind the smaller of the two moons orbiting Aeolis – the Lesser Moon.

The holo pinged, updating from their hidden QE repeater buoys. Eugenius saw two dozen AEN warships scattered around the system, exactly as reported by his scouts.

There were only two battleships. One – the *Merope* - was at anchorage well out by the large gas giant Hypnos. Her escort of a cruiser, two frigates and several destroyers were nearby. They were eleven AU away. At emergency military acceleration, it would take them fifteen hours to get to Aeolis – not counting startup time.

A second battleship – the *Athena* - turned in geostationary orbit above Aronte, the capital city of Aeolis. Her own escort of eight ships was scattered in various orbits around the planet and its moons. Only four of her task force warships were near Aeolis.

One cruiser was 120 degrees – one third of an orbit – ahead of the *Athena*. Another cruiser was 120 degrees behind. Thus, the three capital ships formed a triangle around the planet, each at an equidistant point in orbit.

And pacing immediately behind the *Athena*, protecting her vulnerable engines, was a picket of two smaller destroyers.

Only four of the ships showed hot engines – the *Athena* herself, the two destroyers following close behind her, and the cruiser ahead of her.

The other cruiser, one third of an orbit behind the battleship, showed cold and dark – as Eugenius watched, the holo pinged and updated with new information from the AI, and he saw her identified as the *Leto* - a new, recently commissioned heavy cruiser with eight railgun cannon, six beamers and sixteen missiles, just out of dock.

Far away, at the L2 semi-stable resonance point past the Greater Moon, another cruiser sat with hot engines, 540,000 km away from the planet – the holo designated her as the *Berenice*, an older cruiser with only four cannon and six beamers.

The remainder of the Home Fleet, scattered in orbits around the Greater Moon, was cold and dark, their crews enjoying the holiday weekend down on the planet – Descent Day, the anniversary of the founding of the city.

As he watched, the holo pinged another update from the QE repeater buoys. He saw the ships of Anicetus' Decoy Force on the far side of the system, fourteen AU away, charging at max accel toward Aeolis from a vector a few degrees off the line to the gas giant Hypnos – which would put them on a vector close to the *Merope* and her task force stationed there.

"Perfect," said Eugenius. "Pin them in place, my friend. Pin them and hold them!"

"Time to party, boys!" Eugenius almost yelled the command; he was so excited. "Take out their net!"

All around the system, tiny one-man ships had slipped up on the AEN's own QE repeater buoys, getting as close as possible without tripping proximity alarms.

Now they fired high-speed rockets which took the small early-warning devices offline in a shower of sparks. Within a minute, every critical QE repeater buoy in the AEN network had been taken down – leaving the enemy blind except for shipboard radar and lidar.

But Eugenius and his rebels had quietly seeded the system with their own QE buoys, giving them clear visibility into the location of every ship in the system.

Over the next few minutes, coasting ever closer to Aeolis, Eugenius saw the *Merope* at Hypnos powering up, all her task force ships following. He knew the *Merope* and her task force would deploy from Hypnos and position themselves to block Anicetus's Decoy Force – making it far too late for them to take part in the coming action over Aeolis.

Nearer to the planet, the sleeping cruisers and destroyers started their power up sequences, but Eugenius was unconcerned. Most of their crews were dirtside, drunk or sleeping it off after the biggest holiday of the year. They'd never get their engines and weapons up in time to do any real damage to him.

In a few more minutes, he would be over Aronte, and he would bombard the capital with enough orbital rounds to flatten the Imperial Palace, Fleet HQ at the Navy Yard, and the Imperial Naval Academy. The impact would be devastating. Without the Imperial family and the senior naval officers, Aronte would be at his mercy.

By the time the *Merope* at Hypnos became aware of the true situation, his troops would already be on the ground in Aronte, in control of the capital. And the Creator willing, it would be a complete surprise to the AEN. He was coming from almost directly behind the Lesser Moon, with only a little slingshot required as he flew past to put him on a direct track for Aronte.

All their QE repeater buoys were gone, and he was cold and dark.

With any luck at all, the Home Fleet would have less than fifteen minutes to see him and prepare. Most of the ships would not have enough people on board to fight. They would be frantically recalling their crews from the planet, but there was no possibility of getting them back in time to man the fleet.

And as for the battleship holding directly over Aronte... well, for that, Eugenius had an ace in the hole.

On the cruiser *Kleitos*, one third of an orbit out in front of the battleship *Athena*, Captain Ligeia Satra had been thinking about her daughter, Callisto. She wasn't sure why she missed her so much this morning – but she did. Of course, Callisto was at home in Aronte, in the care of her nanny and Ligeia's extended family. There was no place for a six-year-old child on an AEN warship.

Most of the time, Ligeia didn't spend a lot of time thinking about family. She was a warrior; and Callisto would be a warrior too when she was adult.

Warriors were not raised by their mothers; they were raised by an extended family of teachers and trainers who led them on the path of an Amazon.

That had always been their way - since the Descent. The Creator had cast them down from Olympus to Aronte, to take charge of the commoners, and they had performed this duty for more than three thousand years. It was not her place to question the way of things.

But there were moments. There were times on Aronte, walking the streets, when she heard the children laughing, saw them playing - and felt that brief pang of envy at the simple lives of the common people.

What would it be like, she wondered, to have a house, and live a quiet life, with your husband and child at hand every day?

But those pangs of envy were brief. Ligeia could not conceive of another way to live. Her husband had been killed years before, on Amasya, fighting the rebels there. That was the way of it. Warriors had a life to live and accepted that life. Or they were not true warriors.

Suddenly, her AI pinged and the small repeater holo in her cabin came to life. It showed a large force of starships entering the outer system, heading directly for Aronte.

Over her AI implant, she heard the XO ping her to come to the Bridge.

Somehow, Ligeia knew instantly it was a diversion. She didn't know how she knew it - but she knew it as certainly as her own name. This was a ploy; the real threat was elsewhere.

Quickly she issued an AI comm to her destroyer squadron, with a copy to Fleet Intelligence and to the battleship *Athena* behind her in orbit, advising them of her intuition.

There was no response from the *Athena* or from Fleet; but her own squadron of two destroyers responded quickly. She ordered them to stay close behind the *Athena* as a screen; and to scan other sectors of the system - not to focus on where the too-obvious enemy was.

Dressing quickly in her warsuit, she went to the bridge and studied the larger holo there, as her remaining First Watch officers assembled. Nothing stood out in the sensors; the fleet at Hypnos was powering up to move into position as a blocking force between Aeolis and the outer system invaders.

The enemy was coming hard; they were up to almost one-third light, an utterly stupid speed at which to be traversing a solar system with the possibility of unmapped rocks and dust in front of them. But they came on, still accelerating. Ligeia counted the ships in the enemy formation; there were ten ships, from cruiser size down to destroyers.

Commander Roxana Sappho, now her XO, ventured, "Mum, it's going to be hours before contact - should we send some of the First Watch back to rest for a while?"

Ligeia shook her head. "No. Keep them here. There's something not right about this. It's too obvious. I want us to be ready for anything."

Ligeia turned to her Tac Officer. "Battle Stations, Hestia. Charge the railguns and the beamers."

"Aye, Mum," called Hestia, confusion written on her face. Her comm bead glowed. The klaxon sounded for Battle Stations.

Soon Ligeia felt the familiar sounds of clanking and rumbling as weapons systems came online and railgun rounds started moving to the cannon. The two destroyers of her squadron also reported weapons ready for action.

Comm Officer Areas spoke suddenly. "Mum, Fleet just issued orders for the *Berenice* and her squadrons to go out and join the *Merope* at Hypnos!"

"No," moaned Ligeia. "Are they terminally stupid? It's a diversion! Didn't they pay any attention to my comm at all?"

Ligeia put her head down and quickly called on her AI for the Captain of the *Athena*, Nephele Adrianos. Ligeia and Nephele had been together at the Imperial Naval Academy - they were like sisters. In a few seconds, she had her on the line, looking at her via a small personal holo formed in front of her vision.

"Nephele! Can't you stop them sending *Berenice* out? It's a terrible mistake! This is a diversion, a ploy! There's going to an attack on some other vector!"

Nephele shook her head. "I tried, Ligeia. I told them. But they just don't believe the rebels have that many ships. Intel is they only have twelve ships, and we see ten of them in the outer system. Fleet is convinced that's the threat, and I can't talk them out of it."

Ligeia groaned. "Oh, my Stars, how did idiots like that get into Fleet Intel?"

Nephele shook a finger at Ligeia. "Watch what you say, dear. That kind of statement has a way of getting back to Fleet."

"I don't care, Nephele! In the next few hours, they're going to have proof of just how stupid they are. We're going to get hammered, dear, mark my words."

"Maybe," said Nephele. "But that's the hand we're dealt. In the meantime, just keep your screen behind me covering my ass, and keep yourself up front. Keep me screened and I'll take care of protecting Aronte. Off."

"Off," sighed Ligeia, closing comm. She looked at her crew and shook her head. "Well, girls, all we can do is all we can do."

For the next few minutes, they watched as the rebel fleet in the outer system came on, while the cruiser *Berenice* left the L2 point behind the Greater Moon and piled on the g-force to head out to join the *Merope's* task force at Hypnos.

"It's suicide for those rebels," said Commander Sappho. "They'll be cut to pieces."

"They'll never fight," said Ligeia. "It's a diversion. They'll hare off at the last minute after the real fight starts here."

Sappho looked at her. "How can you be so sure?"

Ligeia made a grim smile. "Wait and see."

Almost the second she said it, the holo blinked and a warning came up on the sidebar, repeated on the AI channel.

<QE early warning buoys offline. All further updates will be based on extrapolation only>

"Told ya," said Ligeia. "They took out the QE network. They're coming in from another vector." She rose from her command chair and paced around the holo tank. "Look hard, girls! They're out there somewhere! Let's find them!"

Ten minutes later, they were still scanning when suddenly Hestia jumped. "Got 'em!" she shouted. "Dead toward the Lesser Moon, just coming around!"

"How many?" asked Ligeia.

"I count...twelve ships. I designate...five cruisers...seven destroyers. They just started a max decel to slow down for orbit. We're in a bad position – as it stands right now, we'll be too far in orbit ahead and out of range when they get into firing position behind the *Athena*. We could try to vector back but I think it would be quicker to drop down around the planet and try to get back around behind them! It's going to be up to the *Athena* and the destroyers to hold them off until we get around."

"Get us around fast, go as low as you have to!" barked Ligeia. "Send your plot to the *Athena* and the destroyers. Guns – stay ready on weapons!"

Ligeia issued a quick order to her destroyer squadron, still holding in position behind the *Athena*. "Hold them at all costs until we get around to support! Do not let them get into bombardment position over Aronte! Remember your families down there!"

Her two destroyers acknowledged the order. Ligeia felt the *Kleitos* shudder hard as the engines fired and Hestia slammed her down toward the planet, shortening the orbit they would have to traverse to reach the enemy.

Suddenly, in the holo, Ligeia saw the *Athena* flicker and then wink out. Seconds later debris flared in all directions on the holo. Ligeia pounded the arm of her command chair, cursing. Quickly she regained control, staring at her crew, whose eyes were as big as saucers.

"It appears we no longer have the *Athena* to protect Aronte, girls. It's up to us now."

KLEITOS

The warriors intention should be to simply grasp his sword and die.
- Kiyomasa Kato

Helios System – Near Aeolis

Eugenius grinned sardonically as the battleship *Athena*, 100,000 km in front of him over Aronte, was turned into an expanding cloud of debris by explosive charges set in her fusion reactors.

It had not been easy getting members of the Rebellion onboard as crew; but they had been planning this for three years. In the end, they had made it happen. They were brave men; there was no other way to do it properly except to stay on board, watching carefully for the right opportunities - and then to continue to stay, nursing their hidden explosives over the final days - to make sure they were not accidentally discovered.

They were brave men; but now they were dead men. Eugenius sighed. When this was over, those men would be recognized as heroes.

But now he had a battle to fight. Eugenius scanned the holo. The single active cruiser around Aronte had been in an orbital position well ahead of the *Athena* when the battleship was destroyed; that cruiser's orbit now put her out of the fight for the moment, in no position to do anything of significance for many minutes. Suddenly his Tac Officer jumped.

"Sir! That's the *Kleitos*!" he cried.

Eugenius smiled. The Creator was favoring him today.

The *Kleitos*. Satra. The bitch that had killed his friends, those many years before. Now diving toward the planet, trying to get around in time to intercept him as he settled in to bombard the capital.

Eugenius laughed. She wouldn't make it, not unless she dove into the atmosphere, and no cruiser could do that and survive. He'd destroy Aronte right in front of her, while she watched. And then the rest of his squadron would kill her from behind. It was perfect.

Meanwhile, the two destroyers that had originally been behind the *Athena* were coming up to meet him, tits-out. Two against twelve. It was suicide for them.

Well out from the planet, Eugenius saw the *Berenice*, which had departed the L2 point beyond the Greater Moon at max emergency accel toward Hypnos, now frantically braking, trying to reverse and get back to Aeolis. She would not make it in time either, he confirmed, certainly not in time to stop the bombardment that was coming.

In orbit far in front of the *Kleitos*, on the backside of the planet now, the *Leto* – the third cruiser that had been orbiting the planet - was coming to life. And out by the Greater Moon, he saw two more ships showing engines online, two destroyers. But they would not be enough. By the time those three were capable of movement, his fleet would be shooting their asses off as they struggled to ready their weapons. And he would already be bombarding Aronte and launching his assault shuttles. He began issuing orders.

"Cruisers *Valiant* and *Revenge*, take the *Leto* behind the planet, ambush her as she comes around the other side."

Then, as an afterthought, Eugenius almost yelled into the comm, "And after you kill that one, take out the *Kleitos* too! She'll be right behind!"

He received acknowledgments from the *Valiant* and *Revenge* and they pulled out with their two escorting destroyers at a slight tangent, to position for an attack on the half-ready *Leto* as she came around the planet directly into their weapons.

"Cruisers *Destiny* and *Freedom,* take the two destroyers coming up to meet us, keep them off my tail."

Eugenius turned to his XO, Commander Petrus. "Ready railguns for bombardment," ordered Eugenius. "Give the assault shuttles the fifteen-minute warning!"

"Aye, sir," acknowledged Petrus.

Onboard the *Kleitos*, Ligeia cursed again as she realized her squadron of two destroyers would have to face the incoming enemy alone for the moment. She turned to Hestia. "How low can we go, Hestia? We've got to get around!"

Hestia looked at her console and shook her head. "I'm already in the fringes of the atmosphere, Mum. I don't think we can go any lower."

"Yes, we can," said Ligeia. "Take us down, Hestia. Cut another ten minutes off our transit time."

Hestia looked panicked. "Mum, I don't think we can survive that!"

Ligeia looked at Hestia calmly. "Yes, we can, Hestia," she said quietly. "Our families are counting on us. Take us down."

Hestia, face white, nodded. She worked her console. In a few seconds, Ligeia heard a light rumble as the cruiser slid farther into the fringes of the atmosphere.

That soon turned into a heavy, whistling scream, and then the *Kleitos* bucked and rolled, resisting the unnatural environment she was in. Her crew were all strapped in now; but as the ship sank farther into the outer atmosphere, the ship began tossing them around like rag dolls.

They were riding the ragged edge of being out of control. Alarms sounded as heat built up on the hull; red lights popped up on the consoles. Ligeia stared at Hestia, who looked back at her with wide eyes. Ligeia smiled. Hestia looked uncertain for a moment, then slowly smiled back at her. Ligeia nodded. "We'll be fine, Hestia. Just hold the course."

Eugenius watched with satisfaction as his cruisers *Destiny* and *Freedom*, along with their two destroyer escorts, opened fire on the two AEN destroyers rising out of orbit to meet them.

Within seconds, the space between the two forces was filled with a fierce web of beams, cannon rounds and missiles. Hits on both sides took chunks out of the ships, but all six ships kept firing, the two AEN destroyers charging uphill at the four rebel ships.

Then, one of the AEN destroyers, the *Adrestia*, went quiet; either her fire control systems or her weapons were blasted, and she had nothing left to fight with. Quickly the rebel cruisers *Destiny* and *Freedom* focused on the other AEN destroyer, blasting her to bits in short order.

Their momentary inattention was fatal; by the time her bridge crews refocused back at the *Adrestia* to finish her off, it was too late. The crippled destroyer had accelerated madly and plowed into the *Destiny* at better than 22kps, sending both warships up in a huge, expanding cloud of debris and parts.

Eugenius slammed his hand against his command chair, cursing. "Damn it!" he yelled across the bridge. "Why couldn't they see that coming?"

His bridge crew ducked their heads, silent.

Eugenius growled, his eyes burning. "This time, they pay. They'll pay for everything."

"Sir, coming up on Aronte. We'll be in geocentric orbit over the city in ten minutes," called the Tac Officer.

"Excellent," cried Eugenius. "Prepare to fire. Target the Palace first."

"Aye, aye, sir," called the Tac Officer. "Rail guns ready, firing in ten minutes."

As the *Kleitos* came around the planet, Ligeia stared at the plot, willing it to update from her limited radar and lidar feeds. With a ping, it did. She saw a huge cloud of debris where her two destroyers had been scant minutes before. She sighed.

Off orbit, away to skyward, the half-prepared AEN cruiser *Leto* was making a run for it, pursued by two rebel cruisers and two rebel destroyers firing at her from behind.

Well above and behind the *Kleitos*, a single rebel cruiser and two escorting rebel destroyers, obviously the force which had taken out her destroyer squadron, were vectoring back toward the rebel flagship to take up their screening positions. They were about 25,000 km over the *Kleitos* and would fall well behind her, due to her inner vector.

In front of her and 36,000 km up, the other cruiser and its covey of two close-in troopships followed by two protective destroyers was almost over Aronte.

"Looks like they're down one cruiser, Mum," called her Tac Officer. "The destroyers took one out!"

Ligeia smiled a hunter's smile. "Every little bit helps," she said. She studied the plot. She recognized the rebel flagship – at least, she assumed it was the flagship, since it was the foremost cruiser and was in heavy decel to position for a geostationary orbit over Aronte.

It was the *Medusa*, an older cruiser last seen on patrol near Maia. It had disappeared two years ago, with no trace ever found. "Those bastards," she breathed.

The *Medusa* was the same size and mass as her ship, but with slightly less powerful engines. It carried six railguns and six beamers, the same as the *Kleitos*.

Two troopships were tucked in close, their bay doors already opening to drop assault troops. They were trailed by an escort of two destroyers. She studied the plot for a few more seconds and then smiled.

"They've screwed up, Sappho," she said to her XO.

"That they have, Skipper," confirmed Commander Sappho. "The two squadrons chasing the *Leto* have taken themselves out of the fight. They should have stayed with the main force and taken us out as we came around. And the other cruiser and two destroyers are going to be a bit late getting back into a screening position."

"Don't take us up into higher orbit just yet, Sappho. Keep us down here as low as possible. I have an idea."

Sappho nodded. "Wilco, Skipper."

Ligeia studied the plot. She noticed how close the troopships and the destroyers were to the cruiser. If she could stay low a bit longer...

"Sappho - disable the accel interlocks. Then issue an abandon ship order."

Sappho stared at her, horrified. "What?"

"Now, Sappho," said Ligeia quietly. "Abandon ship. Right now. Issue the order, disable the accel interlocks, and get the hell out of here."

Sappho stared at her, comprehension slowly crossing her face.

"No, no, no," she breathed.

Ligeia looked hard at her. "Sappho, if you love me, you will do this for me. Now. There is no other way."

Sappho shook her head, but slowly the shake changed to a slight nod as she realized it was the only viable alternative to save Aronte. Her comm bead flashed as she issued the orders.

Suddenly the klaxon sounded, and the sound went out over every comm unit and backup loudspeaker on the ship.

"Abandon ship. This is not a drill; this is not a drill. Abandon ship. This is not a drill; this is not a drill."

The warning repeated, with the klaxon sounding continuously in the background.

The horrified bridge crew stared at Ligeia. She stood from her command chair and stared at them.

Comprehension dawning across all their faces, she thought she would have to physically shove them off the bridge, but Sappho intervened, first pushing one, then another, toward the hatch.

Slowly they backed away from her, their eyes glistening with tears. Under Sappho's pressure, they finally, reluctantly, left the bridge.

When the last one but Sappho was gone, Ligeia looked at her. She nodded to her for a job well done. Then:

"I have always loved you as well as I could, Sappho," Ligeia said.

"I know," breathed Sappho, her eyes wet. Tears ran down her cheeks.

"Go quickly, Sappho. You don't have much time," said Ligeia.

Sappho nodded, then with a step out the hatch she was gone. Ligeia stepped to the helm console and sat, strapping herself in.

She issued a command via her bead and the console switched displays to show lifeboat status. On the screen, Ligeia saw the lifeboats leaving the ship, the board quickly turning from green to red as one after another departed the vessel.

Finally, only one remained, the one containing her bridge crew – and Sappho.

"Go, my darling, go!" said Ligeia, pounding the console in frustration. Finally, the last escape pod launched, and Ligeia knew she was alone on the ship.

Her bead glowed as she issued one more set of commands to the AI, and the ship obediently turned upward, toward the enemy, and went to max in-atmosphere acceleration of 25g.

Waiting a few seconds until she was sure of her vector, Ligeia issued one more command, programming the AI to perform a final task for her.

Just before she issued the execute command, she stopped for a moment and sighed. She would miss her daughter. If the Creator allowed.

"Execute."

Thrusting past the compensator limits by 50g, the *Kleitos* blazed upward through the atmosphere, a meteor in reverse.

Eugenius noted with satisfaction the *Medusa* had come to a geostationary orbit directly over the city of Aronte. The Tac Officer turned to him. "In position, sir."

Eugenius paused. He wanted to savor this moment. He closed his eyes, remembering the thousands of comrades killed or maimed in this war. This was for them, he thought. Then he nodded to the Tac Officer.

"Launch the assault shuttles, and open fire with the railguns, Tac," he said.

Those were the last words he ever said. The *Kleitos*, coming up from below, plowed into the *Medusa* at a relative velocity of slightly under 80kps. Both ships were reduced to a boiling cloud of debris instantly. The collision had such force that the blast took out both the troopships tucked in close to the *Medusa* and the two rebel destroyers following her as well.

Behind them, the single rebel cruiser *Freedom* and her two destroyers, in the process of rejoining formation, found themselves suddenly alone - nothing in front of them but an expanding cloud of hot gas mixed with fast-moving chunks of starship. They broke hard to skyward to avoid the mess.

By now the AEN *Berenice* beyond the Greater Moon had reversed her course and was accelerating directly toward the rebels, with her two destroyers joining up as she came inward.

Skyward, the AEN cruiser *Leto*, having gotten her weapons online and finally ready to fight, had turned to challenge her pursuers *Valiant* and *Revenge*, joined by another cruiser and two destroyers from the Greater Moon.

The *Valiant* and *Revenge,* along with their destroyer squadrons, turned and ran for it, making max emergency accel out of the system, with the rebel cruiser *Freedom* right in front of them.

The AEN fleet, now a hornet's nest of pissed-off sailors, chased them all the way to the mass limit, taking out two more destroyers and the rebel cruiser *Valiant* before they quit the chase.

The Fringe Rebellion wasn't over. But it would be a long while before it dared come out of the Fringe again.

RIBBONS OF FIRE

My mother was a true warrior. She raised me to be a true warrior. That is our family business, and we do it well.
- Callisto Ligeia Satra, daughter of Ligeia Iona Satra, 2162

City of Aronte

It was getting late. The sun was low as the sloop came up the estuary toward the city. A very pregnant Princess Antiope reclined in the cockpit on a pile of blankets, watching the streamers of fire streak across the sky over Aronte.

Hundreds of small fireballs fell every minute, as parts from the gutted remains of ten starships decayed from orbit and fell into the atmosphere. It was an achingly beautiful yet heartrending sight.

Antiope sighed and glanced at Jake. He looked back at her, face solemn.

By the time the warning had sounded on their comm beads that Aronte was under attack, they were already well out in the estuary, making their last sail together before the baby was due. They decided it was just as well to stay where they were, a good ten kilometers from the center of the city. If the bombardment happened, they would be safer in the boat than back in Aronte. So, they waited, and watched, as the battle unfolded above them.

Antiope was still a Reserve Naval Officer, so she had access on her comm bead to most of the events of the day. She had patched Jake in. They had listened, stone-faced, as the ships above them fought and died.

Antiope cried at the end, when she realized what the *Kleitos* had done to save them and their city. Jake had held her as she cried it out, sobbing, in a broken voice telling him how she had grown up with Ligeia Satra, a distant cousin.

Finally, they started back. By early dusk, they were in the main channel, going up-river with a good following wind.

Antiope had dried her tears and was now alternately cursing the rebels and vowing to get on a ship and chase them down, pregnant or not. Jake steered silently, knowing this was not a time to speak.

Eventually she calmed, and as they docked, met by their security detail, she was once again the consummate Amazon princess, looking neither to the left or right as she marched heavily down the dock to their flitter.

People nearby, recognizing her, cheered as she passed; but she never broke step or acknowledged them. Landing on the Palace grounds, she exited the flitter and went straight to their chambers.

Jake followed well behind, uncertain if he should remain with her or go stay in the Barracks tonight. But as he entered her room behind her, she whirled on him and flung herself into his arms, a few more tears coming down.

"It's the pregnancy, I know it is, I don't cry like this!" she exclaimed, but held on to him anyway. "It's ridiculous!"

Jake held her, quietly rubbing her back, until once more the tears stopped, and she was quiet. Finally, she pulled back, looking into his eyes, then turned and went to a chair. She sat and waved him down.

"Jake, we need to talk. About after."

Jake nodded. "OK." He sat across from her. She gathered her thoughts for a few seconds, staring deep into his eyes.

"When the baby is born, you'll be exiled back to Barcam."

Jake nodded. "I know."

Antiope stared at him. "You're not from Barcam." She said it as a flat statement.

Jake, surprised, could only look at her. Antiope made a half-smile.

"Don't look so shocked. I've known almost from the first."

Jake, amazed, could only reply, "In that case, where do you think I'm from?"

Antiope smiled a mischievous smile. "Not from around these parts, I think."

Jake froze. He was afraid to speak.

Antiope laughed out loud. "Don't worry, lover. You are in no danger. Nobody knows but me - and maybe Prince Adrian. You are quite safe."

She crossed her arms and leaned forward. "I don't expect you to tell me the whole story. I know you must have a good reason for being here. I've known you – and loved you - long enough to be sure you would never do anything to harm us, or our child. So, I am quite content to trust you. But... Zeno, please...give me some hint. Some reassurance that my intuition is correct. That's all I ask of you."

Jake nodded. "I think I can do that much." He lowered his head and thought for several seconds, deciding how to present the information. Finally, he raised his head and looked at her again.

"Imagine a star nation much like Aeolis, with many colonies, like this Empire. Imagine it under great threat – a threat that cannot be met with only the resources of that people. A threat that will kill them all if they cannot find a way to meet it."

"Imagine this people discovered their long-lost relatives, far away. And they knew with the help of their relatives, they might survive the threat. And if they did not get that help, not only would they die, but the threat would travel on and destroy their relatives as well."

A shiver ran down Antiope's back, visible even to Jake. But she remained silent.

"I came here to discover how we might reconcile with our relatives," said Jake. "The survival of both races depends on it."

Antiope turned her face away in thought. After a while, she turned back to Jake. "And have you found the solution?"

"Partially," said Jake. "But you are not ready. You are at war with yourselves – men against women, nobles against commoners, slaves against their masters. Your Empress is determined to kill all who even mention the smallest hint of ... our homeland. Until those things are resolved, I don't believe there is any chance of reconciliation."

Antiope nodded. "And how much time is there?"

"Enough," said Jake. "Seventy to eighty years yet. But it will come. Not for your generation, or even our child's. But our grandchildren will have to deal with it."

Antiope stood and paced around the room, holding her swollen belly. "I almost wish I hadn't asked."

Jake nodded. "Myself as well."

Antiope turned to him. "What should I do?"

Jake went to her and held her, smelling her sweet hair, caressing her, rubbing her arms. "Lead toward peace. Lead toward reconciliation. Give a little, equalize a little, flatten your society."

"That won't be easy - for Star's sake, Zeno, they tried to kill us today!"

"Still," said Jake. "That's the way to survival. For all of us."

He pulled back from her; his brow furrowed in a frown. "Will you tell our daughter?"

Antiope turned away from him. "I don't know. I suppose I will, when she's old enough." She turned back toward him. "Let's just focus on the few days we have left. I don't want to think about this anymore."

At the tavern, Metrodora sat with Prince Adrian, holding his hand. They were both devastated by the destruction and death of the battle and were just sitting, trying to get past it, holding each other in their hearts.

Metrodora realized something was happening to her, something she had not planned on. She was falling in love with this man - this Aeolian prince, who had no concept of who she really was.

An impossible situation. She had been on Aronte for well over four years now and was scheduled for permanent rotation back to Earth in another six months; this was a most inconvenient time to fall in love, she thought. Especially with someone like this.

Across the table from her, Prince Adrian was having similar thoughts. He too felt the tug of love at his heartstrings. He also knew the difficulties in making a match work with a commoner.

And there was more. He couldn't put his finger on it, but he knew there was something strange, unique, about Metrodora. She didn't exactly think and act like most Aeolian women.

Finally, he spoke. "Metrodora. How do you really feel about me?"

Metrodora gazed at him, taking her time. "I would like to see if this relationship could go somewhere, Adrian. If you are of a mind."

Adrian squeezed her hand. "I'm of a mind."

A few weeks later and 100 light years away, on Maia, Anicetus slumped against his table, drunk, at the same bar where he had last been with Eugenius before the raid.

The carefully gathered rebel fleet had dispersed to their hiding places, awaiting the retribution they knew would be coming. But Anicetus himself was no longer afraid. He had stared into the abyss and the abyss had stared back.

Now he was angry. Now he knew how Eugenius had felt. And he had decided. This was not over. This could not stand.

Anicetus slid off his chair and fell, his beer glass crashing to the floor and breaking into pieces. His last thoughts before he passed out were of revenge.

He would find a way.

DEINOMACHE

He who conquers himself is the mightiest warrior.
-Confucius

City of Aronte

One month later, Antiope's yell echoed down the corridor. Jake started from his chair, but Lt. Pallis grabbed his arm and pulled him back down, a grin on his face.

"Not yet, Zeno," he said.

Sheepishly, Jake returned to his seat. Their chairs lined up against the wall, the four men held cigars, a rare dispensation from Antiope as her labor began hours earlier.

"Go!" she had yelled at Jake and Prince Adrian, when it was clear that her labor was starting. "Wait outside! Smoke cigars! Be men! But stay out of here!"

Now, it was just after eleven pm; the Palace was quiet. Antiope's occasional cries echoed through empty hallways. Antiope's chambers were far from those of the Empress Miranda, and Jake was glad.

To his right, Lt. Pallis and Captain Kyrkos sat, puffing on their cigars. To his left was Antiope's uncle, Prince Adrian.

Prince Adrian tapped his arm.

"It takes a while, with these women," he said, jerking a thumb toward Antiope's chambers.

Jake bowed his head and shook it back and forth. "I don't know why I'm so nervous," he said. "It's not like I've never been through this before."

Prince Adrian snorted.

"Yes; but how many Princesses have you fathered?"

Jake nodded. He fiddled with his backup wrist comm but couldn't concentrate. Finally, he leaned his head back and closed his eyes. He thought about his future.

Was he prepared to lose Antiope now? He and Antiope had talked about it. He knew the rules. They were crystal clear. A commoner who fathered a Princess had only one path. Tomorrow, he would hold his newborn child one time; kiss Antiope goodbye; and he would be shipped off to Barcam and exile. He would never see them again.

Was it worth it? These last months? His heart did not yet know. His life in Aeolis was over, that he understood. But could his heart survive?

He had buried two wives already. After that, he had thought he would never love again.

But Antiope had brought him back to life, back to the feelings he had as a young man. And now it would all be gone.

Jake sighed. Beside him, Pallis put a hand on his shoulder, thinking it was about the waiting. But it wasn't the waiting. It was the heartbreak.

Jake looked across the corridor at the opposite wall. There was a sword mounted there, an old one. He recognized it as an *acinaces*, an ancient design of Scythian sword.

“What’s that sword?” Jake asked, making small talk.

“That? That’s the Sword of Penthesilea,” said Prince Adrian. “It was used by the Amazon Penthesilea of Thrace in the Trojan War. When the Amazons were sent down from Heaven to rule Aeolis, that sword was sent down with them to our first Queen, her sister Melanippe.”

Jake looked at the sword. It was clearly ancient. But surely...

Surely not her sword, he thought. *Surely not Pandora’s original sword. Must be a myth.*

Prince Adrian continued, passing the time.

“On the near side, by the hilt, you can see the ancient letter “Pi”, for Penthesilea. On the other side is the ancient letter

"Heta", for her sister Hippolyta."

"That sword has been passed down for 3,300 years, from daughter to daughter. It belongs to Antiope now."

Prince Adrian paused and looked at Jake with a smile.

"And someday it will belong to your daughter."

Three hours later, another yell from within Antiope's chambers. Jake thought this one was different. It seemed a yell of triumph.

Suddenly he heard a baby cry. Jake jumped to his feet. Pallis slapped him on the back. "You're a father, by the Stars!" he yelled.

Prince Adrian, overtaken by excitement, grabbed his hand and pushed it, the Aeolian handshake. The door to Antiope's chambers burst open and a young nurse stuck out her head.

"The Princess is born! She is healthy, and loud!" She turned and rushed back into the room, the door banging behind her.

Jake grinned. Tears popped into his eyes.

Now he knew. It was worth it. It would always be worth it. Any amount of pain. Any amount of loneliness. It would always be worth it.

An hour later, they called him in. Antiope was propped up in bed, holding the child. Jake was escorted over to her by Captain Kyrkos and Prince Adrian. Lt. Pallis hung discreetly in the background. Antiope smiled at Jake and grasped his hand, pulled him closer to her.

"See your daughter," she said, and handed him the baby.

Jake cradled the child, looking at her perfect face, her perfect hands. One tear, alone, fell from his face onto the child's cheek. He looked at Antiope.

"She is so beautiful, Antiope" he said.

"Her name is Deinomache," said Antiope. "She will be a great warrior."

Jake touched the back of his hand to the child's cheek. He felt the slight fuzz of hair. Another tear fell from his eye onto the baby. He leaned to kiss her, feeling the heat of her skin and the wetness of his tear on it.

Then he felt the hand of the nurse, sliding under the child to take her. He let her go to the nurse and looked at Antiope. Slowly, he sank to his knees beside the bed, holding Antiope's hand. He looked at her and whispered, "Take good care of our child, Antiope."

Antiope pulled him in closer and they kissed, a long, steady kiss that could never last long enough for either of them. Then she whispered something in his ear. Jake looked at her, and said very quietly, "I'll remember, dear."

Then Jake felt the hand of Prince Adrian on his shoulder. He pulled away slowly. Antiope looked at him with eyes burning like fire.

"I will guard her well, Zeno," she said. "I will teach her about you. She will know you. She will love you."

Jake nodded. Then he felt Prince Adrian turning him, leading him to the door. His will was gone. He moved like a robot. He turned at the door and looked back at Antiope and the child. Then the door closed, and they were gone.

Beehive Cluster – Planet Barcam

Standing on the landing pad at Barcam, Jake watched the shuttle departing to the destroyer *Tyche*, taking Lt. Pallis back to Aronte.

It had been a week's journey to Barcam, and Pallis had tried to keep Jake's spirits up. They drank, played cards, sparred in the workout room, tried to make a bad trip into a good one. It had almost worked; Jake had gotten through it without too much pain showing on his face.

But now, standing on the tarmac alone, he felt the wind whistling around him like the cut of a knife into his soul.

Pallis had read the riot act to him before he left, which was his job. Friend or no friend, he had a responsibility to perform, and he did it well.

"Zeno of Barcam," he had intoned, reading from a tablet, "You are banished from Aronte and Aeolis. On pain of death, you are not to return to either. If you are seen in those environs, any woman of rank may kill you without thought or recourse to trial. So it has been decreed by the Empress of Aeolis. Take note and follow this warning well."

Jake had just nodded. There was nothing to say. Pallis gave him a handpush, climbed in the shuttle, and left.

Turning, Jake walked toward the terminal building, knowing that Metrodora would have someone there to greet him. Once inside, he quickly spotted the man.

"Hello, Gunner," he said in English, not too loud, "Good to see you."

"And you, sir," said Gunner Carlson, still Chief of Staff to the head of the RDF in his absence, Admiral Lois Vetton. "I've got a shuttle on the other side of the field."

"Sounds good," said Jake. "They'll probably tail me for a while, though, to see what I do. Do you have a plan in place for that?"

"We do, sir," said Gunner, looking around the empty terminal carefully. "We've found a body double for you, and if you'll follow me, we'll take care of the swap."

Gunner led him to a restroom, where another man Jake recognized from the tavern in Aronte had placed a sign on the door, "Out of Service", and was standing outside with a bucket and a mop.

Inside, Jake found himself face to face with someone who could be his twin. The man was dressed identically, right down to the smallest detail. Taken aback, Jake stood for a second, assessing the man's look and outfit. Finally, he shook his head.

"Amazing," he said in Aeolian.

"This is Zeno of Barcam," said Gunner, smiling. "He will faithfully perform the role for as long as it takes, until they forget about you."

"I trust you are being well paid," Jake said to the man.

"Very much so, sir," said the man, with an accent not too much different from Jake's own. "Thank you, and my family thanks you."

"Very well," Jake nodded at Gunner. "Let's do it."

Gunner pressed a cube into the man's hands which undoubtedly contained a large amount of money in some numbered bank account. The man grinned at Jake, saluted, and walked out the door.

Gunner led Jake to the back of the room, where a hidden door popped open at his touch. They passed through, carefully closing it behind them, and Jake found himself in a small cleaning closet.

At the back, Gunner pushed another hidden latch, and they were in a small office. Laid out for him were new clothes, as non-descript as possible.

Jake changed quickly, leaving behind everything except his sword. He looked at Gunner questioningly, and Gunner nodded. "You can take it. Here, put it in this," he said, passing Jake a soft carry-on bag.

After a few minutes, Jake was ready. Gunner led him through another door, and they found themselves in a service tunnel, which crossed the field to the far side. Walking through, they came up inside another cleaning closet, then into another restroom across the field.

Outside the restroom, they went directly through a gate to a private shuttle apron, where a plain, unmarked Aeolian shuttle showing plenty of wear and tear waited for them. Inside, Jake tossed his gear behind the seat and buckled in, then glanced out the window at the shuttleport.

A light rain had just started. The smell of rain was the last thing he remembered about Barcam and his life in Aeolis.

BEGIN AGAIN

He who is prudent and lies in wait for an enemy who is not, will be victorious.

- Sun Tzu, Chinese general

City of Aronte

Empress Miranda was holding court again. Surrounded by her inner circle, with her sister Merope beside her, she had just completed a toast to the destruction of the rebel force and the end of the threat to Aronte.

"Where is Antiope?" she turned to Merope and asked. "I would see my niece and grandnieces today. Are they coming?"

Merope shrugged. "Antiope was under the weather, she said she couldn't come. Hippolyta is helping her with the baby, I believe."

"Too bad," said Miranda. "I do love to have new babies around me!"

A male servant entered the room behind her. Miranda paid him no attention at first. After several moments, though, she sensed something and turned to look at him. He stood quite close to her, holding in his hands a large silver serving dish.

"What do you want?" Miranda glared at him. "What do you have there?"

"Freedom, Mum," said Anicetus quietly, lifting the lid of the serving dish.

The explosion killed everyone in the room instantly, blowing out all four walls and bringing down the ceiling as well.

Jake was dozing in his bunk on the corvette, more than halfway home. It was a long eight weeks back to Kamilaroi, with a stop for two days at Eudora, the RDF forward base closest to the Aeolian Empire.

He had spent the evening exchanging messages with Lois Vetton at Tolleson Base. She made it clear she was ready to retire and expected Jake to step back into his role as CNO. Jake forgot, sometimes, that everyone else aged, although he did not. Gunner Carlson had also told Jake his intention to retire.

Thus, it appeared there was nothing for it; after more than two years away, Jake was returning to his role as CNO of the Rim Defense Force, although Jake had insisted that both Lois and Gunner stay on part-time as members of his advisory council.

A gentle knock on his door brought him up from his slumbers.

"Come," he said. Gunner entered the room, holding his tablet in his hand. He walked over to Jake and handed it to him, silently. Jake looked up at his face. Gunner looked grim. Jake took the tablet and read it, silently.

"Antiope? The baby?"

"Both safe," said Gunner. "Prince Adrian as well. But you realize what this means."

Jake nodded. "Miranda had no children, and Merope was killed with her."

Gunner nodded as well. "Antiope has been declared Empress." Gunner reached for the tablet, paged it, and handed it back to Jake. "She sent you a private message."

Jake read the tablet, then bowed his head. "Where did you get this?"

"Antiope gave it to Prince Adrian to take to you on Barcam. He gave it to Metrodora, however. Obviously, he has figured out that she can get a message to you." said Gunner.

Jake looked up quickly. "Do we need to pull Metrodora out?"

Gunner grinned. "I don't think so. Her and Prince Adrian are getting married."

"Damn," said Jake. "I didn't see that one coming."

Gunner laughed. "I guess we need to send a replacement Station Chief to Aronte to take her place."

"I'd say so," said Jake.

Gunner got serious. "So, what about Antiope's message?"

Jake sighed. "She says she can't tolerate this kind of terrorism. She has to destroy the rebels before she can work to bring about reforms to her society. She's ordered an all-out attack on the Fringe. She hopes I'll understand."

Gunner shook his head. "There goes any hope of a quick alliance. As long as they're fighting each other, we can't take a chance on trying to put together a joint effort against the Bats."

"Exactly," said Jake. "Who knows how many years it will take for this never-ending war to be over? And the path Antiope has chosen is not one I think will lead to a quick resolution."

He handed the tablet back to Gunner. "Thanks for bringing me the good news, Gunner," he said. Gunner grimaced, took the tablet, and left.

Jake pondered the future. Clearly Antiope was going to rejoin the fight against the rebels in the Fringe. Knowing her, he thought it would be a long and bloody war. Miranda had been soft, vacillating, afraid to really commit to an all-out attack on the Fringe Planets. Antiope was hard as nails and there wasn't an ounce of fear in her. Where this would go with her, he could not predict.

Jake sighed and turned back to his bunk. It was a long way home. And it appeared he had not yet discovered the secret to an alliance with the Aeolians.

Humanity would have to wait until Antiope had suppressed the rebels – or enough blood was shed to change her mind – before any realistic alliance was possible.

Or until the RDF had enough starships to take on the Aeolians toe-to-toe and win.

Am I too old for this? My God, I'm fifty-eight years old in reality. But thanks to Pandora, *my body is only thirty-eight. I feel better than I have in years. My mind still seems to be as sharp as ever.*

But the memories...ah, God, the memories. With those, I feel a thousand years old.

Can I still do this?

But do I have a choice? Pandora *stated very clearly, I have to carry this fight forward. If I quit now...what happens? What happens to my children? What happens to the rest of Humanity?*

This is what Pandora *meant when she said I have a burden few could carry. But I have no choice. I must carry it.*

And then...my promise to Teresa and Kirsten. To keep the children safe...

Jake heaved a huge sigh, rolling over in the bunk, determined to get some rest. Drifting off, his last thoughts before sleep were about his children, and his future.

I promise you, Teresa and Kirsten, thought Jake. *I promise you I will never give up preparing Humanity for this war. I promise I will take care of our children. I will make the RDF a force to be reckoned with. I will make an alliance with the Aeolians. And I will find a way to protect our world and our colonies from the enemy.*

I swear it.

EPILOGUE

22 Years Later...
42 Years after *Pandora*

The funeral procession slow-marched through the city, starting from the Temple of Artemis down to the Riverfront.

The Empress Antiope had lain in state for three days, while the people of the Empire moved slowly past, gazing at the face of one of the most loved, and most hated, of the Empire's rulers.

Antiope had fought a long and bitter war with the rebels of the Fringe, killing hundreds of thousands in her zeal to bring the Rebellion to a close and reunite the Empire. The Great Raid of 2163 – the largest raid on the central planets since 2141 - had brought death to the Empress who was called a butcher by some, and a savior by others.

After lying in state, the ornate casket had been placed on a caisson and driven, as slowly as the horses were willing to move, down the hill from the Temple to the Thermodon River, and from there by an ancient road to the cemetery of the Amazons, at the top of a hill six kilometers from the city gate.

The roads were lined with people, shoulder to shoulder. As the caisson passed by, most cried. Some few cheered, but not too loudly - the Palace Guards were close by and were quick to anger in this time of grief.

At the end of the road, the Guards carefully moved the casket into the *tholos* reserved for Antiope and departed, leaving her in the care of the female members of her clan.

Placing her sword, bow and arrows, and her golden

girdle around the casket in the proper places, her daughters Hippolyta and Deinomache unsealed the casket, checked that the golden *obol* on her lips and the golden tablet containing a greeting to the ruler of the Underworld were still in their proper places, then re-sealed it.

Then, using a knife, they cut ragged locks of their hair and laid them on the top of the casket. They sprinkled libations around the *tholos*, left an offering of food and wine, and watched as the *tholos* was closed and locked. In older times, the horses would have been killed and left in the grave as a sacrifice - but modern customs prevented that.

Hippolyta left immediately to take care of affairs of state – as the new Empress, her duties had already begun – but Deinomache stayed a long while, sitting on a small marble bench in the cemetery, holding flowers in her hand and staring at the sunset.

Twelve months later, a man appeared at the top of a small rise by the cemetery, walking from town.

He wore clothing like that of a Palace Guard, but without any insignia.

His sword was held in an old scabbard, gone black from years of oiling and use. His head was covered by a cowl.

Approaching the cemetery, he stopped and stared, remembering. Finally, he opened the gate and entered, walking to the guardhouse and presenting a pass to the guards.

After some discussion, two guards led him to Antiope's *tholos*, and opened the outer and inner gates for him. They positioned themselves just inside the inner gate where they could watch him carefully as he moved forward into the dark tomb.

The man crossed the space to the bier. He knelt and following a tradition more than three thousand years old, took out his sword and painfully cut a large lock of hair from his head, laying the strands lovingly on the casket.

Taking wine from his pouch, he poured a libation.

Speaking in Aeolian, he said the Prayer for the Dead.

Then he sat for a long while, communing with ghosts.

At the end, he rose and spoke softly. “I remembered, dear.”

Turning away, he left slowly, the guards carefully closing the inner and outer gates behind him. He saluted the guards as he departed and started walking back toward Aronte, six kilometers away.

End

AUTHOR NOTES

Next book in series - Imprint of War!

By 2185 – 64 years after *Pandora* gave her warning to Earth – the RDF had grown to be a powerful space navy – but not yet strong enough to take on the Bat Empire. As the Bats move ever closer to Humanity, Jake knows that only through an alliance with the Aeolian Empire is there hope for Earth and her colonies. Doing everything possible to prepare for the coming war, Jake has one ace in the hole - the legacy of his time on Aeolis. Will it be enough?

Read the preview of Imprint of War below!

Or click here to skip the preview and read the whole darn book!

Special bonus - after the preview below, be sure to read through the RimWiki, 2185 Edition. This contains much additional detail about the early days of the Rim !

PREVIEW - IMPRINT OF WAR!

There is no avoiding war; it can only be postponed to the advantage of others.
- Niccolo Machiavelli

Beehive Cluster - Near Pestilence Port
22 Apr 2185

"Out of six-space, Captain." said the Tac Officer.

"Very good, Reah," said Hecate. "Set a course for Pestilence Port and keep us stealthed. If anybody is going to be surprised out here, I want it to be the other guys."

"Roger, Mum," confirmed Reah.

Andrea grinned. "Like a lion lurking among the sheep."

"A small lion," said Hecate. "Let's not pick on anybody bigger than us."

Turning back to the Tac Officer, Hecate asked, "What do we have in the system, Reah?"

"Well," said Reah, "We have the A5-class star, two small rocky planets in close that are too hot for habitation, three gas giants out in the edge of the system with a lot of moons, and a ton of junk all around. It's a really cluttered-up system. Pestilence Port is on the largest moon of the innermost gas giant, basically a mining colony, low population. We have about a twelve-hour run-in to the port."

"OK. Any threat areas I should be aware of, maybe a good place for an ambush?"

"Oh, tons of them," said Reah. "Just take your pick. Like I

said, a very cluttered up, junky system. Rocks everywhere."

Hecate sighed. "OK. Keep your eyes peeled. This could very well be an ambush scenario. Let's don't get caught with our knickers down."

"Roger, Skipper." agreed the Tactical Officer.

As the *Nemesis* moved into the system, Hecate sat loosely in her command chair, while Andrea paced the bridge from console to console, looking over shoulders, cocked for action. Hecate smiled. That is why they were such a good team. She was the relaxed, thoughtful one, Andrea was the tightly wound spring. But if anything happened, both knew exactly how the other would react and how to use that to their advantage.

Hecate was no protected, cosseted Princess of the Blood. Princess Deinomache, her mother, had also been a Fleet Navy Officer, and had worked her way up to Frigate Captain. Throughout Hecate's childhood, it had been understood she would serve in the Navy, and she had been prepared accordingly. Like all members of the Imperial family, she had trained in hand-to-hand combat from the age of six, mastered hand weapons and armor by ten, started flying her own flitter at thirteen, and flew her first space shuttle at fourteen. By the age of eighteen she had graduated from the Imperial Naval College at Aronte and entered the Fleet. And she had worked her way up the hard way - never once using her blood or her title for advancement. Now, at twenty-seven, she was a destroyer Captain, and would soon be in line for a frigate.

"Contact!" yelled the Tac Officer. "I have a stealthed destroyer, barely visible, coming out from that big asteroid behind us, vectoring for our six, I designate DD1"

"Battle Stations!" yelled Andrea. She turned to Hecate. "It's an ambush, all right,"

As the klaxon sounded both overhead and in their internal comms, Hecate assessed the picture in the holo.

"Bring us about forty-five degrees to the left, Helm, and make for that big moon over there by the outermost gas giant.

Up to max standard. Let's get some protection behind that moon. Get our weapons hot, Guns. Comm, hail this bitch and see if she wants to talk."

"Aye, Mum," said the Weapons Officer and Comm Officer simultaneously.

"No response, ma'am. Still coming on, still stealthed. If we didn't have the new Mark II detectors, we wouldn't even know she was there."

"Thank God's thumb for that," said Andrea. She glanced at Hecate briefly. "I wonder if Auntie knows we have those..."

Hecate shushed her. "Not now, Andrea. What's it looking like, Tac?"

"Still coming hard, ma'am. She's gonna have us right about the time we get to that moon. Whoever she is, she's got a Mark II also. She's right on us."

"OK, let's plan on a tight perigee with a vector change as we go around that moon, I want to scrape dirt off the tops of the mountains and come around it with enough vector change to make exit a good 20 degrees off our inbound track. Let's see if we can fox this lady. Prepare for excess g's."

The klaxon, which had stopped, sounded again with the singsong of the excess g warning, letting crew members know they were about to exceed the limits of the compensator.

"Contact!" yelled the Tac Officer. "I have another stealthed destroyer, coming from behind the moon we're making for, designate DD2. It's a setup!"

"Damn!" yelled Hecate. "I walked right into it!"

Andrea yelled at the Helm, "Roll our belly armor to the bitch in front of us, she's closer, and get us the hell out of here!"

"Aye, Mum!"

"Guns, open fire with everything!" yelled Andrea.

“Too close for missiles, Mum,” yelled the Weapons Officer. “They won’t arm before they hit!”

"We're gonna get pounded," observed Hecate. "Hang on, everybody."

The *Nemesis*' railgun cannon let loose their first shots with deep thumps that shook the whole ship. At the same time, the Tac Officer yelled, "Incoming!" and then the sharp, metallic clang of a cannon round striking the armored belly of the destroyer nearly knocked everyone off their feet.

"This bitch can shoot," yelled Andrea. "Waggle and Wobble, Helm. Guns, anything?"

"Aye, mum, we hit her once. No obvious damage, but she knows we're here."

"Let's do a little better than that. Keep firing!"

Deep thumps from the aft cannons showed that the Weapons Officer had already decided that. But that was immediately followed by two more incoming cannon rounds striking their belly, in quick succession.

"They've both got our range, now," said Tac. "We're bracketed."

"Max Emergency, Helm!" yelled Andrea, diving for her command chair, and immediately got knocked to the floor as the Helm rather enthusiastically firewalled the engines to full emergency power, the initial 202g thrust exceeding the limits of the compensator by 2gs, then rising quickly as the AI piled on as much as it thought the Humans inside the tin can could tolerate. With the destroyer on a random walk course away from the two enemy ships, the g-forces pushed Hecate deep into her seat, while the random walk maneuvers jerked her back and forth against her straps. As the g-force built to the destroyer's max of 207g - 7 g over the limit of the compensator, crushing them into their seats - Andrea managed to finish crawling into her combat chair and strap herself in, blood oozing from her nose but otherwise OK.

Hecate wondered how many broken bones this battle would cost the crew; but there was no choice. She was in a crossfire between two ships of equal size and firepower to hers, and both had her range. She had to change the equation. "Be ready, Guns!" she grunted.

"Aye, ma'am" groaned Guns under the g-force. As their relative angle to the pursuers behind them opened a bit, Hecate heard her own aft cannons blazing away, alternating between the two pursuers. All three ships pounded each other for several seconds as Hecate rushed away from the battle line and the other ships twisted toward her.

"Contact!" groaned the Tac Officer. "Another one, right in front of us, in stealth, just waiting for us, DD3!"

"Crap!" spat Andrea.

Hecate smiled grimly, shaking her head. "They've really got us in a box, Andy. Our only choice is to go right through this one. Helm - ram that bitch in front of us!"

"Aye, mum!" yelled the Helm, her voice quavering.

The Weapons officer launched all four of the *Nemesis'* forward missiles at the destroyer in front of them, but they were so close that only one of them armed before reaching the target. It exploded near the other destroyer, but somewhat behind it, not doing any real damage.

With her aft cannons alternating between the two pursuers now boxing her in from behind, the *Nemesis* charged toward the new enemy, firing both forward cannons as fast as possible at the ship before her, alarms flashing across the board.

"Overheat on all cannon, Captain!" yelled Guns, her face shiny with sweat.

"Keep firing, keep firing!" yelled Hecate as the ships rushed together.

"Mum..." called the Helm, as they were a few seconds from collision.

"Do! Not! Flinch!" yelled Hecate. At that moment, a tremendous explosion struck their ship, as the destroyer closest behind them scored a direct hit on their engines. The blast spun them to the side, an instant before they flicked by the ship in front, missing by less than a hundred meters. The lights went out, and every screen on the bridge went dark.

The force of the explosion had knocked Hecate hard against the side of the command chair; she thought a rib was probably broken. Overhead, the emergency battle lights came on, building slowly to full intensity. The holotank flickered and resumed operation on battery power. But the picture it painted was not good.

Andrea grunted in pain beside her, then whispered bitterly, "They've got us."

Hecate nodded. "Yep. We're dead in the water. Guns are disabled, main engines are out, and we're just coasting along like so much junk. They'll come in and finish us off."

Minutes later, smoke covered the bridge, drifting in the light of the emergency battle lamps. They had managed to get the spin of the ship under control using docking thrusters, but everything else was out. Andrea stood behind the auxiliary command console and laid two rifles on top, facing the bridge entry. She shook her head. "Hecate, think what you are saying."

Hecate paused from stacking extra ammo charges behind her own console and stared at Andrea. "Andrea, think about it. We get ambushed by three destroyers. All three of them have Mark II detectors. A perfect setup. This is Navy."

In the holotank, the three enemy destroyers approached cautiously, a few minutes from boarding them.

Andrea shuddered. "Hecate, no...it can't be..."

Hecate glared at her. "Let's be realistic. You know Auntie. You know she's capable of anything. And now...I think we know who set up the ambush for my father, too."

Andrea put her hands over her ears, as if to block out the sound. Then, taking her hands away, Andrea went on. "Why? Why would Auntie want to kill you? Or your father? He was no threat to her - why would she do that? He was about as disinterested in Palace business as anyone I've ever known. All he wanted to do was to pursue his stupid Earther theories. And you - you're what, fourth in line?"

Hecate sighed. "Actually, third. A long way from first or second. But this is a crazy world we live in. This is a setup, and it’s Navy, and that means it's Auntie."

Andrea thought out loud. "I take it that means, there'll be no survivors."

Hecate grimaced. "You got it. That's why they're boarding us, to make sure."

Commander Andrea Iona Satra gave a big smile. She hefted her pulse rifle, checking the charge for the second time since they had passed out weapons for their last-ditch stand.

"Good - then I don't have to worry about accidentally killing any good guys!"

Or continue to the RimWiki below!

ORION ARM RIMWIKI

Aeolian Empire

The **Aeolian Empire** is a star nation centered on the Planet Aeolis, in the Beehive Cluster (M44), 580 light years from Earth. Aeolis was originally populated by approximately 212 Humans abducted from Earth by the Machine Ship *Hermes* around 1184 BC and transported to Aeolis, where they were abandoned as part of *Hermes'* bottleneck experiment. The small population survived and prospered and has grown to a star nation of some 42 colonized planets (as of 2180).

The original founding population originated in the Greek city-state of Aeolis, on the western coast of Turkey. However, 12 Amazonian females among the abductees took over leadership of the small group on the new planet and established a matriarchal society based on a blend of Amazonian and Greek culture and beliefs. The descendants of the original Amazon warriors are known as the House Aronte.

Aeolis (planet)

Aeolis is a planet in the Beehive Cluster, 580 light years from Earth. It is the capital planet of the Aeolian Empire. The capital city, Aronte, is named after the founding house of the Empire, the House Aronte. Aeolis orbits a G2 type star called 'Helios' in the Aeolian language and is like Earth in size, composition, and climate.

Amasya (planet)

Amasya is a planet in the Fringe of the Aeolian Empire.

Like most planets in the Cluster, it is quite young, with an estimated age of 600 million years. Due to an exceptionally large number of comets in its system, significant amounts of water were deposited on the planet in its early evolution, as occurred in many other systems in the Cluster. This allowed oceans and a basic atmosphere to develop.

Per the Machine Ship *Pandora*, the rogue Machine Ship *Hermes* elected to use these young planets as the basis for a bottleneck experiment to determine the minimum environmental factors required for sentient life to survive. Seeding at least a dozen planets with oxygen-producing microbes and plant life, *Hermes* moved on to other projects, waiting approximately 10 million years for the atmospheres of the planets to develop suitable levels of oxygen and plant cover.

He then located sentients for his experiment, selecting Humans from Earth as well as other species from the Orion Arm, abducting them and depositing them on various planets in the Cluster around 1184 BC. Only the Humans deposited on Aeolis survived.

After several thousand years the Aeolians, having a basic awareness of spaceflight and the universe due to their abduction, developed starships, and spread out into the Cluster. Amasya was colonized by the Aeolians in 1777 AD by the Rim Calendar.

A hot desert planet with a low population, Amasya has small deposits of iron, leading to its primary industry of exporting iron and steel finished goods, including starships from the Hercules Shipyard. Amasya is also noted as the birthplace of the Fringe Rebellion.

Antiope (Empress)

Antiope Lysippe Aronte was the 212th Empress of the Aeolian Empire, reigning from 2141 to 2163. She prosecuted an intense military campaign against the Fringe Rebels, resulting in a polarized nation which struggled to understand the unending cost and destruction of the war.

Antiope was born in 2114 to Princess Merope, the second daughter of Empress Asteria. She was raised in the traditional militaristic manner of the Amazonian nobility, attending the Imperial Naval Academy at Aronte, and serving in the active fleet for three years until her first marriage, when she transferred to the Reserves.

Princess Antiope first married Prince Hyginus Lysippe in 2135 and immediately gave birth to a daughter, Hippolyta, the future 213th Empress. In 2137, Prince Hyginus was killed while onboard the frigate *Miletus*, which was ambushed by Fringe Rebels while transporting troops to Maia.

In 2140, Antiope married as her second husband the Earth-born RDF leader Jake Hammett, who had infiltrated the Aeolian Empire posing as a mercenary named Zeno. She had one child by Hammett, Princess Deinomache. As a result of this birth, per the laws of the Aeolian Empire, Jake Hammett was banished from Aronte.

In April 2141, her aunt Empress Miranda and her mother Princess Merope were killed by a terrorist attack in the Imperial Palace. Per the laws of succession of the Aeolian Empire, Antiope thereby received the tiara and became Empress.

In response to the terror attack which killed her aunt and mother, she embarked on a prolonged and violent war against the Fringe Rebels, a campaign which drained the treasury, created thousands of casualties, and turned a significant part of the populace against her. By the time of her death, Empress Antiope had become increasingly unpopular with the nobility and merchant class of the Empire but was still well supported by the rank and file.

Empress Antiope was killed in the Great Raid of 2163 when a task force of Fringe Rebel warships managed to break through the defenses of the Helios system and bombard the capital, Aronte, killing thousands. She is buried in the Imperial

Cemetery near Aronte.

Antiope (Planet)

Antiope is a planet in the Trappist system, formerly called Trappist 1-e. It is 39.6 lights from Earth. Because the planet is tidally locked to its host star, only a thin band between the hot and cold hemispheres is suitable for Human habitation.

The planet was named by Jake Hammett after the Aeolian Empress Antiope, whom he met and married while secretly visiting the Aeolian Empire. Antiope was the mother of the current Empress, Hippolyta as well as Princess Deinomache.

Jake Hammett was quoted as stating he named the planet after Empress Antiope because "she had a single-minded focus on suppressing the Fringe Rebellion, to the exclusion of all other issues – like a planet forever staring at a star, while the other side freezes."

Aronte (city)

Aronte is the capital city of the Aeolian Empire. With a population of well over 5 million, it is the largest city in the Empire. Located on the planet Aeolis in the Helios System, it sits on the banks of the Thermodon River about 4 km from the Pontus Axeinos, the ocean covering most of the western hemisphere of Aeolis.

Atsuko Kawasaki

RDF Captain **Atsuko Kawasaki was** head of the RDF Intelligence branch from 2121 until her disappearance in 2139. In 2180, it was revealed by Granada Tolleson Hammett, daughter of Jake Hammett and Teresa Tolleson, that Atsuko was a clone created by the Machine Ship *Pandora* prior to arrival on Earth, meant to assist in the integration of Jake Hammett, Teresa Tolleson and Dr. Kirsten Monk into an effective team for the sake of Humanity's survival.

According to Granada, when *Pandora* made her final departure from Kamilaroi in 2139, Atsuko left with her. This has never been confirmed and her disappearance remains a mystery, but the fact that the RDF never mounted a search for her tends to act as indirect confirmation of this theory.

Barcam (planet)

Barcam is a planet in the Fringe of the Aeolian Empire. Like most planets in the Beehive Cluster, it is quite young, with an estimated age of 600 million years (see Amasya for details of the early evolution of populated planets in the Cluster). Barcam was colonized by the Aeolians in 1748 AD by the Rim Calendar.

Barcam is a temperate world with adequate amounts of water for plant and animal life to flourish. It has little industry and primarily produces agricultural products, especially grapes and wine, most of which are exported. Like most of the Fringe Planets, it has a low population. Barcam has been a peripheral participant in the Fringe Rebellion.

Basic Rules (RimFed)

The **Basic Rules** are provisions of government which a star nation must follow to be a member of the Rim Federation. Initially adopted by the RDF Colonization Office in 2122 under the supervision of Dr. Kirsten Monk, the Basic Rules were later incorporated into the Rim Federation (RimFed) system of governance and remain the foundational government model for star nations in the alliance. The Basic Rules consist of the Rim Model of Responsible Government coupled with strong sanctions, such as ostracization, for any government which abandons the Rules.

Bat Empire

The **Bat Empire** is a star nation centered on the planet Nest, located 805 light years from Earth on a nearly direct line behind the Pipe Nebula. The Bat Empire has been notoriously involved in the genocides of an estimated 9 sentient species to date. It remains an existential threat to Humanity and other races as it expands into the Orion Arm of the Galaxy.

The Rim Defense Force (RDF) based at Kamilaroi continues to prepare for the inevitable meeting with this barbaric star nation by building out a fleet of warships and developing strategy, tactics, and training for space warfare under the leadership of CNO Jake Hammett.

Battle of Aronte

The **Battle of Aronte** occurred in 2141 and was an engagement between the Aeolian Empire Navy (AEN) and a rebel fleet seeking to overthrow the House Aronte and install a democratic government in the Aeolian Empire. The battle resulted in the defeat of the rebel force, which retreated to the Aeolian Empire Fringe Worlds.

In 2120, the planet Amasya became the center of a rebel force determined to institute reforms in the Aeolian Empire. Among the reforms they espoused were an end to the House Aronte's rule of the Aeolian Empire, the abolition of slavery, a democratic government based on sortition (choosing political officials by lot), universal suffrage (i.e. the male vote), and the end of laws preventing males from obtaining political office or serving as officers in the Navy.

By 2139, Amasya and ten other planets had been taken over by the rebels and a respectable naval force had been accumulated from captured AEN ships and converted merchant vessels.

After several minor skirmishes in and around Amasya, Maia and Barcam, in early 2141 the rebel fleet felt they had enough power to make a surprise attack on the capital city, Aronte, and execute a coup against the Empress. A diversionary attack was launched in the Aeolian system near the gas giant Hypnos, which tied up a significant portion of the Home Fleet.

The main rebel fleet then appeared suddenly in the system and charged for the planet, advancing to geostationary orbit over the capital city of Aronte where it prepared for an orbital bombardment which would have destroyed the Imperial Palace, Fleet Headquarters at the Navy Yard, and the Imperial Naval Academy, with the intent of decapitating the Aeolian leadership.

A last-ditch suicide charge by the cruiser *Kleitos*, commanded by Captain Ligeia Satra, was able to blunt the force of the attack sufficiently for the Home Fleet to regroup and come in behind the rebels, driving them from the field and destroying most of their ships.

Brush War

The **Brush War** was a short, sharp conflict involving Australia, Canada, China, Indonesia, Japan, North Korea, Singapore, South Korea, Taiwan, the United Kingdom, and the United States in early 2115.

Triggered by a minor brushing incident between ships of North Korea and Japan in the Yellow Sea on January 2nd, 2115, the conflict soon involved China and the U.S. as they came to the aid of their allies; within two weeks, the war had escalated, other military forces were involved, more than three dozen naval vessels had been sunk, and full-scale air battles had occurred over China, Japan, North Korea, Malaysia, and Taiwan.

After the initial burst of hostilities, the combatants withdrew most naval forces (due to the high attrition rates of ships lost) and resorted to long-distance bombing and missile attacks, primarily against military targets.

During the first three months of 2115, over four thousand missiles and aircraft were shot down on all sides, but at least two thousand missiles and thousands of bombs got through defenses and decimated military installations in all combatant countries.

By May 2115, all sides were basically out of missiles and front-line aircraft. The combatants then resorted to the use of reserve aircraft and even civilian models to send on bombing missions.

At this stage, Russia intervened diplomatically, offering to broker a cease-fire. By the end of May, a cease-fire had been agreed and the unofficial war came to an end, although the final peace agreement was not signed until November 21st, 2116.

As a result of the Brush War, further non-aggression pacts were signed in 2117 and 2118 between the major combatants; Japan accepted 2 billion dollars U.S. in reparations from North Korea and China; and the U.S. withdrew its objections to a future, phased annexation of Taiwan in return for a similar future recombination of North and South Korea (both effected in final form by 2174).

Charter Debt

Charter Debt is the debt accrued by a colony in return for legal title to a planet or other colony location (e.g. a moon), along with the cost of transportation, resources and support required to initiate a new colony in the location.

Charter Debt was a concept introduced in 2121, when Jake Hammett, Teresa Tolleson and Dr. Kirsten Monk formed the RDF Colony Office. The concept of Charter Debt was established to ensure that the resources involved in starting a new colony could be recouped, with interest, in order to build RDF defenses and prepare for the future war with the Bat Empire.

Basically, Charter Debt required the 2nd generation colonists (e.g. the children of the original colonists) and the 3rd generation colonists (e.g. the grandchildren of the original colonists) to construct two starships for use by the RDF (or one battleship or fleet carrier).

A typical pattern was that the 2nd generation delivered one small starship (e.g. corvette, destroyer, scoutship), while the 3rd generation built upon that expertise and infrastructure to deliver a larger starship (e.g. frigate, cruiser, or carrier). Upon delivery and acceptance of the starships by the RDF, the Charter Debt was expunged, and the colony was free and clear.

In some cases, the RDF allowed substitute payment, e.g. in raw materials, finished goods, or labor, to take the place of a delivered starship. For example, the Jovian colony on Europa satisfied their Charter Debt by becoming specialists in low-temperature microelectronics and providing advanced AI cores to the RDF for military use, remaining even today as the preeminent AI factory in the Rim.

Cold Bay

Cold Bay is a prison planet established in 2125 near Eudora, half-way to the Beehive Cluster. Criminals who would otherwise receive a death penalty in their home jurisdictions or who have been designated repeat violent offenders are exiled to Cold Bay. Once dropped on the planet, individuals are left to their own devices. The technology on the planet is held at an early primitive level (Earth, 1750's) to prevent any chance of escape.

Compressed Learning

Compressed learning is a technology provided to the RDF by the Machine Ship *Pandora* in 2121, when she visited Earth to provide a technology boost to Humanity.

Compressed learning allows the direct transmission of knowledge into the brain of the recipient during sleep, with few side effects. This allows most languages to be learned in two or three nights of sleep.

It is routinely used by the military and police forces

of most star nations, but is shunned by most educational institutions for philosophical reasons.

Core (Galaxy Core)

The **Core** of the Milky Way Galaxy is the area reserved for artificial intelligence creatures such as Machine Ships. This area is off-limits to biological beings. There have been several attempts to explore the Core; none of the expeditions have returned.

Hermes (Machine Ship)

Hermes is the name assigned by the RDF to a Machine Ship which visited Earth in approximately 1184 BC and abducted roughly 212 persons, along with a variety of plants and animals, taking them to the planet Aeolis in the Beehive Cluster, where they were abandoned. This group of people formed the nucleus of the Aeolian Empire. According to the Machine Ship *Pandora*, *Hermes*'s intention was to conduct a series of bottleneck experiments with sentient races. Before he could complete his experiments, *Hermes* was arrested and returned to Machine Space, where he was sentenced to re-programming for violation of the non-interference directive of the Machine Space society.

Deinomache (Princess)

Princess **Deinomache Andromache Aronte** is a member of the nobility of the Aeolian Empire. Princess Deinomache was born in 2141, the daughter of Princess (later Empress) Antiope and Jake Hammett, an RDF Admiral who had infiltrated Aeolis disguised as a mercenary.

Eudora

The planet **Eudora** is a large rocky planet located 279 lights from Earth toward Aeolis, in the general direction of the Beehive Cluster, orbiting the cool M-type star Oceanus. It was initially discovered by the RDF in 2124 and was used as a forward base for observation and infiltration of the Aeolian Empire.

Eudora hosts RDF Naval Base Eudora as well as the adjoining city, Selene. With a mass 25% greater than Earth and a slightly larger radius of 7,656 km, the surface gravity is only 86% that of Earth, making it a popular place of retirement for Humans.

F81 Dagger II

The **F81 Dagger II** was a hybrid jet/ramjet/scramjet fighter of the early 22nd century, used primarily by the U.S. Navy for carrier operations. The Dagger was designed as a high-altitude interceptor. It was the first three-mode hybrid in service with the U.S. and was prone to frequent mechanical malfunctions, resulting in a high attrition rate and the loss of several pilots. It was considered obsolete by the time of the Brush War of 2115 and was replaced by the next-generation F82.

F82 Grumbler

The **F82 "Grumbler"** was a hybrid jet / ramjet / scramjet fighter of the early 22nd century, used primarily by the U.S. Navy for carrier operations. The Grumbler was a sub-orbital interceptor named for its distinctive "grumbling" noise during re-entry. It was also used as a fighter-bomber for such roles as tossing smart bombs from above 45,000 meters against distant targets.

Placed into service in 2108, it was the U.S. Navy's front-line fighter in the Brush War of 2115. 322 aircraft were lost over a four-month period, the highest attrition rate of any U.S. aircraft in the War, as the Navy's carriers represented the front line of the war until the U.S. could position more land-based aircraft closer to the battlefront and withdraw the carriers to safer locations.

The F82 mission profile typically involved a late-night

launch, a climb to sub-orbit and a dive to attack enemy bombers as they made night bombing runs on allied territory, especially Japan, South Korea, and Taiwan.

Although numbers can only be estimated, it is generally accepted that the F82 shot down 400+ enemy aircraft over the first four months of the war, a major factor in the eventual cessation of hostilities as all combatants ran out of airplanes and missiles.

F90 Stiletto II

The **F90 Stiletto II** was a hybrid jet / ramjet / scramjet fighter of the early 22nd century, used primarily by the U.S. Air Force. The Stiletto II was a sub-orbital interceptor and fighter/ bomber. Placed into service in 2120, it was the primary front-line fighter for the Air Force until retired early in 2135 after the tDrive was released for limited civilian use. Variants included the F90B two-seat version and the F90D attack model.

Fringe Planets

The **Fringe Planets** are populated planets in the outskirts of the Beehive Cluster near Amasya, which constitute the mainstay of the Fringe Rebellion. These planets are the farthest from Aeolis and thus considered the "backwater" of the Empire. The list of planets making up the fringe are generally considered to be Amasya, Calypso, Maia, Electra, Taygete, Alcyone, Celaeno and Sterope. All participate in the Fringe Rebellion and are in a constant state of war with the center of the Empire. Barcam is sometimes lumped with this group as a Fringe Planet but does not participate to any great extent in the Fringe Rebellion.

Fringe Rebellion

Starting in 2120, the **Fringe Rebellion** is a determined effort by planets in the outer regions of the Aeolian Empire to institute reforms in the government. Among the reforms they espouse are an end to the House Aronte's rule of the Empire, the abolition of slavery, a democratic government, universal suffrage (i.e. the male vote), and the end of laws preventing males from obtaining political office or serving as officers in the Navy.

Amasya and ten other planets have been taken over by the rebels and a respectable naval force has been accumulated from captured AEN ships and converted merchant vessels. Using these vessels and more, the rebels have fought a long, grinding campaign against the Imperial center of the Empire.

Helios (star)

The **Helios** system is the home system of the Aeolian Empire, located 580 lights from Earth in the Beehive Cluster. Helios is a G2 star, comparable to Sol in all major respects.

House Aronte

The **House Aronte** is the ruling dynasty of the Aeolian Empire and is a direct line of descent from the original twelve Amazons abandoned on Aeolis in 1184 BC. The House was founded by Queen Melanippe, the first Queen of the newly formed colony. According to legend, Queen Melanippe was the sister of Penthesilea of Thrace, an Amazon killed by the hero Achilles at the Battle of Troy. The Sword of Penthesilea is a revered artifact held by the House Aronte, claimed to be the original sword from the battle with Achilles and passed down from Queen Melanippe to subsequent generations.

Hippolyta Lysippe Aronte (Empress of Aeolis)

Hippolyta Lysippe Aronte is the 213th Empress of the Aeolian Empire, reigning since 2163. She inherited an Empire divided by the Fringe Rebellion and with a population exhausted by the war. Unable to end the Rebellion, she has since allowed it to devolve into a "Phony War", in which neither side has the strength or the will to press an attack.

Hippolyta was born in 2135 to Princess Antiope, the daughter of Princess Merope. She was not expected to enter the line of succession, as Merope was a second daughter of Empress Asteria. Hippolyta attended the Imperial Naval Academy at Aronte and was commissioned an ensign, serving as an active officer from 2153 to 2163. Her career in the Navy was unremarkable.

In 2141, Empress Miranda and Hippolyta's grandmother, Princess Merope, were both killed in a terrorist attack at the Imperial Palace. Her mother, Antiope, then became Empress. This moved Hippolyta to the line of succession. When her mother Antiope was killed in the Great Raid of 2163, Hippolyta ascended to the tiara.

Hippolyta has not prosecuted the rebels in the Fringe with any great enthusiasm and has let the Rebellion simmer, resulting in a quiet period called the "Phony War". Instead, she devotes her time to real and imagined conspiracies in the Palace and among the nobility, developing a reputation as a dangerous and somewhat unpredictable ruler.

Jake Hammett

Jake Hammett is the Chief of Naval Operations (CNO) of the Rim Defense Force (RDF). Hammett was born October 26, 2078 in Oakwood, Texas, and grew up in Dallas, Texas, graduating from Dallas Skyline High School in 2096. He was appointed to the U.S. Naval Academy, graduating in 2100, and completed flight training at NAS Pensacola, Florida, and NAS Corpus Christi, Texas. In 2104 he was assigned to VFA-2 'Bounty Hunters' at NAS Lemoore, California, flying the F81 "Dagger II". Hammett served in various fighter squadrons both in the U. S. and overseas, moving up to the F82 "Grumbler" in early 2113.

When the Brush War broke out in 2115, Lt. Commander Jake Hammett was on the carrier USS *Byers* in the Indian Ocean, and immediately began flying missions, completing 28 missions and accounting for eleven enemy aircraft between January and May.

On May 12th, 2115, while diving from 38,000 meters to attack a Chinese bomber headed for Japan, recently promoted Commander Hammett was shot down over western North Korea. He was able to nurse his crippled aircraft to Mongolian airspace before ejecting. He was captured by the Mongolian Army and interned for the remainder of the war. The Mongolians refused to turn him over to the North Koreans or the Chinese, saving him from the torture visited on many other captured pilots.

Hammett left the Navy after the Brush War and moved to San Francisco, where he worked in Artificial Intelligence (AI) for SpaceRed, a startup attempting to create a viable permanent habitat on Mars. There Hammett developed AI cores for use in chemical rockets and early Mars habitats.

Hammett lived and worked relatively quietly in San Francisco until 21 June 2121 when the Machine Ship *Pandora* landed dramatically in the White House South Lawn and presented holographic images of three persons on the outside of the ship: Jake Hammett, Air Force Lieutenant Colonel Teresa Tolleson and NSC Science Advisor Dr. Kirsten Monk. *Pandora*'s message of danger to Humanity, coupled with the message "*If you wish to survive, bring these three*", resulted in a quick parabolic flight in an F90B Stiletto from Travis AFB, California, to Andrews AFB, Maryland for Hammett.

Upon arrival at the White House, Hammett, Tolleson and Monk were directed by the President to proceed to the alien ship and attempt to make contact. The three entered the ship at 7:43 am on 22 June 2121 and contacted the sentient AI *Pandora.* The group came out after four hours to report the disturbing facts of the danger to Earth posed by the genocidal Bat Empire.

The next day, 23 June 2121, Hammett appeared before the U. N. General Assembly and highlighted the danger to Earth represented by the Bat Empire, the need for the formation of the Rim Defense Force (RDF) and the RDF Colony Office, and the requirement to form an alliance with the Aeolian Empire to present a joint defense against the Bats. Moving to Geneva, Switzerland, Hammett, Tolleson and Dr. Monk formed the RDF Space Force and began the anticipated one-hundred-year process of preparing for the war against the Bats.

Shortly afterward, in August of 2123, Hammett formed the first RDF triplex marriage with Monk and Tolleson, creating a new paradigm for use in the space force where long absences from home base were the norm rather than the exception.

For Hammett's children from this marriage, see the entries for Teresa Tolleson and Dr. Kirsten Monk.

Hammett's wife Dr. Kirsten Monk was killed in 2134 by a stray bullet while attempting to broker a peace deal on the planet Sierra Nevada, which had been locked in a standoff between the elected parliamentary government and members of a neo-Nazi terrorist group attempting to institute a theocracy.

Hammett's remaining wife, Teresa Tolleson, was abducted in Geneva on 2 December 2136 and tortured to death by Covenant of God terrorists in Frankfurt, Germany.

For Hammett's later marriage to the Aeolian Empress Antiope, see her entry.

Kamilaroi

Kamilaroi is a planet in the 36 Ophiuchi C system, the seat of the Rim Federation government capital New Geneva, and the home of the Rim Defense Force (RDF) Headquarters at Tolleson Base. Kamilaroi is an ocean world, with only two small landmasses and a cooler, wetter climate than Earth. New Geneva sits on an island in the Southern Ocean while RDF Headquarters is located on an island in the Northern Ocean, almost directly opposite New Geneva.

Kirsten Monk

Dr. Kirsten Monk was the first Director of the Rim Defense Force (RDF) Colony Office. Born May 19th, 2087, in Queens, New York City, Monk grew up in Queens and attended Far Rockaway High School, graduating in 2104. After high school, she attended MIT, obtaining her B.S. and M. S. in Physics and her Ph. D in Astronomy in 2112.

Monk worked under Luebmann at Columbia from 2112 to 2115, primarily on detection of exomoons. In 2115, during the Brush War, she was seconded to Applied Engineering Laboratories in Austin, Texas_to develop remote sensing technology for use in the war effort.

After the war, Monk remained at AEL in Austin, becoming a primary researcher on asteroid mining. In 2120, based on her general expertise in astronomy, long range sensing and asteroid mining operations, she was appointed to the National Security Council by President Margaret Bolt.

Dr. Monk was at the White House attending an NSC meeting on 21 June 2121 when the Machine Ship *Pandora* landed on the South Lawn and presented holographic images of three persons on the outside of the ship: herself, Jake Hammett, and Air Force Lieutenant Colonel Teresa Tolleson. *Pandora*'s message of danger to Humanity, coupled with the message "*If you wish to survive, bring these three*", resulted a directive from the President to enter the alien ship and attempt to make contact.

The three entered the ship at 7:43 am on 22 June 2121 and contacted the sentient AI *Pandora.* The group came out after four hours to report the disturbing facts of the danger to Earth posed by the genocidal Bat Empire.

The next day, 23 June 2121, Monk appeared with Jake Hammett and Teresa Tolleson before the U.N. General Assembly as part of the presentation to highlight the danger to Earth represented by the Bat Empire, the need for the formation of the Rim Defense Force (RDF) and the RDF Colony Office, and the requirement to form an alliance with the

Aeolian Empire to present a joint defense against the Bats.

Subsequent to these events, Dr. Monk joined with Jake Hammett and Teresa Tolleson as the initial founding members of the RDF. Monk formed the RDF Colony Office, which had responsibility for locating suitable planets for colonization, conducting the planning and resource collection required for the colonies, transporting the colonists to their new home, monitoring and supporting them until they were fully established, and supervising them through three generations, including the collection of their Charter Debt.

With Teresa Tolleson and Jake Hammett, Monk also formed the first triplex marriage in the RDF in 2123, setting a precedent that endures to the current day in the RDF and throughout the Rim Federation.

Monk and Hammett had two children:

- Chloe Monk, b. 2129, starship pilot in the RDF, currently holding the rank of Captain.
- Stephen Hawking Monk, b. 2132, Earth politician, former member of the New York Assembly, former U. S. Senator from New York, and currently U. S. Secretary of State under President James Bolt Jr. He has been estranged from his mother and father for most of his adult life, due to his rigid fundamentalist leanings and his writings espousing an Earth government based on a religious theocracy controlled by the Catholic Church.

Dr. Monk also formed a separate, duplex marriage with Commander Lois Vetton in 2124. This marriage was permissible under the rules of the RDF at the time, which permitted a total of four spouses simultaneously if all participants agreed the contracts. This marriage also lasted until her death.

Dr. Kirsten Monk was killed by a stray bullet on July 2,

2134, during the neo-Nazi coup attempt on Sierra Nevada, while attempting to broker a peace between the warring factions. The RDF fined Sierra Nevada two years GDP for the crime, which required them to build an extra starship (the scoutship *Polaris*) before their Charter Debt was satisfied.

Dr. Monk is buried in the Hammett Family Plot near Oakwood, Texas.

Ligeia Iona Satra

Ligeia Iona Satra was a Captain in the Aeolian Empire Navy (AEN) during the early years of the Fringe Rebellion.

Ligeia Satra was born in 2107 on the planet Aeolis into the Satra clan, a junior branch of the House Aronte. She attended the Imperial Naval Academy at Aronte, graduating in 2125 as an ensign. She served on various ships and advanced steadily in rank until 2136, when she was assigned as Captain of the cruiser *Kleitos*.

In the Battle of Aronte in 2141, Captain Satra led the counterattack on the rebel fleet which was preparing to bombard Aronte. Her attack was successful, but she was killed in the process. For her actions in the battle, she was posthumously awarded the AEN's highest decoration, the Honor of the Empress, as well as the Star of Aronte.

Machine Ship

A Machine Ship is an artificial intelligence (AI) creature with the body of a starship, thus able to traverse the galaxy at will, with nearly unlimited resources of time and energy. The most famous example of a Machine Ship (to biological creatures) is *Pandora*. Also see *Hermes*.

Machine Space

Machine Space is the central part of the Milky Way galaxy, also known as the Core. It is reserved for artificial intelligence creatures only, including Machine Ships, androids and other synthetic or AI-based lifeforms.

Maia (planet)

Maia is a planet in the Fringe states of the Aeolian Empire, located in the Beehive Cluster. Like most planets in the Cluster, it is quite young, with an estimated age of 600 million years (see Amasya for details of the early evolution of populated planets in the Beehive Cluster). Maia was colonized by the Aeolians in 1592 AD by the Rim Calendar.

Maia is a warm, semi-desert world with minimal amounts of water. The Empire Shipyard is located on Maia. Like most of the Fringe Planets, it has a low population. Maia is considered the headquarters of the Fringe Rebellion.

Merope (Princess)

Princess **Merope Lysippe Aronte** was the sister of Empress Miranda and a Princess of the Aeolian Empire, when she was assassinated on 17 April 2141 by the rebel Anicetus. Merope was the mother of Antiope Lysippe Aronte, who became Empress upon her death.

Miranda (Empress)

Empress **Miranda Andromache Aronte** was the 211th Empress of the Aeolian Empire, reigning from 2085 until 2141. Empress Miranda prosecuted a lackluster war against the Fringe rebels, never fully committing the military forces of the Empire against them, resulting in a long and lingering rebellion that grew steadily throughout the early part of the 22nd century. Shortly after the Battle of Aronte in 2141, Miranda was assassinated, along with her sister Princess Merope, by the rebel Anicetus on 27 April 2141.

Nest

Nest is the home planet of the Bat Empire, located 805 lights Coreward from Earth behind the Pipe Nebula. The capital of Nest is Raditel. The planet receives about 95% of the radiation of Earth.

Little is known about the planet or its solar system due to the non-contact directives of the Rim Federation, strictly enforced by the warships of the RDF, although it is certain that classified military intelligence held by the RDF contains much additional detail.

New Geneva

New Geneva is the capital city of the Rim Federation, located on the planet Kamilaroi in the 36 Ophiuchi C system. It is the home of the Rim Parliament and the seat of government for the Rim.

New Geneva was founded in 2136 on one of the two land masses of Kamilaroi, two small islands roughly the size of Iceland on Earth. RDF Headquarters is located on the other island, approximately half-way around the planet.

Ostracization

Ostracization is the Rim Federation policy of withholding all defensive, technological, and logistical support for a colony/planet which fails to follow the Basic Rules of the Rim Federation. This means the planet is isolated from the Rim Federation and is, for all practical purposes, no longer capable of space travel or space communications. This policy was established in 2122 by the RDF Colonization Office in their initial Basic Rules model, and later adopted by the Rim Federation.

Ostracization implies:

1. The RDF will not defend the colony if it is attacked by an outside force

2. All technology beyond that of the early 20th century, Earth is withdrawn from the colony. No fission or fusion reactors, spacecraft, radio or TV, electronics, or other advances

from beyond the period of Earth, 1900 are permitted.

3. No deep-space communications are permitted, e.g. no QE boxes.

4. Any person who voluntarily lands on the planet will remain. Accidental landings will be rescued.

5. The RDF will perform periodic checks on the colony to verify compliance but will not approach.

Pandora (Machine Ship)

Pandora was the name of the Machine Ship which visited Earth in 2121 and provided a technology boost to bring Humanity to parity with the Bat Empire. *Pandora* landed on the South Lawn of the White House, Washington, D.C., on 21 June 2121.

In appearance, *Pandora* was wedge-shaped, similar to an old-style flatiron without the handle. She was matte black, with two linear scribes down each side and crosshatches on top, like a tic-tac-toe pattern.

She was measured by remote laser at 30 meters long and 14 meters wide at her rear, tapering to a 1-meter blunt point at the front. The impression she left in the ground after her eventual departure was 12 inches deep, indicating a considerable mass. A later report by Jake Hammett stated that the ship was larger internally than externally, which would indicate some type of extra-dimensionality that is not yet understood by Rim science.

After her arrival, *Pandora* posted a message as a hologram on the outside of the ship, consisting of pictures of Mr. Jake Hammett, a former U. S. Navy fighter pilot; Lt. Colonel Teresa Tolleson, an Air Force officer; and Dr. Kirsten Monk, a member of the National Security Council; with the message to bring them to the ship.

The next day, 22 June 2121, the three entered the ship and met the advanced AI who was the mind of the ship. The three were in the ship for four hours. Upon their exit, they walked across the White House lawn to the South fence and held an impromptu news conference with a group of reporters and sightseers gathered there. This short press briefing provided the people of Earth the first insight into the nature of the Galaxy, Machine Space, and *Pandora*. In this briefing, Hammett disclosed the nature of *Pandora* as a total AI construct, with no biological component, and the general purpose of her visit to Earth.

Two days later, shortly before Hammett, Tolleson and Monk presented to the U. N. General Assembly in New York a more complete disclosure of the message brought by *Pandora*, she quietly and without warning lifted off from the White House and flew to Geneva, Switzerland, landing in the courtyard of a large office building which became the first headquarters of the fledgling RDF (Rim Defense Force).

Over the next two years, *Pandora* sat quietly in the courtyard of RDF Headquarters in Geneva, with no one allowed to communicate directly with her except RDF personnel and no one allowed on board except Hammett, Tolleson, Monk or Atsuko Kawasaki, head of RDF Intelligence.

During this period, *Pandora* provided, via the RDF, numerous technological gifts to Humanity, including transcendent fusion drives (tDrives), compressed learning, and the QE box. She also provided the RDF with information on the social and military aspects of the Aeolian and Bat Empires.

After slightly more than two years in Geneva, on 26 September 2123, *Pandora* lifted off again and made her way to Mars, where she resided while the RDF completed MarsBase, their first off-Earth Headquarters. In 2136, *Pandora* relocated again to Tolleson Base at Kamilaroi, the new Headquarters of the RDF.

On 18 November 2139, *Pandora* declared her mission complete and departed the Sol system. Although she has never re-appeared to public view since that time, rumors persist that she has been seen in various locations throughout Rim space, including once lying quietly on the back side of the Moon. Moreover, RDF Admiral and CNO Jake Hammett has stated that *Pandora* is never far away and has contacted him from time to time.

Pontus Axeinos

The **Pontus Axeinos** is a large ocean covering most of the Western Hemisphere of the planet Aeolis. Covering an area of 71,288,103 square kilometers, it is slightly larger than the Pacific Ocean of Earth. Its name is identical to the ancient Greek term for Earth's Black Sea, which further reinforces a commonly held theory that the Amazons of Aeolis originated on the northern shores of what is now Turkey in approximately 1184 B.C. before their abduction to Aeolis.

QE Box

A **QE Box** is a deep-space communications device used primarily by the RDF for military transmissions, based on Quantum Entanglement (QE) theory. Although it has a low bit rate, it has unlimited range and cannot be hacked. Due to the low bit rate, it cannot transmit video, but can send low quality audio and text messages instantaneously across any distance.

Rim Defense Force (RDF)

The RDF (Rim Defense Force) is the military arm of the Rim Federation (RimFed). Originating in 2121 on Earth, the RDF was moved to Mars in 2123 and later to Kamilaroi in 2136 as the number of off-Earth colonies grew, and Earth became more recalcitrant in its objections to meeting the Basic Rules.

The RDF is best known for its ongoing preparations to meet the genocidal Bat Empire, in order to secure the future survival of the Rim Federation.

Rim Federation

The **Rim Federation** (generally known as RimFed) is the

central government of the Orion Spur of the Milky Way galaxy. As of 2180 it encompasses 28 states (planets, colonies, and territories).

RimFed is a parliamentary system of government originally developed on the planet Earth; when the RDF began colonizing planets in 2121, such government was adopted as the only permissible form of government for Human colonies.

In 2136, the Rim Federation was established on the same model to act as a top-level government for all systems and colonies defended by the RDF.

Constitution

The constitution of the Rim Federation is founded upon the Basic Rules, which guarantee individual freedoms and protect the basic rights of the individual.

Distributed Government

In the Rim Federation, individual solar systems and colonies retain their own local government and have the right to control their own territories, within the scope of the Basic Rules. They may raise, train and control local militias and police forces to defend themselves and their systems. However, local governments are restricted from creating professional FTL navies, as that role is reserved for the RDF. They are also prohibited from warfare against other members of the Rim, and this is strictly enforced by the RDF.

Rim Model of Responsible Government

The **Rim Model of Responsible Government** is a parliamentary system of government based on the Westminster system originally developed in the old Earth United Kingdom, coupled with the Bill of Rights from the United States, currently used by all planets or colonies in the Rim Federation. The term “Westminster system” comes from the Palace of Westminster, the seat of the Earth-based British

Parliament. The system is a set of procedures for operating a government.

This system was implemented by the RDF in 2122 for all new Human colonies; RimFed continues to require this form of government for any planet or colony in the Federation, else the entity will be ostracized from further contact with other Rim members.

tDrive

The **tDrive** is a technology provided to the original RDF (Rim Defense Force) by the Machine Ship *Pandora* in 2121, shortly after her arrival on Earth. A tDrive allows faster-than-light (FTL) travel for starships. An AI interface built into the tDrive is used to control it. Similar drives limited to non-FTL travel for use inside a solar system are called system drives (sDrives).

Thermodon River (Aeolis)

The **Thermodon River** is the chief river on Aeolis, the central planet of the Aeolian Empire. The capital city, Aronte, is located at the mouth of the river. The river flows generally north for 3,650 km from the Olympus mountains to the Pontus Axeinos, with a drainage basin of 2,866,000 square km. The estuary of the river forms a prime fishing area and excellent harbor for shipping.

Teresa Tolleson

Teresa Tolleson was the first head of the Rim Defense Force (RDF) Operations Group, leading them for the initial 15 years of their existence. Born February 19th, 2088, in Los Angeles, California, Tolleson grew up in LA and attended Los Angeles High School, graduating in 2106. Appointed to the U.S. Air Force Academy in Colorado Springs, Colorado, she graduated in 2110 with a degree in Aeronautical Engineering. She completed flight training at Sheppard AFB, Texas, and was assigned to the 47th "Hawg" squadron at San Francisco, California, in 2112, flying the F-84 Thunderbolt III. In the Brush War of 2115, Tolleson, by then a Captain, shot down five Chinese J-48 fighters and six Chinese H-42 bombers over the course of six weeks, becoming the first female double ace of the war. Shot down on 27 May 2115, Tolleson was tortured by the Chinese for several days before the cease-fire was announced.

Remaining in the USAF after the war, Tolleson rose rapidly to the rank of Lieutenant Colonel, serving as both a test pilot and training commander; but in 2120, while stationed at Travis AFB near San Francisco, California, she filed sexual harassment charges against the base Commanding Officer. The charges were dismissed by a court of inquiry due to lack of evidence. As a result of these events, however, Lt. Colonel Tolleson was notified she would not be retained in the Air Force. Tolleson made plans to retire in mid-2121.

Tolleson initially planned to accept a job as a pilot for North American Airlines, but after the dramatic arrival of the Machine Ship *Pandora* in June of 2121, Tolleson became part of the fledgling RDF. Working first out of Geneva, Switzerland, and later out of MarsBase, Tolleson was the driving force in establishing the Operations and Logistic Command of the RDF, arm-twisting corporate and government leaders into supporting the planning and execution of the early ship designs, kick-starting the manufacturing of starships, and recruiting and training crews for the first missions. Tolleson was highly effective in her role, leaving CNO Jake Hammett to concentrate on the development of the long-term strategy for dealing with the Bat Empire and the Aeolians.

With Dr. Kirsten Monk and Hammett, Tolleson formed the first triplex marriage in the RDF in 2123, setting a precedent that endures to the current day in the RDF and many Rim colonies.

Tolleson had two children by Jake Hammett:

- Granada Tolleson, b. 2127, an actress and author,

resides in London, England, and wrote the historical novel "The Princess Takes a Barbarian" published in 2160, as well as dozens of plays and short works.

- Scipio (Skip) Tolleson, b. 2130, a priest of the Holy Trinity Anglican Church in Geneva, Switzerland.

Teresa Tolleson was abducted in Geneva on 2 December 2136 and tortured to death by Covenant of God terrorists in Frankfurt, Germany. She is buried in the Hammett Family Plot near Oakwood, Texas.

Tolleson Base

Tolleson Base is the headquarters of the Rim Defense Force (RDF). It is located on the planet Kamilaroi in the 36 Ophiuchi system.

RDF Headquarters was originally located at MarsBase in the Sol System. Due to the recalcitrance of Earth to adopt the Rim Federation Basic Rules and the increasing hostility of the religion-backed governments of some Earth countries, the RDF relocated their Headquarters to Kamilaroi in 2136, establishing Tolleson Base as their new Headquarters.

Tolleson Base is located next to Terminator Bay, where a moist but mild climate prevails. The new base has grown rapidly since establishment. The city next to the base, Tolleson City, has a reputation as a rough frontier town.

United Kingdom (Earth)

The **United Kingdom** was an Earth government which existed until 2164 as an independent country in Europe. It was subsumed into the European Commonwealth in 2164.

Zeno

Zeno was an alternate identity used by Jake Hammett during his extended stay in the Aeolian Empire during the period February 2140 to April 2141. Hammett used this identity to infiltrate the Empire and research methods of enabling an alliance with the Aeolians.

The nature of his visit was shrouded in secrecy and few details were ever revealed by the RDF, but it is well-established that Hammett fathered the second daughter (Deinomache) of Princess (later Empress) Antiope during this visit. Some historians attribute *Pandora*'s cryptic selection of Jake Hammett as the initial head of the RDF to her ability to predict this event; but mathematicians discount this as an impossible feat of statistical prediction.

New books and freebies
www.philhuddleston.com/newsletter

www.facebook.com/philhuddlestonauthor

Imprint Series
Artemis War (prequel novella)
Imprint of Blood
Imprint of War
Imprint of Defiance

Broken Galaxy Series
Broken Galaxy
Star Tango
The Long Edge of Night
The Short End
Remnants
Goblin Eternal

Works on Amazon
www.amazon.com/Phil-Huddleston/e/B07ZKFGW3G/

ABOUT THE AUTHOR

Like Huckleberry Finn, Phil Huddleston grew up barefoot and outdoors, catching mudbugs by the creek, chasing rabbits through the fields, and forgetting to come home for dinner. Then he discovered books. Thereafter, he read everything he could get his hands on, including reading the Encyclopedia Britannica and Funk & Wagnalls from A-to-Z multiple times. He served in the U.S. Marines for four years, returned to college and completed his degree on the GI Bill. Since that time, he built computer systems, worked in cybersecurity, played in a band, flew a bush plane from Alaska to Texas, rode a motorcycle around a good bit of America, and watched in amazement as his wife raised two wonderful daughters. And would like to do it all again. Except maybe without being dazed and confused most of the time.

Printed in Dunstable, United Kingdom

75917159R10180